COWBOY AWAY

Part Two of the In the Reins Series

Carly Kade

Cowboy Away
A Novel by Carly Kade
Excerpt from, *"Reluctance" by Robert Frost, from* A Boy's Will *(London: David Nutt, 1913);* used courtesy of the public domain.
Author Photograph by Melanie Elise Photography
Cover Design by Joshua Jadon
Edited by Ann Luu
ISBN: 9780996887922
ISBN: 099688792X
Library of Congress Control Number: 2017916372
Carly Kade Creative, Phoenix, AZ

Carly Kade Creative
Phoenix, Arizona
http://www.carlykadecreative.com

Praise for EQUUS Film Festival Literary Award winner for Best Western Fiction and two-time Feathered Quill Book Award winner *In the Reins*

"If you love horse stories and are looking for a book to draw you into its pages and not let go until that last page is read, check out *In the Reins* – you won't be disappointed." – **Feathered Quill book reviews**

"*In the Reins*, a Western book by Carly Kade ... was a great book, and I was sad when it was over (and wanting to read the second book)." – **Horses & Heels Equestrian Lifestyle site**

"*In the Reins*, by new author Carly Kade, has it all: new beginnings, fun characters, beautiful horses, and plenty of enticing, steamy scenes at the stable!" – **Maryland Equestrian Lifestyle Guide book review**

" ... if you're tired of waiting around and hoping for some tall-dark-and-handsome mystery cowboy to jingle his spurs on into your barn (and, believe it or not, that was NOT intended to be a metaphor for anything), go ahead and pick up a copy of *In the Reins* to live out your fantasy in fiction." – **Eileen Cody, Horse Nation's Resident book reviewer**

"A book that will feel like coming home, complete with a sexy cowboy, a strong female lead, and beautiful horses." – **Heather and Horses book reviews (5 out of 5 horseshoes)**

"I'd suggest adding *In the Reins* to your beach bag or throwing it in your trailer to read and unwind after a long day at a horse show!" – **Brittney Joy, author of Red Rock Ranch book series**

"I highly recommend this book to all fellow equestrians, no matter your discipline! I may primarily ride English, but I have a cowgirl heart and this book definitely calls to it." – ***Booking Around book reviews***

"This story is great about getting the horse facts straight! It's like watching a movie where people can actually ride their horse without flopping all around. Reading accurate descriptions of horse training is refreshing. And if that isn't good enough here, there is a sweet, fiery romance complete with horseback kisses. This is one I'd highly recommend to grab on a beach vacation and read with your toes curled in warm sand." – ***SSwriter.com book review***

For DD,
I'm still following my dream.

IN THE REINS EPILOGUE
MCKENNON

Devon didn't know that I had worked it all out with Sophia. I wanted her to arrive after I'd shown Star so she could be there to support me whether we had won or not. I remember how it felt. I was warm and happy for the first time in such a long while when I told Sophia that I realized I needed Devon to be there no matter what happened.

But that was then …

Now I just sit here idle, been this way for a while, rearview mirror adjusted, so I can watch her go round and round in the pen on that painted pony. I know she knows I am watching her.

Boy, had they gotten good! Because of me, they got good because of me.

Devon and Faith reminded me that I still had something left to give, a will to train again. Looking away from Devon's image spinning in the mirror's reflection, I splay my gloved hand in front of me. I rest it on the steering wheel while my truck vibrates and chugs diesel beneath me. Slowly, I ease off my soft lambskin glove, one finger at a time. And I just stare at it, that left-hand golden band. It still means everything to me, but now it also means nothing.

I glance up again to make sure she is still going round and round. I wiggle the wedding ring off my finger and expose a calloused white ridge where it had always been. Running my thumb over the raised groove it left on my skin, I hesitate at my ring finger's tip. I feel my pulse accelerate as I think about its loss, no longer having it be a part of me.

The past and future hover together and collide in this single decision. I turn the ring over and over in the palm of my hand, rub the calloused ridge with my thumb again, and, with a sigh, force the ring back to its rightful place.

I just can't take it off.

Lifting my hat, I run my fingers through my hair and shake my head. I see JD saunter up to Devon in the rearview. He takes the place at the rail that I should be occupying right now. JD tosses his arms across the top railing and rests his head on them. Disgust, jealousy, indecision and questions of loyalty blaze through my veins. Too many emotions are blinding me, confusing me.

I have to get out of here.

Ramming the truck into drive, I jam my boot to the gas pedal and speed off, kicking up gravel behind me. I know I am making a scene. I flee down Green Briar's drive, heading for the easy choice. I realize I am taking the easy way out. When the going actually got going or tough, I always got going myself.

Squeezing the steering wheel, my knuckles white, I look up and see the beautiful pair minimizing. Devon and Faith are no longer in harmonious motion. Now they are merely a stopped speck, watching me go again. I feel sick. I know that JD is telling Devon, 'I told you so,' and reaffirming to her that I am broken, that I won't ever get over it.

Maybe I am … and maybe I won't.

My heart races when I think about being with Devon, but at the same time, my heart is broken being without a different "her."

I am to blame. I pushed that damn animal too hard. It was all spurs, battles and pinned ears with the horse because of my wanting to win so bad. I rushed it all. I had forgotten my roots, everything I'd learned.

How could I have put her on top?

I risked and lost everything with that decision.

My eyes begin to blur, hot tears building, ready for rupture, under the excruciating memory of her pinned under that damn horse, JD shrieking for an ambulance, those last words …

'Ken, I love you.'

Ken. She was the only one who ever called me Ken.

PROLOGUE
DEVON

It all seems like forever ago, starting with the spun-out-side-of-the road scene in my car that altered my future. Fate healed me – it led me to Faith, to Green Briar, to McKennon. For once, I am really living, not in the pulling back, but in the trusting, in the going forward. It just isn't in the reins.

As my relationship with McKennon developed, I realized he was right there with me and often one step ahead. For the first time in my life, I actually feel appreciated … *seen*. I am in awe of his empathy for the animals … for me. He is selfless, confident, lets others be just the way they are, and it never impacts him.

For me, that's the sexiest part about McKennon … his inability to be impacted. I fell in love with his calm, (of course, his good looks hadn't hurt either). McKennon possesses the ability to just be. He is peaceful, rooted and secure in his manhood. McKennon doesn't do temper tantrums like the selfish men who once defined my relationships, and that alone feels like freedom.

I am able to be me … to be just as I am.

With McKennon, things were different from the start, ever since that first electric jolt crossed between us. It expanded to a shared appreciation of beauty in the human form (we can't take our eyes off each other), in the world of art (music, poetry, art, his books, my writing) and nature (the horses, gardening, trail riding beneath the sky). We enjoy each other without reservation, judgment or even words. In our short time together, I've come to understand the brilliance of McKennon, and he makes me feel brilliant.

Michael was terrible at all of it. With him, the best parts of me ended up frozen, cold. We were like two ships passing in the night that happened to dock at the same pier. On the contrary, McKennon tunes into me like a radio station going from fuzzy to a clear channel.

With JD's muffled voice as background noise, I lean over Faith, stroke the sorrel heart-shaped spot on her neck and watch McKennon pull away.

I expected this.

I can't help but think of the last verse of Robert Frost's poem *Reluctance* ...

Ah, when to the heart of man
Was it ever less than treason
To go with the drift of things
To yield with a grace to reason
And bow and accept the end
Of a love or a season

After we came together and shared that first kiss, I contemplated what the future might hold for us, and I figured McKennon would get spooked by our new relationship when so much remained unresolved about his last one. Even so, I still wonder aloud, "Is he leaving already? Leaving before this thing between us has even begun?"

Am I going to have to yield with a grace to reason and accept the end of our love now that McKennon had reached the end of his show season?

JD begins to answer. I hush him.

"I know the answer, JD," I murmur.

Yes. Yes, he is leaving. And I'll be OK with it. I have to be.

I've always felt different. I have this weird ability to see things before they happen. I have the inclination to finish people's sentences and read other's thoughts just by watching their body language. I wouldn't say I'm psychic; rather, I'd say I have a gift for sensing things. I think I acquired this higher sensitivity from having more animal relationships than human ones in my youth. I preferred their silent communication through body language to empty or difficult human conversations. Still do. With animals, it is all about feeling out the other's energy and respecting each other's space.

I can sense McKennon needs to heal. His loss runs deep. I decide then and there, from the back of my horse, that I will respect his space. I'll wait. It is fate helping me again. Only time can tell what our next chapter will be.

I'll wait while he works it out. However long it takes. I will wait for McKennon.

CHAPTER 1

MCKENNON

I've been living my life like I've been shot out of a gun since she died.

What is the point?

Being on my own is the only thing that's made sense since she's been gone. But, when Devon showed up on the ranch, I realized that I was still breathing, still lusting for something. I felt blood, warm, in my veins again.

Yeah ... cool, composed McKennon – that's how I'm supposed to be.

That's who I am for them. I always leave Green Briar when I feel a bender coming on – our wedding anniversary, the anniversary of her death, all the moments in between. It can be anything. Something small, a single memory, will set me off, and I'm no longer a man in control.

I don't want anyone to see me like that, not Sophia, not the staff, certainly not Devon. JD is the only one I'll call if I get really bad – a fistfight, an unpaid tab, waking up not knowing where I am. He's her brother after all. We are family. Family is all you can count on in times like those.

The whiskey bottle tumbles out of my grip, startling me awake. I'm alone on top of some crude, red velour bedspread, all velvety and crusty, in this dive motel room.

Hazy, I watch the ceiling fan rotate slowly above me and think about the kiss with Devon. Devon is the real deal. I didn't think a man could find two of those in a lifetime. I like how I would walk into the barn, see Devon, and the dynamic would immediately change.

Was it curiosity, energy, a common spirit, her innocence or the newness that began our relationship?

My heart pounds as I recount my fingers tangled in her auburn hair, her breath sweet and her lips hungry. All of that pent up want surging between us finally let loose after months and all at once. I toss my arm over my eyes, headache blazing fire in my mind. Devon's warm, big and beautiful doe eyes fade. I see my wife again. She's pinned under that damn animal.

I need help. I know that. I'm stuck, and I can't move forward. JD is mad at me for thinking of moving on with Devon. The boots may have been a mistake, but it's been years now.

I should be able to move on. Shouldn't I?

The problem is – I can't.

CHAPTER 2

DEVON

O *K... "however long it takes" ends up being approximately 14 hours, 28 minutes and 3 seconds. So much for waiting.*

A night of tossing and turning behind me, I head straight to Green Briar because what little patience I had wore thin overnight. Sleep starved and in need of answers, I peel open the heavy barn doors to find JD tending to his morning chores. He is shirtless and in jogging pants. His baseball cap is turned backwards, and his skin is still glistening from a morning run. For a moment, I ponder his muscled torso. I admire JD for the dedication it takes on his part to acquire a physique that allows him to make a living riding raging bulls.

This cowboy certainly is committed – to his body and riding bulls that is, certainly not to women.

Taking notice of me hovering between the doors, JD addresses me with a nod and a once over before dumping a scoop of grain into Faith's feeder.

"You're looking so hot this morning, I wish I were an oven mitt," he calls from mid-aisle.

His comment annoys me, but I give myself permission to look anyway. JD has the type of body that romance novels are made of and certainly not the kind of sculpted male form a woman gets to see very often in reality. My appreciative eyes sweep over him.

Catching my gaze, JD turns his shirtless torso toward me. With a sinister grin, he flexes his arm muscles, twisting just right so a wave of ripples cascade over his washboard stomach. I look away quickly, but not fast enough.

"You like these?" he asks, running a finger over each abdominal muscle, tracing their peaks and valleys. "You do … don't you, Devon? Caught 'cha lookin'. Didn't I now? Why don't you come on over here? Let me carry you outta this barn." JD opens his arms, waistband of his sweatpants hanging dangerously low, and starts strolling down the aisle toward me.

"Knock it off, JD," I scold, strutting into the barn toward Faith's stall. Putting JD's body out of mind, I place a palm to my mare's forehead as she devours her breakfast. I feel a little mean when JD's megawatt smile fades.

"What's with the sour mood, Devon?" JD grunts.

"Where is he, JD?"

"I can't say," he responds, shrugging his shoulders then making his way down the aisle, dumping the rest of the grain rations as he goes.

I follow him.

"Do you really want to send me out there on a wild goose chase? I'm going after him no matter what. I *have* to talk to him, JD," I press.

"Why do you keep wasting your time on him, Devon? He's broken. Somethin' snapped when Madison died. He's not the same guy."

I tense. It is the first time I've heard anyone say her name. I didn't even know it until JD uttered it just now.

Madison. That was her name. McKennon's wife's name was Madison.

"I don't want the man he was, JD. I want the man he is for me *now*," I continue, putting her name out of mind.

JD shoves his hands in the pockets of his sweatpants, pulling the elastic even lower, exposing a chiseled 'V' and a tuft of hair that turns my cheeks pink. The exposure forces me to look away again.

"You're breakin' my heart, Devon. Don't know why you wanna put yourself through the agony. I shouldn't even consider helping you on this."

I know my friend well though. There is hope. I can tell he is mulling it over because he is gnawing on his cheek like he always does when he's considering something.

"Please, JD," I plea.

"Fine," he huffs. "Don't know why I even care anymore anyway. He's at the Tumbleweed Inn. It's not far from here, just off of the interstate."

"What's the room number?"

"Ah, come on, Devon."

"Cough it up, JD. I know you know where he is."

"You wanna see me skinned?"

I tap my foot impatiently.

"He's not gonna like this," JD continues, adjusting his baseball hat. "I don't think you should go after him. You don't know how he can get."

"That's not for you to decide. I need to see for myself the condition he's in. He can reject me or accept me when I get there. You didn't tell me any of this when you probably should have. You did your best to warn me off from McKennon, but now I am invested, JD. I can't just turn it off."

"Aw, shucks. I told you it wasn't my story to tell."

"Tell me now." I stare at him, hands planted on my hips. "What room is he in, JD?" JD chews his cheek again.

"He's gonna have my hide for this. The room's 323. You probably should know that the number represents the month and day of their anniversary. He always asks for that room number. There's something else," JD pauses and clears his throat. "Figurin' I should tell you that I am McKennon's brother-in-law, too. I'm the one he calls when he's off on some bender."

A pang of pain reaches my heart, and I swallow hard. Now I know her name, the date she married him, and why it always occurred to me that McKennon and JD had a mysterious connection. She was their common bond. Pushing off the thought, I hug JD.

"Thank you," I mutter near his ear.

"I'll be here when you need me," he responds. I hear the want. It is heavy on his lips.

Suddenly, I am very aware of my palms on the hot bare skin of his muscular shoulder blades. I shame myself for our proximity. I never intended to encourage any advances.

"McKennon … he … he just left you here. He'll do it again and again. Me … I could be good for you," JD whispers, hopeful. I resist as he pulls me to him a little too tightly. I can feel his warm biceps flex around me and the firmness of his naked chest as he takes a deep breath of me in.

This has to stop.

I wiggle from his grasp, hold him at a distance by his broad, tanned shoulders, and shake my head slowly, sadly, from side to side.

Maybe in another life. Maybe at a different time, but now … no. No, JD can't be good for me. Not now, not ever because my heart is with McKennon. I only want McKennon. Today, tomorrow, forever … wherever he is.

"OK, Devon. Have it your way," JD mumbles, folding his arms around his torso, gripping his elbows.

"I'm always going to be your friend, JD. Just nothing more. I'm sorry." I am a little sad and a lot relieved when he won't meet my eyes. "I'm always going to be your friend," I repeat. "I promise you that." I start to leave, but stop to give JD's shoulder a reassuring squeeze, then I jog out into the daylight toward my car.

I know what I have to do to bring McKennon back.

CHAPTER 3

DEVON

Coasting off the freeway, I spot the Tumbleweed Inn at the bottom of the exit ramp. It's not the sort of place I thought I'd ever visit. I swallow hard, surveying the trash-littered parking lot lined with semi-trucks. There'll be no luxurious chandelier lobby or ornate carpeted hallways in this place. Visions of highway murder movies flash though my mind. Clenching my teeth, I muster my confidence and pull in.

If I'm going lose him, I might as well have him at least once.

I circle the motel, studying the corroded plaques adhered to each exterior room. Spying room 323, I glide my little import into a parking space just outside the royal blue metal door, paint chipped and peeling. My pulse increases when I notice it is severely dented on the bottom. My imagination clicks into action, and suddenly I'm envisioning the steel-toed boot of an angry ax murderer trying to kick the door in to get to McKennon.

Stepping out onto the potholed asphalt, I assess the landscaping overrun with weeds and tighten the waist belt of my trench coat. This isn't exactly how I'd imagined we'd spend this particular moment together. I pop the collar and steal a moment to peek inside. The smooth satin strap of my fire engine red bra reminds me of what I've come here for. I realize that it doesn't matter where we are, just that we do. I smile as the wash rack incident floods my memory. I close my eyes for a moment and bite my lip remembering McKennon's rugged body pressed against me.

Yes … this will jolt his memory of us and bring him home to Green Briar!

Heart racing, I step to the door, an electric current creeping at my skin inside the long coat, and let my knuckles fall on its cool exterior.

McKennon is in there.

CHAPTER 4

MCKENNON

I thread my fingers through her hair and stroke the peach skin of her soft shoulder. She hums the lovely sound. That blissful purr she always makes at my touch. Her scent is alive and well in my bed. She begins to roll over, coming ever closer to me, and I feel my constricted heart expand. I long to see her face as she shifts in the sheets. I wait patiently watching her silky tresses fall across her back in waves with her slight movements.

I anticipate this moment every time. Just as her face lifts above her shoulder, and I hope to meet her lips with mine, the covers become a dark, angry whirlpool, folding her in until a spiraling ocean at the center of the mattress engulfs her. The evil tide pulls her from my grasp, from our bed, and the black sea opens, pouring out onto the dirt floor in that damn show pen.

From the eye of the hurricane, I see her, expression still soft and sweet. Until her eyes meet mine in the shadows of his hulking belly. She is crushed beneath him. Her lovely, icy irises expand and contract melting into clear tears. They stream from her eyes and dampen the ground around them, feeding the rushing ocean that steals her from me time and time again. She pets the beast, a slight smile on her lips and a faraway look in her eyes. She whispers that she loves me. The words sound the same as they did the last time, and they echo and echo in my mind until an angry tidal wave crashes into me.

As I am dragged from the bed, I lose sight of her. I flail in the riptide and am sucked back, thrashed in many directions. I can't find my breath. The relentless current lashes me to and fro until I am thrust to the surface. I am gasping for air, grasping for her. Suddenly, I've landed, and I'm on a stagecoach running away, wild and blind. I notice the reins are in my hands, and every horse from our barn is on the other end. I finally see her again. She is in her white flowing wedding dress, her feet hovering above the grass, directing our runaway horses toward cliffs.

I know it isn't her. It is her ghost. I charge our horses forward anyway. The leathers crack on our show horses' backs. Faster. I want to catch her. Just as I am within reach, she disappears again. She flutters away like a bird to the clouds. We go over the cliff. I let go of the reins and take all of our horses with me. I should care about what will happen to them, but I don't feel anything as their loose leathers whip my face until we are all bunched up crashing into the rocks. I hear our horses cry out, but I am silent. I welcome death. It is the only way I can see her again. I wait for the warm nothing to come, but it doesn't.

I've awakened. I always awaken. The dream keeps coming. The same dream over and over. I constantly hope that one day the dream will end – that I won't wake up, and maybe Madison will finally be there. Only then will I see her again. Until then, I am afraid my key might always be in the ignition.

CHAPTER 5

In my haze, I vaguely realize there's a rasp at my door. I swing my heavy legs off the bed and find the floor. It's hard to swallow … the alcohol is thick, leaden on my tongue, the dream still alive and real in my pulsing head.

"Just a minute," I call out. My voice is hoarse. I whisk the small plastic alarm clock from the nightstand and focus my dry eyes on the red digital numbers. I've slept all day again.

"Who could be here?" I wonder aloud.

I dive into the bathroom. I stick my mouth under the faucet and take a long drink. The water is lukewarm and tastes metallic. I splash some of it on my face, smooth my hair, and hover in the mirror for a moment, not recognizing my reflection. I look terrible, my eyes bloodshot and yellowed.

I'm not the cowboy I used to be.

Spying the little bottle of mouthwash by the sink, I crack the top and swish it around in my mouth. I pull a white shirt over my head. It smells like Green Briar, and my gut turns. I spit the green minty liquid down the drain. The knock comes again. This time more intensely.

Who could be here? Had I gone off and done something in my stupor? Should I prepare myself for a pop in the nose if I open that door?

I figure whatever's coming my way, I surely deserve so I crack the door open, barefoot, still in last night's blue jeans. I am stunned at what is on the other side.

What is she doing here? How does she know where I am? God, it's so good to see her.

Suddenly, I'm angry, embarrassed and moved all at the same time. I open my mouth and start to speak.

"Did JD –" I begin. I don't mean to sound panicked, but my surprise at her arrival is evident.

"Shhh," Devon responds. I hover there as her eyes wander over me, and I register the slight bewilderment in her expression. She's never seen me like this before. I struggle with the chain on the other side of the door. My fingers are trembling. I can't wait to let her in. I never dreamed I would feel this way about a woman ever again while on this earth.

I fling the door open ready to speak, to defend myself, to explain, to apologize, to make excuses for my bad behavior, for the condition I'm in, but she just puts a finger to my lips and slips up close to me. Her smile is sweet, her energy is warm, and she smells like flowers and sunshine. She is fresh air in this awful space. Suddenly, there is a lump in my throat that I can't seem to swallow. I don't know what comes over me, but I have to hug her. We don't speak and are idle in our reunion for a tick of the clock. Then I can't control myself any longer. I dive at her, leading us into a wild kiss. Her lips are just as I remembered, only more urgent this time, her breath sweet.

She's missed me … I think.

I fist a hand in her long, soft hair and wrap an arm around her waist, clutching her diminutive frame closer. My heart swells when a tiny gasp escapes her. Her hands wander up beneath my T-shirt, nails smarting my skin in the best kind of way, and I feel a wave of desire rise. Thunder in my veins, my fingers fumble toward the belt at her waist. It's clear she has come here for something more than an explanation of where I'd gone, why I'd left her. I grin, letting the realization set in. Devon's big brown eyes grow large, a little bashful even, at my discovery. I loosen the knot hastily, hardly in control of myself, a surge burning through the front of my jeans.

She has come here to seduce me.

I take a deep breath and open Devon's coat. Peeling the trench coat away, I push it from her shoulders, and it falls to the floor, puddling around her ankles. There she is, standing in only her bra and panties. My eyes widen as they walk all over her. At once, I am taken aback and turned on by her brazen actions. I graze my fingertips across her stomach, up and over her bra, soft, red, lacy. The memories from our early days at Green Briar rush at me like the water in that wash stall did.

Speechless, I inhale, tip my head and dive toward her again. I can't help but kiss her deeply, urgently, all of me wanting her, wanting to be lost inside her. I can tell her lips can't get enough of mine as we twist our mouths in warm, welcomed unison.

"Daring Devon," I say, momentarily breaking from her lips and brushing her hair behind her shoulders, taking her in. I let my fingers slip through her tresses and lightly trace her shoulders. She doesn't say a word. She simply holds my stare. Devon's quiet confidence is enticing. I feel like I can see her soul. She is so beautiful standing there in her red under things and determined to unravel me.

My eyes trail her body appreciatively. This is the first time I've really unabashedly looked at this woman. Her cheeks are flushed, her lips slightly parted, her big eyes warm and dreamy. As my gaze sweeps over her sweet, peach skin, I fight to contain myself. It is almost too much to bear when I take in the sight of her breasts, two perfect swells supported by her lacy, racy lingerie.

Fully in the moment for the first time in a long while, I realize I want this to happen more than anything. I want to pick her up and feel her wrap her strong, lean, equestrian legs around my waist. I want to take her to the bed and lay her down. I want to remove those lacy things so I can slowly press my lips to every part of her beautiful body. I want to become one with her, take her as mine for the first time.

I ache to turn my belt loose as my eyes continue their journey, traveling over her stomach, around the curve of her hips, across the red satin of her panties, down her athletic legs, ending in cow-girl boots.

Those boots! Why did she have to wear the damn boots? Why had I even given them to her in the first place?

I feel a fierce electric jolt to my heart. I back away from Devon as Madison returns to me.

"I – I – I can't do this," I sputter as the shame returns. I scan the dive motel room I've been holed up in. I remember my wife, recall the dream and become present to the alcohol still on my breath.

"Oh," Devon whispers. I sense she's suddenly embarrassed, unsure of her decision to come here. Her eyes search the floor.

Frozen, I just look at her lovely exposed body, her trim waistline calling to me. I want to grab her hips and draw her petite frame to all of mine again. I want to lay her down so badly. But … I know I have to send her away before things get out of hand. Still, I owe her something, some sort of response.

"Not now anyway," I manage through clenched teeth. "There's somethin' I have to take care of." I scoop up the coat at her feet. I have to cover her up, or I may not be able to hold out. I drape it over her exposed shoulders, and she fists her hands around the collar, pulling the material closed around her body. I can't be with Devon like this, not in this awful place, not in this negative state of mind. She deserves something more, special, better …

"I have to go," she murmurs, hurt evident in her eyes. "Coming here was a mistake. I am going to try to believe it's not forever. It's just for now."

"Wait," I croak, hooking her by the elbow as she scrambles to leave. I have to hold her back. I need to try and explain. She tenses at my touch, but then she sighs and turns to face me. Relief washes over me.

"There's somethin' I have to do," I repeat, reaching out to touch her cheek. Cupping her face, I caress her skin with my thumb, hoping she realizes that I'm not rejecting her. I am rejecting the time, the place. Frustrated, I recognize I don't have the words to make this right. I'm not able to say the things I know she needs to hear.

At least there is some comfort in knowing that Devon feels as strongly for me as I do for her. I want to try on life again with her so desperately, but I need to put the demons away. I'm not free. I quickly, gently kiss her flushed cheek. She closes her eyes and removes my hand from her face. Flashing me a ghost of a smile, she turns to go.

"Goodbye, McKennon," she utters, twisting the doorknob.

I am immobile as I watch her leave. I didn't ask her what she really wanted. My heart tells me to catch her and beg her not to go, but my head tells me it isn't the right thing to do. Not now anyway. Right now, I have to create as much space between us as I can. I am being cruel to be kind. I have to let her go just like she said, 'not forever, but for now.' The beating organ behind my chest clenches as she slips through the crack and closes the heavy door behind her. I hang my head and slide the chain back in place to keep myself in. I am alone again with my heavy heart in this musty, old motel room, air stale with spilt liquor and the filth of past cigarettes filtering through my lungs.

I may be turning her away now, but I know I will eventually come back to what I need – Devon.

CHAPTER 6

S itting in the saloon's parking lot, neon lights flashing, my cell rings for what feels like the 50th time. I recognize the number. I sigh and throw the phone into the glove box.

Right now, I'm looking to get lost, not found.

I just sent away any hope for a future and the best thing that happened to me since I lost my wife. I'm in no mood for talking. I slam my truck door behind me and march toward the front door. It feels good to get out of that dank motel room, even if I am only a few miles up the road.

I put my Stetson upside down on the bar top. I place it on its crown just like my uncle taught me. It's an old habit, drilled into me. 'It's good luck,' he'd tell me. 'It ruins the bend in the brim if you set it down the opposite way.' He was the only father figure I'd ever known, and I'd been slapped silly a time or two for forgetting that last part in his presence. I order a whiskey and see her coming from a mile away.

"Hi there, cowboy," she purrs, batting her heavily blackened lashes.

"Not interested," I reply.

"Oh, don't worry. I see your wedding ring. Just wonderin' what you're all somber about is all. You look so lonesome, and I'm good company. So tell me, what happened?" she presses, running a finger under the collar of my shirt.

The bartender delivers my drink. I eye her and slump over my glass, pulling it closer to me, a message that she should back off.

"Oh, you're a prickly cowboy, aren't you?" she asks, tapping a finger to red lips. "Let's see now. She left you tonight, didn't she?"

I can't believe she actually has the nerve to ask me this. My blood pumps behind my eyes. Devon's retreat is all too fresh in my memory.

"No!" I holler at her. "Like I said, not interested in you or in talkin'!"

I shoot my drink.

"Hey cowboy," calls the bartender. "Keep it down or I'll have Big Bart over there escort you outta here." He pumps his fat thumb over his shoulder, toward the bouncer coveting the front door.

I examine Big Bart.

No way.

I decide to cool it. I smile and figure it wise to apologize to the barfly.

"Apologies, miss," I say with a jut of my chin, hoping she'll move on.

"Oh. Now I've got it," she spews. "Good looking fella like you? Probably have fillies throwin' themselves at you all the time. Couldn't resist that sweet young meat, could ya?"

Now she's waving a fluorescent orange traffic cone fingernail at me?

"Threw you out, didn't she? You bad boy! You dirty dog! Just look at those baby blues on you!" I grit my teeth as she sucks through hers, all jagged, making the *tisk, tisk* sound of a disapproving mother.

I have no desire to explain myself to a pleather-clad lounge lizard, so I just glare at her and call for another drink. Shifting my attention from the intrusive wench, I instruct the bartender to leave what's left of the bottle. It's a lot. Hesitating, he eyes me then Big Bart.

"You'll have no trouble from me, sir. Just leave the bottle," I growl, sliding him a large bill. Slipping my spot in his grimy apron pocket, he obliges and leaves the whiskey. I fill my glass to the tippy top and turn a cold shoulder to the broad who started all the commotion in the first place. I suck the drink down then pour another and another in silence. She finally gets bored with the lack of dialogue.

"Your loss," she grumbles, bashing me in the back with her boney elbow as she passes. A lesser man might be tempted to backhand her. This is the sort of thing that happens often in this kind of establishment though, so I've come to expect this type of interaction here. No skin off my knee. It's kinda why I like the place. It reminds me that I'm not the only broken one wandering around these parts. I chuckle watching her move on to a beer-bellied bearded man in a trucker cap at the other end of the bar.

Poor chap.

Once the buzz settles in, I feel content. I am alone at last. I drag the glass bottle toward me, and the brown liquid sloshes inside. All I want are my memories and this bottle of booze. I'm only interested in drinking whiskey until my mind's gone. I'm puttin' my emotions to the side tonight – women, family, love, horses – the intention is to make it all blur, at least temporarily.

CHAPTER 7

I 'll never forget the first time I spoke to my wife. Oh, I'd seen her around, way before we ever exchanged words. No doubt, the woman was impossible to miss.

She looked like a supermodel. She had long, thick blonde hair falling down her back. It landed just above her waist. The woman had big pouty, plump, perfect, pink lips. Any cowboy would clamor to kiss them. And those icy blue eyes of hers were showstoppers indeed. If they happened to land on you, they'd freeze you stone cold in your tracks, then melt you to mush in the same instant. She had the kind of stare that you'd fantasize about, but when those eyes finally fell on you, they turned a confident, cocky cowboy straight coward and all hot under the collar in an instant. The first time Madison's eyes happened upon me, I wanted to slither away fast like a rattler diving into its hole.

She was the queen of the horse show scene, always adorned in one-of-a-kind outfits and seated on the best mounts. She looked like she was from another place, somewhere exotic. Even though I'd taken notice of her looks, it was actually the quality of her animals that I'd noticed and truly appreciated first.

She had a different horse, (a different and obviously very expensive horse), for each event: showmanship, hunt seat, Western, trail, and even the speed classes. Yep, the cowgirl did it all. And apparently had it all, too.

Madison McCall was born with the Western silver spoons of silver spoons in her mouth. It was just there, dangling out of her perfect lips for all of us lesser beings to drool over. Her daddy owned the country's largest Western apparel company and the biggest auto dealership in the county. He sold the kind of clothes and the type of trucks I always dreamed of owning.

I quickly learned that her father, Sterling McCall, was the kind of man that I'd never be. I wanted to write his daughter off as spoiled, unapproachable and not my type. Her blood ran too rich. It was in my best interest not to pursue someone like Madison McCall. Trouble was the woman intrigued me. I knew all too well that, to a family like the McCalls, I would probably appear a penniless ass, all rodeo and ego, too fresh off the circuit to take a relationship, (or anything else for that matter), seriously.

It was kinda true, too. I'd just given up bronc bustin' to take a real, more steady shot at training Quarter Horses. A buddy of mine, Brody, had gotten out of rodeoin' and landed a pretty good gig with an up-and-coming training facility. He was getting lucky doing it, and he was willing to hook me up with an opportunity to give an apprenticeship a go.

Hadn't been in town more than a month or two the first time I spoke to my future wife. I spotted Madison perched on a barstool at a local watering hole. She looked trapped, semi-circled like prey by a crowd of men, hovering over her, looking for their way in. I was pretty sure they were hitting on her. Why wouldn't they be? She had it all: beauty, deep pockets, family businesses, nice ponies. As I approached the gathering, it appeared that she looked uncomfortable.

As usual, McKennon to the rescue, or somethin' like that anyway. I figured it couldn't hurt to do a temperature check by interjecting a little good ol' boy humor.

"Don't you know only the best goes between those legs, boys?" I asked, angling myself between the sharks and Madison. "Think y'all might be a little outta your league here," I continued, stepping up to the bar, separating the crowd of men from the stool Madison was seated on with my physical presence.

Madison shot me a 'how dare you talk about me like that' look. It was the type of look that could cause a scuffle if one of her admirers felt compelled to defend her.

I sized up the other cowboys, preparing for a possible rumble. Bull riders. I could tell by their stature. Short, cocky, drunk. I felt confident I could fend for myself against this gang. I was tall and lanky, a size better suited to bronc bustin' than taming bulls. With my wingspan, I'd be able to connect with at least a couple of their jaws before they even saw me coming.

"And how do you figure you know anything about me, cowboy?" She questioned, eyes like darts.

I liked the glint in her eyes. For me, it started there. It made me feel hot. That look of hers was enough to hook me, make me want to know more. She was interested, too. I knew it so I dropped my best line, the one that's worked dozens of times before.

"What kind of horse do you have, miss?" I asked.

Of course, I already knew which horses she rode. I admired all of the perfect specimens she owned. Against my better judgment, I'd been studying Madison from afar, growing increasingly more intrigued. Though it appeared she was an expert at every event *and* I never grew tired of seeing her in those skintight English breeches, it was watching her run the barrels that I loved most. Barrel racing was when she was all wild, free and unrestrained. It was when she was turning them that I thought this stranger looked most beautiful in blue jeans. A grin would always tug at my lips when she hollered out 'Get!' pumping her rein hand, clutching the saddle horn then blurring past me on the way home from the barrels to the finish line. Watching her in that event sent a shiver up my spine. Never felt like that about a girl before Madison McCall.

What struck me most was how her mounts always sensed her, ears pricked, tails flowing out behind them. I was in awe at how the horses seemed to intuitively know what she wanted. Her barrel mount never failed to bring the speed when she asked for more. I preferred Madison that way rather than the buttoned up, regal, polished version of herself that she most often presented.

"How do you know I have a horse?" she demanded, straightening on her stool.

"I can smell it on ya," I lobbed back, raising an eyebrow.

"I'll have you know my brother over there won't like hearing that you've been disrespecting me," Madison warned, gesturing to a pool table off in the distance.

Paying her threat and the brother no mind, I leaned in closer near her cheek. "I'm not disrespecting, miss, just tellin' it like it is. I've seen you around. Know who your daddy is. Know the pedigree of the horses you ride. I figured it was good karma savin' these poor chaps a few bucks. It's not fair for them to spend their winnins' on something they'll never win."

The bartender delivered my drink. I raised my glass to Madison's admirers with a smirk.

"You don't know a thing about me, cowboy," she huffed, visibly bruised by my assessment.

"No, ma'am, you're right. Don't know a thing about 'cha, and I intend to keep it that way." I tipped my Stetson, sucked back my drink, placed my shot glass on the bar and smiled at her.

"Screw you, cowboy," Madison said, hopping off her stool to size me up. I almost took a step back, but didn't want to give her the satisfaction. This girl wasn't tall, but her presence was *big*. I looked around to see if anyone was paying us any mind. The bull riders had meandered off while Madison and I were crossing swords.

"Give your brother my regards," I said, bending my brim. "I don't think those boys will be bothering with you anymore. You can thank me another time." I pulled my wallet from my back pocket and raised a finger in the air signaling for my tab. I didn't even want another drink that evening. I did my best to pretend I wasn't interested in her reaction, but I couldn't help noticing that something about Madison's expression seemed both relieved and peeved.

"Didn't ask for your help, kind sir. Please, keep it to yourself next time will ya, cowboy? I don't need savin'. Got a daddy and a brother for that kinda stuff. That's enough male dominance for me," she barked over her shoulder, marching toward her brother at the pool table.

I paid my tab, left the bar and went straight for my truck. I clutched the steering wheel, mulling over what just happened. I wasn't sure why I did what I did or said what I said to Madison. I only knew that I felt a strange desire to look after the woman and maybe to bed her.

I was satisfied that I had moved the undesirable gang away from her, but there was also an unrecognizable fear, too. I wondered if my words had created more space than I had actually intended between us. I turned the key over in the ignition, and my truck roared to life. I was torn. I wanted to know more about this woman yet wanted nothing to do with her. I could smell the money and the trouble. It was like there was a toxic yet enchanting perfume to her skin, inviting but poisonous. I couldn't compete … didn't want to … especially since I was new to town, fresh off the rodeo circuit. Small towns had politics. I didn't know the lay of the land here. Didn't know how long I'd actually be around. I wasn't really interested in a challenge or in settling down for that matter. I was used to having buckle bunnies falling all around me.

I wouldn't know what to do with something as pristine as Madison. I was more at home with heavy makeup and broken souls.

I could tell Madison was different. She acted cowgirl tough, but something told me inside she was soft, fragile and perfect. I could break her, but I swore to myself I wouldn't because I promised myself I wouldn't even get to know her.

At this point in my life, I just wanted to feel good, no strings, be totally and completely detached – myself broken like the women I chose to be intimate with. I was bruised, broke, poppin' pills and soakin' my pain in whiskey.

This one, Madison, wasn't my type. She was too fancy and likely way too much work. Historically, I liked all natural country girls, back when I was interested in relationships. These days, I was more prone to choose the rodeo groupies. It was easier that way. No one got hurt, and we both got to feel good. I never had to explain that I didn't want a girlfriend. They knew it was just a good time. Rich girls never did it for me. High maintenance didn't interest me. I wanted to write Madison off, but something inside called to me. It told me that maybe she was different than she appeared. Maybe she could understand me.

I remember shaking my head at the thought of anyone understanding me, dragging the lever into gear, and hitting the gas to hightail it out of that parking lot.

But that's neither here nor there right now because she ended up being 'the one' and now she's dead. I killed her.

I am tortured. I can't forget the life I thought I would always have. I just want to drift away with the liquor and bathe in what is left of my wife. I lay my head in the crook of my arm and start to sob. I sure as hell don't care that I'm in a bar right now.

CHAPTER 8

"Hey, buddy. Can't do that in here. I'm gonna have to ask ya to leave."

Pulling my face from the crook of my arm, I wipe my eyes with the back of my hand and focus on Big Bart standing over me, arms crossed in front of his chest. He doesn't look mad. He almost looks empathic that I am so pathetic. I figure Big Bart's probably seen plenty of broken down men drinking at this bar. Come to think of it, maybe I've done this here before once or twice. I appreciate his empathy, find myself thanking heaven that he doesn't hand me a tissue.

"OK ... OK ... I'm movin' on." I raise my palms to show my surrender.

"You got someone to call, or am I gonna have to chuck you in the backseat of a cab?" he asks.

"Yeeesss, I've got someone ta call," I slur. I clench my eyes shut at my response.

I'm a mess again.

"Best be sure, I'll be watchin' you 'til you make that call, mister."

"Phone'sss in my truck," I respond.

"That's fine, but those keys enter the ignition, and I'll be callin' the cops before you know what hit 'cha."

"Roger that," I reply and slither off my stool.

I am back in the flashing neon light cast over the parking lot. I'm sitting behind the wheel with a more than half a bottle of whiskey in my gut. I rummage through the glove box for the phone and hit the only number I have saved on speed dial.

"Dude, are you OK?" JD answers, concerned.

"Can't drive," I mumble into the receiver.

"Did Devon come to see you?" he asks.

"Don't know … sure … she didn't drive my truck – *hiccup* – here." I'm not making any sense. The words won't come out right.

"McKennon, go back inside and sit down. I'll come get you."

I stagger back into the bar, battling a round of hiccups. Of course, JD knows where I am. It's where I always go.

Big Bart clutches me by the back of the neck when I come through the door again.

"Thought you were goin'," he barks.

"Ride'sss comin'," I manage.

"Fine. Sit here," Big Bart orders, slamming my wobbly body down in a corner booth. I rub the back of my neck and look up at him.

Man, he's a big man.

"Where's your keys, guy?"

I don't answer. I just produce the keys and hold them out for him to take. Big Bart swipes them from my fingers and clips them to the mass of keys linked to the thick leather belt beneath his protruding belly. It feels like ages later when JD appears, wearing his concern on his sleeve.

"This yours?" Big Bart asks, leading JD to me slumped in the corner. There's a pool of drool on the table.

Big Bart drags me out of the booth by a limp arm that I can't feel, and JD maneuvers himself under my other one. Together, they half-lead, half-drag my inebriated body out to my truck. Big Bart hoists me into the passenger seat and tosses JD my keys.

"Good luck, kid," Big Bart calls to JD before slamming me inside.

JD stares at me from behind the steering wheel. "Oh man, McKennon. Why are you doing this to yourself?"

"Don't know," I spit with effort.

"You can't keep doing this to us, to Devon, man. I'm worried about you."

I shrug and rest my forehead on the cool passenger side window.

"Don't act like you don't care, McKennon. I know you better than that. And you know she deserves better than this. They both do. What would Madison think about your behavior?"

I ignore him and put a hand over my mouth.

"Never mind," JD says, shifting my truck into gear. I reach over and grip his upper arm. He grabs the back of my hand in return. "It'll be OK, brother."

I fold my arms over my chest and beg the tears back. JD knows that, of course, he's going to deliver me to the same dump as usual. He manages to haul me into the motel room, number 323. I hear him call for another cab and close the door behind him. Hoping to have consumed enough alcohol to avoid the dream, I fall face first onto the crappy red comforter and fade to black.

CHAPTER 9

With the light of day, I return to consciousness from my miserable whiskey-soaked evening. I wake and roll off the lumpy mattress, tossing the mangled, sweaty sheets and the excruciating memories of Madison to the side. Taking a seat at the motel room's shifty, cheap two-top table, I twist the lid off a fresh bottle, pour myself a shot and throw it back.

"Hair of the dog!" I yell, flicking the liquor bottle. I show it my long middle finger, punctuating my hate for the stuff, my life and the situation.

I still can't deal with this even after so much time has passed. I have to realize she isn't ever coming back.

But can I?

The truth is death hit me like a freight train. It was the unexpectedness of it all that made it so unfathomable. The loss of my wife leveled me to the point that I feel almost dead myself. I'd give anything for just one more night with Madison. If I could have a last night to love all of her properly, just one more time, perhaps I wouldn't be so haunted. I'd whisper the words of love men sometimes forget to say out loud when they think they'll have endless tomorrows with their women.

"I promise if I had another chance, I'd recite the words I should have been saying all along to Madison. I'd say them all night long," I confide to the bottle. I pour another shot and point to the ceiling.

"Give me another chance," I holler to no one, nowhere. It isn't a prayer because I don't believe anymore. I put my palm to my heart, look up and clasp the glass. I toss another down the hatch. The alcohol is hot in my mouth and burns my throat all the way down. I hate it, I hate me, I just hate. It tastes terrible, but I want so badly to be numb to this pain. I welcome the warm nothing.

I have nothing.

Mornings are bad, but nights are always the worst. When I slip into sleep, the awful dream comes for me. Most often though, sleep simply eludes me. I lie there, turning over and over in my head the things I worry that I never said to Madison, the love I likely withheld. Then, even worse, I needle on the words I did say. The nasty words I buried and pretended I never uttered. I wasn't a perfect man. Madison knew that when she married me. There were times when I couldn't control my temper. I regret all those times because I also couldn't control my tongue. There were so many harsh words I never apologized for before I lost her. Worst of all, I regret the hatred I held for her father that I undeservingly punished her with.

Why couldn't he just have accepted me or tried to like me? Why couldn't he tolerate me even a little once I married his daughter? Why didn't he see I loved her more than anything?

Now I know why. It's crystal clear. It's because I wasn't good enough for her, never was. I didn't take care of her. I broke my vows. I let her down just as her father expected I would. And then I killed his daughter.

I'll never forget the ring of Sterling's voice in my ears when Madison told him I was the one.

'I'll not have you be with the likes of him and have my empire ruined! He's nobody from nowhere and not good enough for this family or for my daughter! He's a drifter, Madison. I'll bet he gets bored with you and is back on the road in under a year. Believe me, I know the rodeo boys. They can't be trusted with a woman's heart because they don't care about their own.'

When I think of his speech, the feelings of fury rise up like it happened just yesterday. He said all this with me standing right there in his barn, holding his daughter's hand. Those words where the hatchet that broke me, and he buried them deep in my chest.

Sterling was right after all. Thinking on it now, I was pretty hard to love back then. The rodeo circuit was a tough lifestyle. I lived on luck and winning, event to event, day to day, life was a blur of highways, truck stops and fairgrounds. If I wasn't winning, I was barely eating and took to sleeping in my old truck. I couldn't afford luxuries if I didn't finish my rides and make the placing with the paycheck. The lifestyle took its toll on me. I became angry, stern and, to be honest, I knew I wasn't much fun anymore. It's why I came to their little town in the first place. I was ready to start a new chapter training horses instead. In my not-so-distant rodeo days, the only times I actually felt good was when I was satisfying my own needs alone in a rest stop bathroom, magazine propped on the toilet seat, or in cheap motel rooms like this one with women I hardly knew and could quickly discard. With the ladies, I was always walking away, and with my competitors, I was always ready to pick a fight. I wasn't responsible for my actions. I put the blame on others for a poor ride, for an event lost, or for my missing the mark; then I went to bed with liquor or a lady. I didn't much care which one it was, just as long as it numbed my pain. That's why I tried to turn a new leaf taking the training apprenticeship Brody set me up with, and that choice eventually led me to Madison.

Madison – she changed everything about me.

Madison made life fun again. She was the breath of fresh air I didn't even know I needed, but somewhere deep inside lurked a feeling that I'd end up breaking her spirit. Madison's love helped me become a better man, but the bad boy in me always sneaked back into our relationship. When I was frustrated, the old side of me that so easily raised its voice would return. Each time, I knew whatever irked me wasn't her fault, but my pride would keep me from apologizing to her.

I wish I could change all of that now.

I was a lucky man. Madison knew how to forgive. Her forgiveness was the glue that held us together. She didn't hold grudges or make up stories. The woman knew that everything was temporary, that storms come and go. Like in any marriage, we basked in the good times and weathered the bad. In the heat of an argument, Madison would always tell me the same thing. I can still hear her clear as day. 'Not everyone or anything is perfect all the time – if ever, Ken. I don't have to like how you're being right now, but I love you anyway.' I just couldn't understand how she remained so controlled when we bickered, especially when I was all wild with emotion and loud with my words.

Madison allowed me my humanness and loved me despite my inadequacies. It was during our disagreements that Madison taught me to be a man most. She wouldn't engage with my episodes of rage. Our relationship was built on trust, on talking things through. It was rooted in the safety we discovered in each other's arms when we held each other close at night. We'd created our own family. We took care of each other. Our dreams, wishes, secrets, hopes, fears were shared, discussed. I had her back, and she had mine.

That is until I killed her.

I hate myself for telling her to shut up and ride the afternoon I put her on that damn horse. Against my better judgment, I urged her on when I knew she sensed the horse wasn't quite right. I plain ignored her intuition about horses. It was the sole reason why I fell for her in the first place, and then it became the sole reason why I lost her. Those awful, ugly, negative words of mine were the last she heard.

Madison was my home. I'd broken our trust. I paid the ulti-mate price. I wish I'd been different and told her that I was proud of her and that damn horse no matter what happened in the show ring, but I didn't. I was bitter toward her father and I wanted to win – so much so, that I put our love on the back burner and Madison in jeopardy on the back of that animal.

I was satisfied for the first time in my life after I married Madison. No more need for burnin' it down with just anyone. My wife had all the heat I needed and more. After Madison, I never had any interest in sowing my oats. I'd been there, done that dur-ing my rodeo heydays. She was it for me – a simple, imperfect man who happened to hit the lottery when she chose to take up with the likes of me. I relished the way I felt as her husband.

Whole. Complete. For once.

I loved the ritual and routine of it. In our union, I knew my duties and my place. We were partners in life. She was mine, the guesswork gone, but the passion never waned. I wanted her more every day. I still want her now even though she's gone.

A lesser man might try to replace his wife straight away, but not me. She was my life. She is my life still. I put my heart on the shelf the day I watched Madison take her last breath. I vowed to never love again. The thing with Devon came as a surprise. I thought I'd shut down the part of myself that is capable of love. I know Devon is the real deal, but she is competing with a ghost that will never go away. This may haunt me always.

Can Devon possibly live with that? Should we move forward, can she have room in her heart for Madison, too? What about a memory of my dead wife that might spark a smile across my face? What if it's one I may not want to explain? Is Devon that strong? Is that too much to even think of asking? Won't she think that I'll never fully be hers?

I pour another shot in hopes of eliminating my conflicted feelings. I want to avoid remembering the day I left Devon in my rearview or seeing my wife and that horse again and again in my mind's eye – all tangled in the reins.

For more than two years, my life has been charging ahead without me like in the dream. I'm on a spooked 12-horse stagecoach that's lost its driver, reins flailing out behind, galloping to nowhere, driven by a ghost. That ghost is Madison. She holds the whip. Just before she passed, I could actually see her pupils expand and contract. My heart hammered as she looked up at me. I watched the last bit of life leave her body until she was gone. It haunts me. Her death ruined me. I am afraid that I've fallen in love with the only thing I have left – reliving my memories of loving Madison.

Can Devon compete with a ghost?

I'm smart enough to know that when you can't get yourself in order, people leave you. If I were to even have a shot with Devon, I'd have to find my way back to the light after everything about me has turned dark … my thoughts, my mind, the conversations I have with myself, my views. I don't want Devon to reconsider her feelings for me, not now that I am ready to finally force myself to think about moving on, but I'd already left her twice in the most awful ways. I drove out of Green Briar without an explanation, then I left her standing there, exposed and untouched after her beautiful offer.

Am I still able to love? I am still able to love. I think.

I'm still breathing after all. Madison will be with me … always … somehow … for the man she helped me become. She is woven into the very fabric of who I am. Now I have to move forward and take the reins back from her ghost. Take the reins and control my life. It's been out of control for far too long. I need to try on this thing with Devon.

Is she waiting for me still?

CHAPTER 10

The next day, I call JD with a renewed sense of direction. I know what I have to do in order to free myself.

"Glad to hear you're still alive, dude. Need me to save you again?" JD teases.

I sense he is in good spirits and not holding a grudge about last night, but I'm in no mood for teasing. Today I am serious, so serious. I mean business.

"I've gotta end that animal, or this will haunt me forever, JD," I blurt into my cell.

"Your head ain't clear right now, McKennon. You're still in a whiskey haze. You don't know what you're sayin'."

"JD, listen to me. I haven't had a drink since last night."

"Ooooh. Big deal," he razzes. "Heard that one before."

"Listen ... I ... I can't live anymore if he's alive, and she's dead."

"Ken." JD's voice is heavy with concern.

When he utters the nickname, I grip the phone harder and clench my teeth.

"You know where he is, JD?" I ask.

"No. No. I don't know where he is. I did what you said. I just loaded him up and drove him to the first livestock auction I could find. Did it as fast as I could, too. Didn't even take a second look at the sign. All I could think about was getting back to you, so I dumped him there. Asked 'em to send a cashier's check and the sales receipt to Sophia."

I let his response linger for some time. I have to find the monstrous horse that murdered my wife. I'll track him down and put an end to this once and for all. However long it takes, even if I lose Devon in the process. I've kept her waiting long enough already. I'm not going to waste any more of her precious time. I consider my next response carefully.

"You there, bro?" JD asks

"Tell Devon I'm not coming back. Tell her I'm not ready."

"What? McKennon … don't do this. Hey, I'll come with you. How 'bout that? Tell me where you're goin'."

"Goodbye, JD." I hang up and spring into action before he can come after me.

With urgency, I pull out the contents of the motel drawers and stuff my sparse belongings into a duffle bag. I fish my pistol from the safe and open the chamber.

Empty. I slam the motel door behind me, march to my truck, toss my bag into the backseat, and turn the key in the ignition. I'm in need of bullets.

Outside of the gun range, I reload the chamber of my pistol in the parking lot. I'd taken the time to check my aim before hitting the road. At first, I felt out of practice, but once I shot the flimsy paper target many times through the chest and a final time in the head, I felt ready. Now there is only one thing on my mind, and it's revenge.

Sweet revenge will be mine.

I'm no longer thirsty for numbness. It's retribution I long for now. I'm finished looking for answers at the bottom of bottles. I've done that enough times. I finally understand there aren't any answers there. Sliding the safety on, I slip my piece beneath the

36

driver's seat, hit speed dial for the second time today and shift my truck into gear.

His phone rings only once before the pick up. "McKennon," he answers flatly.

"JD," I respond, matching his tone.

There is an awkward silence for a moment. I think we are both recollecting on how we'd left things the last time we talked. JD speaks first.

"I swung by the motel to check in on you, but it seems you've turned in the key to your room."

"Yep," I confirm. I'm being difficult for no reason.

"You comin' home then?"

"Nope. Not yet anyway."

"So … where you heading then?" JD asks. The boy has learned to be cool as a cucumber with me.

"Where's the place you dropped him? I need you to try and remember now." Instinct tells me that JD knows the name of the joint, but is withholding it in hopes I'll come back to Green Briar without causing a scuffle anywhere.

"McKennon, when are you going to stop? She's gone, man. Finding that horse and doing whatever it is you want to do to him ain't gonna bring Madison back."

"JD." I grit my teeth. "The name? I need to turn up the bill of sale to see who bought him."

"Why go all the way there, McKennon? Sophia's surely got the receipt. I told them to send it to Green Briar."

"This isn't her affair. She's not to be bothered with this. You clear about that, JD? I won't have Sophia upset, and I don't want it getting back to Devon either. I know how you like to share my whereabouts."

"Fine. Have it your way, McKennon. I took him to the Sugarville Livestock Auction. There. You happy now? Saddest thing you ever asked me to do. There have been some low moments between you and me, but that horse didn't belong there even after what happened. And you know it."

"Don't needle me, JD. This isn't your business."

"This is as much my business as anyone's. Madison was my sister, and Devon is my friend. Wish she were more, but all she cares about is you. I still don't get it. Guess I never will. What am I supposed to say if she asks me if you are ever coming back? I wouldn't know what to tell her. I'm certainly not telling her what you told me to tell her the last time we spoke. Those words will cause her heartbreak, and I won't be doing your dirty work on this one."

My thoughts darken as I picture JD telling Devon I'm not coming back and then consoling her. "Don't tell her anything," I bark, a jealous fire rising in my gut.

"Don't act like you don't care about her, McKennon. We can all see that you feel something again. Underneath it all, I reckon you want to love again. When are you gonna forgive yourself?"

"I'll be seein' you, JD." I hang up the phone.

CHAPTER 11

I resented the damn stallion from the beginning. Madison was the one who found him, and maybe I was a little jealous that I hadn't spotted a winning prospect for our new business as quickly as she had. She liked his bloodlines, so we went to scope him out. He was a surprisingly big yearling. We watched him for a while as he navigated the pasture. I was immediately repelled by the way he roughhoused with the smaller yearlings in the herd. Madison always encouraged open communication in our relationship, so I wasn't shy about sharing my aversion to his dominance before they even brought him out of the pasture. She told me she saw something in him though and urged me to consider him.

"We don't have to take him home today, Ken. Just look at him," she said. When I hesitated, she gave me her pouty lips and fluttered her eyelashes. "Pleeease." I grunted my acceptance, but wore a scowl. She planted a kiss on my disapproving cheek.

Of course I caved.

I wanted to give Madison everything she desired and prove I could give her better than her daddy did. Back then, I was more into proving myself to myself (and everybody else) rather than just loving my wife. I realize now maybe that was what I had right all along, my authentic, unwavering love for Madison McCall. If only I could have let go of the relentless need to affirm I was good enough for her.

"Ah, welcome to High Raven Ranch, Mr. and Mrs. Kelly," the portly owner said, putting his hand in mine. "I see you've been watching our latest crop. They are in need of some manners, but I think you'll be pleased with the prospects."

I didn't like the man's sunken eyes. Something hiding behind them made me uncomfortable. Still, we asked the breeder to bring the young stallion in from pasture for a closer look.

"That one?" he asked, concern touching his brow.

"He's the one I phoned you about," Madison added.

"Oh! Yes, yes," he said brightly, shifting gears. "That's right. You did mention him over the phone. Henry?" He nervously motioned to his head trainer, offering him the lead rope in his hand.

Without hesitation, Henry stepped forward and took the rope from the shaky hand of his boss. When he walked confidently into the pen, I relaxed a little, but the energy of the animal still made me uncomfortable. The horse flicked his ears forward and back as he eyed Henry swiftly approaching him. Something just didn't feel quite right. It was like the horse was readying himself for a battle to begin. I tried to loosen up, but my collar felt very tight. I remember tugging it away from my throat as I looked over to Madison up on her boot tips, arms tossed over the rail and wide-eyed. I attempted to busy myself with being distracted by her smile. I knew she was excited about this one.

Unfortunately, my hunch was confirmed, and it all happened suddenly. The horse came unraveled when the trainer closed their distance. His glossy coat gleamed in the sunlight as he tossed his head up then pinned his dark ears flat against his muscled neck and bared his teeth. In a furious burst, the animal, fierce and wild, reared up on his hind legs and lashed out his hooves. I was aghast as his front feet, one at a time, collided with the head of his trainer. The horse delivered a first and then a second blow to the man for merely attempting to clip the lead to his halter. The gashes later required 25 stitches each, and it took three lassos around the neck to drag the damn horse in from the field.

The wranglers pulled the resistant colt within reach and restrained him on the ends of their ropes. The trainer, holding a rag to his bleeding crown, threaded a stud chain through his halter with his free hand and over the horse's nose. In anger, he thrust down on the lead shank repeatedly, looking to inflict the same pain on the animal that no doubt he was feeling. The force with which he reprimanded the horse caused the colt's eyes to go white around the edges. As they rolled back in his head from the affliction, the colt released a guttural moan. Madison gasped, a hand to her mouth. The crash of that chain on bone made me cringe.

"Stop it! Please!" Madison called out.

I stepped forward and touched the man on his shoulder. I got him to cease his yanking, but he glared at me over his shoulder for the interruption. I removed my hand and took a step back as red flowed down his forehead.

I wondered what kind of operation they were running there. I could only assume by how easily Henry allowed his men to demonstrate such cruel behavior in front of guests that this type of punishment was a regular thing around the facility. It explained the aggression the horse asserted toward his peers in the pasture. His actions were probably an attempt to dominate other horses the way he was being dominated by the humans who interacted with him. The horse was all fear, flight, fight and instinct. He was clearly strong-willed.

After a lengthy explosive battle between horse and human, the colt finally stopped fighting. His coat was slick. His sides were expanding and contracting from exertion. My stomach twisted when I noticed blood trickling from his right nostril below the stud chain strewn over his nose. He stood stone still, darkened by sweat from the struggle, ears pinned. When Madison looked to me, I saw the plea in her eyes, so I hesitantly approached him. When I was within arm's length, the horse turned his head, an angry eye on me, and lunged. He snapped his jaw ready to take a piece out of me. I stopped in my tracks. I didn't need to see anymore.

It was then that I told Madison the horse was a monster in the making. I felt bad for the poor animal, but I didn't know if I could undo the trauma it seemed he'd already experienced in his short life at the hands of his so-called trainer. I didn't think a horse already demonstrating issues with people would make a good fit for our fledging new business. I was taken aback when she laughed me off with a wave of her hand, indicating she thought we could save him.

"He's just young, honey. And you, my handsome hubby, are a horse master. You've apprenticed with the best. I didn't wait all those months while you were away on your horse training world tour for nothing. I waited for you to learn what you felt like you needed to learn so we could start this business right." I'll never forget the look in her eyes as she gripped me firmly by the chin and planted a pillow-lipped kiss on my slightly open mouth. "I want this one. If anyone can tame him, it's you, Ken."

She was right after all. She had waited patiently. 'Give me three months, and I'll be back to make this business work,' I'd told her. We were barely newlyweds when I'd said this. And I *had* trained with the very best. I wanted a foundation in multiple disciplines. I studied the craft under their supervision in hunt seat, Western pleasure, reining, team penning, you name it. I worked mostly with professional Quarter Horse trainers, but it was under the supervision of an Olympic dressage trainer in Southern California that I felt like I had learned the most. As I developed my own training playbook, her method became the underpinning. Working with a trainer of that caliber never would have been possible without Sophia's introduction.

Thank heaven for Sophia. Always thank heaven for Sophia.

With this yearling, Madison meant business. I didn't protest. Flattery always worked on me, so my wife won that day. If Madison believed I could train the horse, then I'd give it all I had ... hell, maybe I'd even teach him how to pirouette and passage, some of dressage's toughest movements, just to show off in front of Sterling. I didn't have to like the animal; all I had to do was get the job done, although I would've preferred to like him at least a little. I had the same sour taste for the horse as I did for her father, and that frightened me.

I wanted Madison to have this horse, but my stomach turned when I handed over our money and was given his papers in return. His registered name was The Devil's in the Details. Even his name reflected his personality.

"We just bought the freakin' devil," I groaned, showing Madison his registration certificate. Madison just shook my comment off and put her hand under his chin.

"You're not a devil. Are you, handsome?" she said.

"So what are we gonna call him then?" I asked in return.

"What should we call you?" Madison purred to the horse.

"Devil ..." I said under my breath. "Devil horse. Perhaps Satan? Hold on. I've got it! How about Demon?"

Madison shot me a look.

"Well, that's what I'll be callin' him anyway," I affirmed. I wasn't budging on this one.

"He's just misunderstood, Ken. I can't believe you can't see that. It's not like you," Madison said, turning her back on me with a flip of her blonde ponytail.

"I'm not interested in seein' anyone get hurt, Madison. Not me. Certainly not you. He's a fine horse, but I don't know if I can change that temperament. Something's just not right with him. It's like he's all locked up in his mind. I can feel it."

"Oh, stop your worrying, Ken. Once we get him home, I think he'll turn into our little prince. In fact, I think he has a rather royal look to him."

I watched Madison tap her nail on her lips.

"Maybe we'll call him Prince. Wait. Let me think." Madison tapped her boot and ran a hand beneath his mane. The colt pulled away, uncertain of her, but not as violently as he had treated me or the other men that handled him. "Yes! Yes, that's it!" she exclaimed after a beat. "I'll call him Charming."

I shook my head and put my arm over my wife's shoulder.

"OK then. Charming it is. Anything for you, Madison."

We brought the monster home a week later, made a dang mess out of our horse trailer doing it, too. Took me weeks to weld the interior paneling back to original form. There were so many dents from that wicked beast's hooves. I reminded myself to trust Madison's intuition though. She had a special bond with horses, and I didn't see how this unruly one would be any different.

Boy, was I wrong about that.

As I started to work with him, there was nothing charming about Charming whatsoever. I stuck to calling him Demon.

CHAPTER 12

I roll down the window and spit out my stale gum. The air blasts my face, and I pass a ranch that reminds me of the McCall place. My mind flickers back to my first date with Madison and the first time I saw her family's spread. Sterling was on a business trip. The only time I was near Madison in the beginning was when her father was at work or out of town.

Cruisin' down the driveway of the McCall property in my beat-up truck, I couldn't help but whistle at the miles of rolling pasture, some lazy cattle lingering out in the distance. I came to later learn that Sterling only liked bulls for one thing ... as his steaks, and he liked them bloody. He made sure to keep a few beef cattle for his pleasure. He practiced his roping with them before they ended up on his plate.

The McCalls and their riches made me nervous. I wiped my hands on the thighs of my jeans to soak up the sweat in my palms as I approached their porch. The front door was open. When I got near enough, I heard a Johnny Cash tune. I looked up to see a second story curtain billow on the breeze. My heart fluttered when the flesh of the woman I was about to take out for a date flashed across the open frame. She was wearing only a white bra and jeans. Not willing to risk the label of voyeur, I looked away, took the front steps quickly and knocked on the screen door.

"Come on in," she called.

I opened the screen door with a creak and let myself in.

"Hey," she said from up the stairs. I couldn't see much of Madison. The only visible part of her was the drape of her long, yellow hair hanging over the railing edge.

"Hey," she said again, a little breathless. "I'm so sorry I'm runnin' late. I just can't seem to find a thing to wear. Mind takin' a seat on the couch, and I'll be down in a minute?"

"Uh … no problem," I said, looking around for a sofa. Nervously, I unbuttoned and rolled the sleeves of my newly-purchased and pressed plaid dress shirt up to my forearms.

I meandered into the room adjoining the parlor and sank down into a deep recliner. I set the cellophane-wrapped bouquet of daisies I'd purchased at the corner grocer on the table and examined the room from my seat. A gun case displayed several rifles in the corner, an enlarged photograph of her father with a shotgun at his shoulder holding up some dead birds, a set of Angus horns hung above the entrance and perhaps the same poor bull's hide was made for a rug under a thick mahogany coffee table, a huge flat screen television was mounted on the wall, beneath it shelves with framed photos of the family. In one of the frames, Madison as a little girl stood next to her childhood pony, several blue ribbons and a couple red down its reins. In another, her ghost-faced brother gripping the scruff of a sheep's neck fleece. It was a mutton busting shot at its best. There was a stiffly-posed family group picture that could have been taken in a department store's photography studio, and finally a picture of a man six feet in the air on the back of a bull. I didn't recognize that gent.

I still couldn't believe I was sitting in her house. Madison was the best damn thing I lucked into. It was not by my doing that I ended up there. A rodeo had come through town the weekend before, and I had gotten a call from a friend of mine, Sallie Mae. She told me she could get me into the competition on a bronc, guaranteed for a sure ride – more importantly, one that would get me in the money. But to do that, she'd need a favor in return. Never one to turn away quick rodeo money, I agreed to the favor without asking what it was. Little did I know, I would wind up in a charity cowboy auction where *I* was one of the prizes. I ended up going for a nice price, too.

Who bet on me? Well, it wasn't Madison exactly.

I'd seen her around after the bar incident, and it wasn't pretty. I'd acknowledge her with a tip of my hat. She'd give me the bird in return. At that time, it was clear that Madison McCall had a bad taste in her mouth for me. No matter though, my eyes always sought her out, hoping one day she'd return my gaze.

It was her friend Penny who cast the winning bid then transferred ownership of me over to Madison. Penny was a nice girl, too nice. She was always gawking at me during horse shows. After the whole thing was said and done, I just stood there as she cashed out, wondering what she had in store for me. I didn't know what I'd do with a girl like Penny. She barely reached my waist and didn't look a day over 14. I figured she'd never had a drink in her life. She must have noticed my uncertainty.

'Don't worry, cowboy. You're not for me. You're for my friend,' she'd said, pointing a munchkin finger at Madison whose eyes went wide when she caught us discussing her. My heart started to thud in my chest when my future wife looked away with a twist of her lips and a flip of that long blonde ponytail. I wondered what had I gotten myself into. Penny continued on to tell me that she had a 'feeling' about Madison and me, so she decided to intervene and set us off together.

What was a cowboy to do?

It was for charity and all, so there I sat on her couch, in Sterling's house, looking at all their expensive things, wondering what was destined for me. I shook my head. When I came to their little town, my only goal had been to stay as far away from the girl and her family as I could, but that was then. When I heard her gallop down the stairs, I was immediately up on my boots, flowers in hand.

"I hope this will do. I just couldn't decide on what to wear," she said, giving me a little smile and a spin. My eyes trailed her body. She looked perfect in red boots, a vintage tour T-shirt and hip-hugging jeans studded with blingy little jewels on the back pockets. My heart hammered as her eyes slivered. It seemed she already knew she'd hooked me. "Those for me, cowboy?" she asked, spying the daisies.

"Why, yes. They are," I said, turning the flowers toward her.

"Want some lemonade?" she asked, taking the bouquet.

"That'll do," I lied.

Lemonade?

I was hoping for something a little stronger, a little something to dull the nerves.

She took a deep breath of the flowers and peered at me through her long, dark lashes. "Daisies are my favorite," she purred. "How'd you guess?"

"Just lucky. I suppose," I answered, shrugging my shoulders. It was pretty much the least romantic response a man could have. I immediately wished I'd said something more suave.

Madison slivered her eyes again and nodded. "Hmm. Let me just put these in some water. I'll be right back." I watched her as she trotted off toward the kitchen, a wry grin spread across her red-stained lips just as she turned to go. I couldn't take my eyes off those back pockets.

I knew then I was a goner.

CHAPTER 13

When Madison came back into the room with our lemonade, I was still standing in the foyer with my hands shoved in my pockets, teetering back and forth on my boot tips and heels, and whistling to myself.

"So what do I call you?" she asked sweetly, handing over my glass.

It bit at my insides that she might not know my name. "Name's McKennon. McKennon Kelly." I took a sip of the lemonade, and my eyes widened at the taste. It was about half vodka.

"You like?" she inquired. "Didn't figure you for a tea and pastries type, cowboy."

She was sinister. I smiled at her. I was grateful to have a little liquid courage in my gut.

"Come on, Ken. I want to show you something."

I furrowed my eyebrows at being called Ken. No one had ever called me that before. I wasn't sure I liked it, but I let it go when she drained her drink, put her hands on her hips and tapped that little red cowgirl boot of hers on the wooden floor.

"Come on now. Never figured I'd out-drink you, cowboy. What 'cha waitin' for? Down the hatch!" she demanded. I eyed her and my full glass of said lemonade. "Don't worry, there's more where that came from," she assured, pulling a flask from her back pocket and shaking it at me, one eyebrow raised.

I liked this girl. Taking her cue, I chugged my drink and followed her lead out the front door into the summer sunshine.

"Where are we going?" I asked as the screen door banged behind us.

"I want you to meet my horses," she said simply.

The comment made me smile. I felt compelled to take her hand, but I didn't. Little did she know, this kind of date was my idea of perfection. I looked forward to meeting her super horses. I'd been studying them from afar for so long now. I couldn't wait to get up close to one of her beauties, let alone all of them.

We crossed the manicured yard to the McCall's crimson red barn flanked by lush green pastures. They definitely knew horses and how to maintain the integrity of their land. I could see the McCalls, (or whomever they paid to maintain the property), made sure to rotate the grazing. The pasture grass was plentiful. I felt my heart soften a little, taking in the picturesque landscape as we crossed the gravel drive to where the horses were.

The scent of hay and sawdust was heavy on the air as we entered the stable. Inside, 12 spacious box stalls housed the McCall herd. It wasn't a big barn, but it had all the bells and whistles: a wash rack, multiple trophy cases overlooking a silver laden tack room, a full service bathroom, chrome appendages at every stall front for leather halters engraved with each horse's name to hang from, and a covered arena for Madison to practice in. It extended off the back of the building, the dirt freshly turned, not a track in it. I was envious. Madison lived on a slice of horse lover's heaven. It was the kind of spread I had always fantasized about calling my own one day.

"These six are mine," Madison said, her fingers gliding down the shiny varnish of the stalls on the left side of the aisle.

Transitioning to the opposite side, she continued, "These three are my dad's. One is his Western pleasure prospect, one's for roping, and one's for trail riding. This one is my mom's, and this one is my brother's, but he doesn't ride much anymore."

"Oh?"

"JD likes bulls better than horses. He's always had rodeo dreams ever since he was a kid." My mind reflected back to the framed shot of her brother clinging to the sheep in their living room. "So we just put our guests on old Bell now. That mare is about as broke as they come. Anyone can ride her," she continued.

I sauntered up to Bell and put my hand under her chin. She blew breath in my face, and I smiled. "She's older, huh?" I asked, scratching the horse's neck.

"Yes. Bell was his childhood horse. Think she's in her 20s now. You know horses, huh?"

I nodded. She smiled then crossed back to her side of the aisle. *Did I just get Madison McCall's approval?*

"This one here is Remy. He likes his forelock groomed ... a lot," she explained, fishing something from the grooming kit near his stall. Remy's ears pricked to attention at the sight of the purple plastic in her hand. He stretched his head out and rested his chin on her shoulder as Madison ran the comb through the tresses between his ears. After a minute or so, she giggled and tucked the grooming utensil into the same back pocket that held the flask. She rubbed Remy's forehead. "There'll be more for you later, buddy. I've got a tour to do."

I happily trailed behind her as she excitedly guided me from stall to stall introducing me to Rosie, Pumpkin, then Trey. I took in how she stroked each one differently, and in turn, they each responded to her differently, just like each was specially trained for a different event. I wasn't even interested in the bling on her rear pockets anymore. I was interested in her, not bedding her, but *her*. Her expression was pure glee. Innocent. I was already in love with her because of the way she loved her horses. She was as at home with them as I was.

"And this one is Cash," she beamed, approaching the last stall in the row. In it, a solid bay Quarter Horse. He poked his head out of the open top portion of the stall door and softly nickered as she approached. "I know I'm not supposed to have favorites, so don't tell anyone I told you so, but he's mine. One of the reasons I picked him was because his registered name is Johnny's Ring of Fire. I just adore Johnny Cash. I have all of his albums. Cash here won me my first championship," she said, one hand resting on Cash's muscled neck, the other pointing toward the tack room. I followed her finger to the top shelf of one of the several trophy cases lining the walls of the room. My pulse raced as I eyed the golden spheres encircling a bronze horse statue topping the mammoth trophy.

Yes, Madison McCall certainly had it all.

"They all have their own personalities," she continued, massaging Cash's neck. The horse's eyes were hooded, relaxed at her touch. "I think they are more human than we give them credit for," she said, moving the forelock from Cash's eyes. I looked at her and felt a heat expanding from me reaching out toward her. We were eye-to-eye. I was disappointed when she suddenly looked away, bashful. It surprised me. Madison occurred to me as so cool and confident. This was her private space though, likely the place she was most herself, no façade, no way she had to be, just a girl with her horses. This was not the kind of place or girl that rodeo boys got to be in or near. Yet here I was, standing toe-to-toe with the goddess in her most private of cowgirl places.

"Want a sip?" she said, backing up a step and pulling the flask out of her rear pocket.

Maybe the girl needed some liquid courage like I did?

"Sure," I said, taking the silver container from her and putting it to my lips.

Whiskey this time? Was she looting her parent's liquor cabinet on account of me?

I couldn't help but wonder. I handed it back to her after taking a proper mouthful, feeling the burn as it slipped into my gullet. She took a fast pull herself and looked around nervously as she slipped it back into her pocket.

"I don't usually drink alcohol around my horses. They are all the buzz I need," she said, eyeing me carefully.

"We don't need to drink," I responded, again feeling that strange desire to hold her. I think she liked my answer because I saw a slight tug at the corner of her lips.

We continued to walk leisurely down the aisle, peering into the stalls one at a time admiring the horses. It was quiet, serene. That is until I broke the peacefulness, of course. "So who'd your father hire to find these equine masterpieces?" I had to ask. I knew I had a tinge of resentment on my tongue and didn't like myself for it.

"What do you mean, Ken?" she asked, rubbing her manicured, but unpainted nails on her thigh and examining them.

"You mean you picked them all out yourself?"

"Yes, I picked them myself. Are you shocked that a lady might have an eye for things equine? My daddy had nothing to do with it. I worked hard for these horses. Granted, my dad has a facility that helps me afford to keep them all, but I went to their breeders, to auction and analyzed them all myself, picked the ones with quality that I could afford from tending bar."

Madison McCall works?

I didn't see that one coming. I was impressed that she had earned them. They weren't just given. I couldn't help but wonder what bar she tended to. I didn't like the idea of that much, but decided to hold my tongue for another time.

"I'm impressed. Didn't mean to disrespect, miss. Ever."

"I am struggling with this one though," she said, leading me to another stall. "I could use some help with her. Penny said you've got instinct. I like instinct. Wanna help me with her, Ken?"

"Me? I'm just some guy off the rodeo. I'm just startin' out in horse trainin' for the show pen."

"I heard you taught that horse they asked you to train to do flying lead changes in a day and a half. Is that correct?"

"Well, yeah."

"I'd call that instinct and true talent. What would you call it?"

"Connection."

"Connection, huh? Even better. Come on. Let's get going with this connection stuff then," Madison said, tugging me by the elbow toward the stall.

I swallowed hard. I had just gotten myself involved with the McCalls.

CHAPTER 14

"Her name is Lyric," Madison said, putting a hand on her hip, pursing her lips and tilting her head slightly in examination of the animal. "And I haven't been able to get a hand on her. I'm hoping she'll grow up to be my new Western pleasure mount and eventually a broodmare like her mother. I'd like to retire Cash one of these days. He's earned the right to just take me on leisurely trail rides in his golden years. After all, he's spent years and years racking up points on the circuit. I've held him to a really strenuous show schedule."

I sauntered up behind Madison and stood close enough that I could almost feel her against me. Madison stood a little straighter at my proximity, but didn't move away. I peered into the stall, leaning over Madison's shoulder just enough to be able to see her smile. I knew that smile was going to be the one to nail me down. Taking notice of a tiny foal quivering in the corner behind her mother's bulging belly, I made a kissing noise with my mouth, and it sent the filly scurrying around the stall, scattering the shavings until they fluttered through the air like snow.

"Jumpy little thing, isn't she?" I said, tipping my cowboy hat back on my head.

"I can't get her to trust me. I've tried treats. I've tried just about everything I can think of. I'd like to start working with her before that fear of hers gets any worse. Think you could help me get a halter on her? Maybe teach her to lead? Lessen that instinct to run?" Madison asked, hopeful.

I looked at the tiny dark filly, all legs and lashes, blinking at me from behind her mother and pondered the request. "Ever consider just being with her?" I asked.

"How do you mean?"

"Just be with her," I repeated. Madison looked to me confused. I was always better at showing than telling. "Here like this." I moved from behind her then reached out and took Madison's hand. She immediately pulled it from mine. It was a reaction. I just stood there with my hand extended, palm open. I could sense she was working my touch out in her head. I was still as a statue watching her. Madison's recoiled hand hovered between us, then she thought the better of it, placing her warm palm back in mine. A smile tugged at my lips.

"Like I said, ever consider just being with her?" A glint of understanding crossed Madison's face.

"I'm sorry," she said, squeezing my hand

"Don't think anything of it, miss," I said, trying not to think of how soft her hand was in mine or how soft other parts of her might be. "Come," I assured, bringing her along as I opened the stall door with a squeak.

The filly took flight and raced a circle around the stall, kicking bedding into the air. I ignored the fearful actions of the young equine and led Madison to the opposite corner of the stall. I motioned toward the ground with a jut of my chin. Silently, we sat down in the deep bedding. After the filly settled back next to her mother, we chuckled to each other. Lyric peeked at us from behind her adolescent lashes, hiding beneath her mother's tail. I smiled at Madison, and the shared moment stretched. She bit her lower lip and dusted the brim of my cowboy hat. Following her lead, I picked out the stray pieces of shavings that had landed in her long blonde hair then brushed her hair over her shoulder.

Again, I felt compelled to bring her to me. I'd made out with cowgirls in barns before, but this time my heart thudded in my chest. This feeling was unusual. I contemplated shifting toward her in the bedding. Just as I was ready to make my move, Madison spoke, breaking the heaviness between us.

She took a deep breath and met my eyes. I was honed in on her. "My dream is to start my own breeding, buying and training business. My daddy thinks horse business is no business for a woman. I want to prove him wrong. Do you think that's crazy?" she asked. It was a whisper.

"I reckon you can do anything you set your mind to, Madison McCall." It was the truth. I was certain this woman could run a successful horse business of her own and so much more. And I liked her name on my lips. I put my hand on her thin shoulder and gave an assuring squeeze. "I'd bet on you."

"With a father like mine? Would you really?" she asked, shrugging her shoulders. Twisting her lips into a frown, she began again, "According to him, he owns this town, everyone and everything in it. No one goes against my daddy, especially not one of his own children."

"He sounds … err … intense," I said. Sensing her disappointment, I continued without thinking, "How about you never mind him. How's about I help you get that business going? We can start with this little lady here." I motioned towards Lyric who had started to explore a little farther from her mother.

"Really? You'll help me with her?" she responded, gleefully before the frown returned again. "My father's complicated. He doesn't much like men coming round the ranch … for me *or* for the horses."

"Well, what about when he's not around?" I asked.

"You mean it?" she asked with an arch of her eyebrow.

Hell yeah, I meant it. I'd muck every stall in this barn for free every day for the rest of my life just to be near Madison McCall.

"Yes," I said, trying to keep my voice cool.

"OK, Ken." I clenched my teeth at her calling me Ken again, but held my tongue.

If Madison wanted to call me Ken I could get used to it ... eventually.

"You be here every Monday and Thursday morning by 6:30 a.m. My dad holds early morning sales calls on those days with his staff. He'll be out the door by 6 a.m. We can work with her then."

"I can do that," I said with a smile.

"Can you get used to calling me boss?" she asked.

"Maybe," I said with an eyebrow arch of my own and a tip of my hat.

"Oh, and Ken? I don't really like to drink," she said, turning those clear and innocent eyes on me.

"I know," I answered.

"Do you want the rest of this?" she asked, holding the flask out to me.

I took it from her hand, twisted off the top and poured the contents into the sawdust next to me. I'd be content to sit here in this stall with her forever, but I knew it would come to an end. Handing the container back to her, I extended my other arm across Madison McCall's back. In return, she leaned into me, and I got that heavenly smile again.

"How's about we go on a proper date?" I asked.

"What? A real date? You don't like hanging out with me in a horse stall?" she teased.

"What are you doing tomorrow?" I pressed.

"Hmmm. Let me check my planner." She dragged her finger-tip across the palm of her hand. "Well, it says here that I'm going out with you, cowboy."

That's when it began. Madison and me against the world, the start of something beautiful. I didn't drink again except on the special occasion of our wedding day. I didn't have a desire for alcohol with Madison in my life.

That is until she died.

CHAPTER 15

"Where are we going?"

"It's a surprise," I said, helping Madison into my run-down truck. "Someday I'll have a better vehicle to chauffeur you around, miss. I promise." I tipped my Stetson and gave her a little grin.

"I'll hold you to that," she replied, holding my gaze a little longer than necessary. That look meant something. I couldn't be sure what though, so I took a step back.

Her eyes on me were so intimidating. My heart was pounding. I reminded myself that it was just conversation. When she winked at me, adjusting the rearview toward her to add some lipstick, I was finally able to let my breath go. I hadn't even realized I'd been holding it.

"I want to show you where I come from. What I used to do," I mustered once her attention was diverted.

"Oh, rodeoin'?"

"How'd you know I was planning on taking you to the rodeo?" It really was no secret that a rodeo was passing through town, but I feigned offense by putting my hand over my heart.

"I asked around about you, cowboy. I have friends in low places. I know you were a regular on the circuit. I know more about that lifestyle than you think."

"Is that so?" I asked, tipping my hat back and blinking at her sitting pretty in the front seat of my rust bucket. She didn't look like she belonged in there. Hurriedly, I shut her in and went to the other side. When I was situated behind the driver's seat, she continued.

"My daddy's family cut their teeth in the horse business through rodeoin'."

"Really? I'm interested, Miss McCall. Do tell."

"My daddy will have my hide for hanging around the likes of you. I can't wait for you to take me to your rodeo."

"I'm not scared of your father," I said through clamped teeth.

"Of course you aren't, Ken. You haven't met him yet. How about we save the sad story for another time."

"OK, Madison. We'll wait until you're ready to share." Her aversion to talking about Sterling McCall made me shift in my seat and grip the wheel tighter. I'd hold my tongue until she was ready to talk about it.

What had this man done to her?

We pulled into the busy lot, and my excitement to show Madison my world grew. I helped her out of my sad truck and led her through the bustle to the stands. We watched a few events, and I whispered the ins and outs of each one into her ear. She seemed to enjoy the rodeo, and it made me happy to answer her questions. I couldn't tell if she was asking me about the events because she didn't know the answers or if she just wanted to hear my take on the nature of things around there. She *had* mentioned that she knew a thing or two about rodeo. It was no matter to me what the truth was. I didn't really care one way or the other because she was interested in what I had to say. Madison McCall and I were really getting on, conversing.

"Now tell me, Ken, what's the event you were known for?"

When she shortened my name again, I furrowed my brow then quickly shifted my expression to a pleasant one. I was still getting used to the "Ken" thing, but it didn't bother me *too* much.

"My brother's got a thing for bulls, but something tells me that you're a little too tall to be riding bulls," she continued.

"Smart girl. You are correct. My build is better suited to the saddle bronc riding event."

"Oh, do tell me! What happens in saddle bronc riding?"

"Well, it goes something like this," I said, shifting on my pockets to face her. She smiled slightly and scooted a little closer to me. I could feel her thigh pressed against mine. I wanted to put a hand on her knee, but figured the better of it.

"The event evolved from the Old West days when true cowboys fought to tame wild horses to use on their cattle ranches," I told her.

"Do you agree with that kind of treatment of horses?" she asked, taken aback.

"No, no, not at all, miss. That way of dealin' with horses was back when most men worked against nature rather than with it by breaking horses rather than training them to work with us through connectedness. I chose saddle broncin' 'cause it is the most challenging rodeo event to master. I want to remember what they used to do to 'em so I never become that."

"They don't hurt the horses here, do they?" she asked. Madison looked down and smoothed her skirt in a sad sort of way.

"No. It's mostly for show, and the horses are wild, so they like the buckin'."

"OK. I guess I'm all right with it then," she said, meeting my eyes with her icy ones again. "How's it work though? How do you win?"

"Well, there is an element of style involved for the cowboy in order to get a good score. You see, a rider has to keep his toes turned outward, make a spurrin' motion consistently from shoulder to saddle, and appear to maintain balance. Y'know? A cowboy has to look like he is in control of his horse even when he's not. The horse is also judged on how well he bucks. It's all calculated into the overall score. Actually, it is similar to bull riding scoring if you follow it with your brother at all."

"Hmmm," she purred.

Turned on by her sexy sound and her interest in the subject, I babbled on. "If the rider touches any part of the horse or his body with his free hand at any time during his ride, he'll be disqualified."

I heard the loud speakers click on.

"Next up will be rodeo's classic event, saddle bronc riding!" I smiled as that familiar rodeo adrenaline kicked in, controlling me, begging me to gamble with my life for money. I loved the high I got from the try.

"You wait here, OK?"

"Wait. What? Where are you going?" she asked, brow furled. "You can't just leave a girl? If you haven't noticed, we are on a date here, Ken."

Suddenly, I felt bad for my way of thinking. I just wanted to impress her with one last saddle bronc win. I wanted Madison to see me in action at least once. As far as I could see, this was my last chance. I had an inkling that for her, I would hang up my spurs for good, at least my rodeoin' ones. There would be no more one-off rides after this one.

"Uh. I'm not leavin' you. I'm hopin' to show you what I can do. That is, if you'll let me." I smiled at her and bit my knuckle.

"What? Have you entered an event?" She looked around and put a hand to her chest.

I just smiled and nodded my head.

"You're gonna go ride one of those beasts? Now?"

"Yep. The horse training is going well and all, but I figured I'd make some fast cash off a good purse in the bronc bustin' event tonight. I suppose a little part of me wants to impress you, too. If it's all right with you, that is? Guessin' I shoulda asked if you minded before I entered. Note taken for next time, miss." I watched for signs of disapproval, readying to scratch my ride at the first blush of it. I was relieved when I saw the corners of her mouth turn up and her face brighten.

"Actually, I'm intrigued by all this, but mostly by you, cowboy. By all means, go. In fact, this makes me kind of hot." She arched an eyebrow, tipped her head to one side, pouted her so pretty lips and fanned her neck with the program.

"Hot?" I asked, tipping my Stetson to the back of my head with my finger. I knew my eyes widened at her response. I was sure it was exactly the reaction she had hoped for.

"Yes. Hot! I kinda like the fact that word of this will really piss off my daddy, too. First my momma, then JD, and now me all stolen by the big bad rodeo! Funny, I never figured I'd actually be goin' with a cowboy who does *real* rodeo." A little red flag went up in my mind, but I decided to ask about the family stuff later. More important things than her past were brewing between us at the moment. We were starting to talk about the future.

"Goin'?" I asked, getting kind of hot myself at the thought of Madison McCall as my steady. Amused, she stayed silent, simply sending me off with a smile and a flick of her wrist.

I pecked her on the check, and we both blushed before I loped down the steps, leaving Madison in the bleachers. I had to get my gear and win some money so I could win the girl.

CHAPTER 16

After a series of stretches, I zipped my chaps and rolled up my sleeves. The scores from the riders to go before me had been pretty good, but nothing exceptional. I was feeling confident because the numbers they put up were nothing I hadn't been able to beat before. I knew I'd pulled a good horse so coming out on top felt possible.

"You're looking limber, McKennon. Your go coming up soon?"

"Why, yes, it is," I said, pulling Sallie Mae into a big bear hug.

"Thought you hung up your spurs, cowboy," she said, lightly punching me in the chest. "We miss you around here. How's the big fancy world of horse training treating you?"

"I have to admit, not so bad," I told her, jutting my chin towards the stands where the beautiful woman sitting like a daisy in a field of cowboy hats caught my eye and gave me a hesitant wave.

I felt a slow authentically happy grin take my face and spread from ear-to-ear. I lifted my hand preparing to wave back, but before I could reach full elevation, Sallie Mae caught me by the crook of the arm and grimaced.

"Hey now! Stop smiling like an idiot, McKennon. If you ask me, you'll come off better with that filly up there by being your usual brooding self. Girls like her seem to love that stuff," Sallie Mae said, elbowing me in the side with twisted lips as she examined Madison McCall out in the crowd. "How could you leave a pretty thing like that up there alone with all those stand rats anyhow?"

"Aw, I'm pretty sure she can fend for herself. She's a toughie, Sallie Mae."

"And by the sound of you, I can see that you've gone all softie on me over said toughie," she teased, sticking a finger in my belly.

"Think I found *the one*, Sallie Mae."

"What's this one's name now?"

"Her name's Madison … Madison McCall," I said, standing up straighter, proud.

"McCall? As in Sterling "King of the County" McCall?" Sallie Mae made air quotes, and I nodded. "You're seeing McCall's daughter?" Sallie Mae quizzed. She was surprised. "As in *the* Quarter Horse Queen?"

"Yup. That'd be her," I replied, tucking my thumbs in my belt loops.

"I'd be careful there, cowboy. This town is big enough that you can remain anonymous if you try hard enough, that is, but it's small enough that people start talkin' if you have any mild success or, say, start dating someone like Madison McCall," Sallie Mae said, rubbing her hands together and looking out towards the stands. "Word around here is Sterling's got a mean streak. Seems he doesn't much like us rodeo folk, not since his brother was killed by a buckin' bull, and his pretty younger wife ran off with a roper."

My eyes went wild with the new information as I looked out at Madison in the crowd. Her earlier comments were starting to make some sense now.

"Before you came around – wait a minute, you toured the Northern circuit in your younger years, right?"

"Yes, ma'am. That's right."

"I thought so. Anyways, Sterling used to be a regular around this Southern circuit," Sallie Mae continued. "He was the premiere stock contractor in those days. He always had the best bulls. His son ... JD's the name, if I remember correctly ... well, he was quite the little man out there mutton bustin', then he started winning on some of Sterling's young steers. Madison turned barrels when she was just a wee thing, too."

"Ah," I said, rubbing my chin and remembering the photos of the McCall youngsters framed in their living room. "I was wondering if she knew rodeo. Seems so from what you're tellin' me."

"Oh, yes. That girl knows rodeo," Sallie Mae said, putting her hands on her hips. "There's no doubt about that, McKennon. Rodeo was a family business for them back then, you see. Elder McCall won Stock Contractor of the Year several times."

I whistled. That type of title came with a big paycheck and repeat wins were unusual.

"Everything changed the day Sterling's brother was killed. He was a bull rider, a pretty good one, too. He was frequently in the money and racked up enough points to earn a spot on the National Bull Riders tour. He was even starting to teach JD a thing or two ... like I said, it was a family business."

"What happened, Sallie Mae?" I probed.

"Sterling's brother drew one of the McCall Company's prized bucking bulls. The bull had him off his back in less than two seconds, then he spun around and came down on the brother's chest. Crushed him to death right there in the rodeo ring. That was before the days when wearing protective vests and helmets was the norm. I heard the accident was just a bloody mess," Sallie Mae continued, lowering her head sadly. "Sterling ... well ... he just walked into the ring and shot several rounds into the middle of the poor beast's forehead. Left that bull dead next to his brother in the middle of the arena ... just left them both there to turn cold together."

"That's awful," I said, shaking my head.

"Here's the craziest part, cowboy. Rumor has it that Sterling had a taxidermist pick up its remains, and the animal was made into a rug for the McCall living room. Sterling wanted to be able walk all over it again and again."

My stomach turned thinking back to the day I waited for my date with Madison.

"Think I might have met that rug," I grumbled. I shoved my hands in my pockets, vividly remembering the huge hide spread under their big mahogany table and the massive horns hung above the doorway.

"Guessin' that's when Sterling went cold and mean. Word is he started roughin' up his wife, and she left him not long after the accident. The woman abandoned the poor kids, too. After that, Sterling put all his energy into work and built up that Western empire of his. He blamed the rodeo lifestyle for his losses."

"I didn't know all of that, Sallie Mae. What I do know is that Madison has quite the silver spoon lifestyle," I said, kicking at a pebble in the dust.

"Shoot! You're in the money, McKennon. Consider yourself lucky! I'd date the kid, JD, for a shot at a piece of that Western apparel company. Hell, I'd simply lay him just to be able to drive one of those trucks from his daddy's dealership. Can you help me out there? Maybe set me up?" Sallie Mae asked, wiggling her eyebrows and jutting me in the side with her elbow.

"It's not like that, Sallie Mae. I don't want anything to do with her father's money." I cleared my throat and lifted my hat to run a hand through my hair.

"Well, I'll be wantin' to meet her if you actually found a keeper this time around." Sallie Mae didn't seem as convinced as I was that this was the real deal, the one that would settle me down.

I don't blame her for thinking that way. I hadn't exactly created the best reputation for myself with the barrel racers. It's just that I wasn't ever one for saying 'no' is all. I never meant to hurt anyone's feelings. I couldn't figure out why they were always so willing all the time anyway. I didn't have much more than the shirt on my back, an old truck, my horse and his trailer. Nonetheless, I certainly wasn't known for sticking around, and Sallie Mae knew that.

"Good luck in the ring, McKennon. I'm off to check on my horses. Got some barrels to turn before I'm too old to pull myself into the darn saddle."

"You'll never be too old, Sallie Mae," I said, swatting her backside as she idled by.

"You watch yourself, McKennon Kelly. That's no way to treat a lady, especially one that's looked out for you on this circuit all these years. Some of the cowgirls that you've loved and left would have you strung up to die if it weren't for me mending the fences you've ripped through. Lucky you're such a looker," she said through her grin, giving me a lingering once over and a wink.

"Maybe I've changed my ways."

"Uh huh ... sure ... Think you're up, cowboy," she said with a smirk, thumbing over her shoulder into the pen. "Good luck, McKennon." I gave her a bend of my brim and grimaced, not thrilled with the reputation I'd created for myself. I never meant to be the 'love 'em and leave 'em' type, just sort of ended up that way I guess.

The loud speaker clicked on. "Up next, we've got our final rider, McKennon Kelly. He's no stranger to the saddle bronc scene, folks. Today, you're in for a real treat! He'll be riding one of our rankest broncs, Hasty Pete. Pete's an angry animal indeed. He's bucked off his last three fellas!"

I climbed up into the bucking chute and settled onto the back of Pete. I could feel his heat on my calves, the steady expanding and contracting of his sides. He knew what was coming ... just like me. I could feel his pent up energy surging below. I knew he was ready to explode.

The announcer continued, "Not to worry though, rodeo fans! This cowboy's been a Circuit Champion three times over now. Glad to have you, McKennon. You ride him good for us now!"

Addressing the announcer's booth with a nod, I adjusted my protective vest, pushed my cowboy hat down low, sat deep on my pockets and looked out into the crowd one last time before I'd signal for the gate. I needed to see her before the clock started its countdown. At my glance, Madison scooted forward on her seat and pressed her fingertips to her lips. The gesture indicated she was interested. I had to show her I was good ... that I was good enough for her. Gripping the end of my rope tight and pushing my heels down, I bellowed, "Let's fly!" cueing the gatekeepers to let my beast go. I was ready for the ride.

The gate of the bucking chute swung open, and my horse burst out, a furious twist of angst and strength. It was happening in slow motion. I had to stay on the horse for eight seconds without touching him with my free hand. I reminded myself that the first buck was always the most violent and the most important one. My breath hitched, gritting my teeth, I squeezed my thighs with all my strength. Beyond the staying on, I had to make sure I marked the horse out, that is, get the heels of my boots to touch the grunting, whirling, spinning, jumping horse above his shoulders, before his front legs touched the ground again. I always told myself if I could make it through the first buck, then I could last the next seven seconds. The seconds stretched like they always did, feeling more like eternity than a slice of time.

The dirt arena whirled and became a blur as I used all the strength and agility I could muster to spur in rhythm with Hasty Pete's bucking motion. My hand was tight around the woven rein attached to Pete's halter, and my legs snapped forward over his shoulder before his front hooves struck the ground.

Success!

I kicked my legs back in a sweeping motion, finding my rhythmic stride, spurring Pete on. It felt as if Pete and I had become one. We were harmonized in movement. I felt the win in my gut. It would be an earned win. This was one of my toughest runs. Pete was giving his all, but I was, too. My muscles burned with each counter move; I had something bigger than just a win at stake. I had something to prove to the woman waiting for me out there in the stands.

Finally the buzzer sounded. It was sweet music to my ears as a pick up rider galloped up alongside us. I leapt from Pete to the other horse's back, smiling to myself as he loped me away to safety. I felt a wave of pride wash over me as I witnessed the effort with which Pete was still bucking up a storm from the center of the arena. I could tell from the spectacular manner with which he was throwing his hind legs into the air that Pete would earn me more than his fair share of points. This horse wasn't bucking in a straight line; he was all over the damn place. This meant a higher score.

Finding my feet again, boots back in the dirt, I awaited our score. With each of us rated on a scale of 0-50, we would need a combined 85 points to move into the lead. Scores in the 80s were very good, but I was hoping to break into the 90s. That would be exceptional.

"Ladies and gentlemen," the loud speaker boomed. My heart skipped a beat in anticipation. "We've got somethin' spectacular here now!"

I lifted my cowboy hat and mopped my brow.

"Spectacular?" I mouthed up to a comrade perched above me on the railing of the chute, eyebrows raised. I swallowed hard waiting on the results. I knew the ride felt really good, but I needed some assurance. He gave me a gloved thumb up.

"The scores are in, folks, and I'll be darned. I've not seen something like this in all my days on this tour," the announcer paused, dragging out the results and building the anticipation. "Well … ladies and gentlemen … it seems that Mr. McKennon Kelly here just earned himself a perfect score on the back of Hasty Pete!"

The crowd went wild, and the cowboys hooted as I was dragged into the center of the ring. The announcer continued, "It's the first 100 ever earned on this tour. Reckon it's McKennon's first, too. Perfect scores only come around once in a lifetime, if ever, in this business, folks!"

The crowd roared, but as I looked out into the stands, suddenly all the celebratory activity around me went silent. I had tunnel vision. I still felt backslap after backslap between my shoulder blades, popping when they made contact with my protective vest. I still blinked as the flash of the bulbs went off around me, but everything in my head was quiet when my eyes fell on her.

Madison was up on her boot tips cheering … for me. She was cheering for me. I never wanted someone out there rooting for me before. This feeling was new, unexpected even, and images of a real future with the woman flitted through my thoughts. I returned to the present when a velvet box was shoved into my hands. The sound around me came back slowly until it felt like the whole arena was shaking with applause. Opening the lid, I looked down at the gleaming belt buckle and rubbed my thumb over the engraved word 'Champion'. Realizing that right then I actually felt like one, I dropped my knee in the dirt, pulled my cowboy hat from my head, put it to my chest, raised a hand to my forehead and thanked the heavens for a job well done, a clean, safe ride and for the woman waiting for me in the stands.

Maybe there *was* some kind of future for a man like me after all. Rising from the arena floor, I loosened the worn-in leather belt from my jeans and threaded the big, new buckle into the older one's place.

CHAPTER 17

I burst out of the stock contractor's trailer, stuffing the winnings that Hasty Pete just helped me earn into my pocket. The bulge of bills felt heavy in my jeans as I raced to get back to Madison. She hadn't moved an inch from where I left her. It made me proud to see her waiting for me there. When I finally reached her, she penetrated me with those icy eyes of hers and revealed a dazzling smile. I put my hands on my hips to emphasize my newly won championship belt buckle and returned the smile with a megawatt one of my own.

"It's *so* big," she commented, arching an eyebrow and ogling my nether region. With a giggle, she threw her arms around my neck and whispered near, "Now that was something, cowboy." Her lips brushed my earlobe, and every hair on my body stood on end. It was time to go.

I guided her away from the commotion, placing a palm to the center of her back. Congratulations still going on in the stands, I nodded in acknowledgment to one person after another as I led her to the carnival area where I could be anonymous for a while. All I wanted was Madison alone, fast.

Once away from the bustle, we wandered along the fairway in comfortable silence looking at the booths and taking in the sights, attraction lights whirling around us, the scent of fried food and livestock heavy in the air.

"I know I'm repeating myself, but that sure was something, Ken," Madison said, blinking at me through her lashes. I briefly stiffened at the nickname, but just as quickly accepted it.

"I made the eight for you, cowgirl," I replied, nudging her gently in the shoulder. She slid her hand into mine. My palm set on fire.

I pondered a pop-up bar as we passed it. It startled me that I didn't even feel like having a celebratory whiskey. This girl was changing me, and I actually liked it.

"Are you hungry?" I asked, swinging our joined hands. This was definitely not the sort of action that earned points on my man card, but I didn't care.

"Not hungry," she said, tugging me toward one of the vendor's tents. I happily trailed behind. When we reached the display, she ran her unpolished nails over a necklace featured at the booth. I saw the glimmer of want in her eyes.

"Do you like that necklace?" I asked.

"I just wanted a closer look is all. It's pretty," she said, shrugging her shoulders.

"Didn't ask you if it was pretty. I asked you if you wanted it, miss. So do you? Do you want that necklace?"

"Yes. I guess I suppose I do," she said shyly, meeting my eyes with her ice blue spheres.

"Well then, I reckon you should have it," I decided. She came from money, and I didn't have any … yet. I was a man making ends meet picking up events here and there while trying this horse training thing on, but I wouldn't let any of that stop me, not when it came to Madison McCall's happiness.

Determined, I went to the booth and asked the merchant the price. He flipped the small white tag toward me so I could read it. I nodded, and he took it from the black velvet display. He held it up and invited Madison to try on the strand. She bit her lip and turned her back to the salesman, shifting her long blonde hair to the side, allowing him to hang the necklace around the soft curve of her slender neck. A wave of warmth washed over me. I was doing something to make this beautiful creature, the one who chose to keep me company, happy. After closing the clasp, the merchant stepped away. Madison shook her hair out around her shoulders and adjusted the jewel at her nape with a smile.

"Ah, let me bring a mirror," he said, disappearing behind the heavy velvet drape of his tent.

I stepped toward Madison and said, "It's perfect."

The vender reappeared from the recesses of his little booth and handed me a mirror. I took a step behind Madison and held the looking glass out in front of us. She felt perfect pressed against me. I liked seeing myself reflected behind her. It caused my heart to pound at a frenzied rate beneath the pocket of my shirt.

"Looks perfect on you ... both of us. I mean ... me ... *and* the necklace."

Madison put a warm palm to the top of my arm, holding our reflection out in front of us. I couldn't resist stealing a kiss of her neck. I was rewarded with her smile.

"Beautiful," I said. "We'll take it, sir," I called to the vendor. With a nod, he retreated back into his little booth. I felt gratitude when he gave us our space.

Madison began to protest my impulsive purchase, but before words could leave her lips, I swung in and kissed the perfect pink pillows. Her eyes went wide at my bold move, but then her long lashes fluttered closed. Returning my kiss, she pressed her lips and all of her body into me. It was oddly innocent and highly intimate all at the same time. I had to control my tongue from darting into her mouth.

"Ahem." The merchant cleared his throat as he returned to the scene.

I didn't want to pull away from Madison's mouth, so I fished a wad of cash from my jeans, most the evening's winnings and gladly handed the money over to the salesman's eager palm. My other hand stayed tangled in her hair, holding her head at the base of her neck. Madison hummed and took her lips from mine, her eyes like icy daggers through my soul. I couldn't stop staring at her. I dragged a single finger from behind her ear, down her throat, across her chest to the large turquoise stone set in silver and embellished with diamonds I'd just purchased for her. I smiled because I'd made her happy. That first kiss was a promise for more. I proudly accepted the sales receipt and handed her the necklace's satin box.

I wrapped my arm around her tight – proud to be her man, showing ownership. No one else was going to get near this girl. I knew everyone would want to try to talk to her if I left her side for a moment.

Not on my watch.

We continued our stroll through the lighted fairway – boot to boot. The necklace gleamed as the smile I'd created on Madison's mouth beamed.

CHAPTER 18

"Don't know what it is … I just like the look of you – and I'm going to fall in love with all of you. Might already be, Miss Madison McCall," I whispered near her cheek once we reached the quiet of the parking lot.

It was early enough that all the wranglers were still out playing games up on the fairway or at the makeshift carny bars sipping whiskeys and trying to get lucky. Even though I didn't stay on the grounds anymore, the RV lot felt like home. I always parked my truck here rather than the boisterous and crowded public parking lots. As we got to my truck, all was calm except for the occasional nicker from the barn area. Leaning to Madison, I swept her up into another innocent kiss. I sensed she was taking this slow. It didn't matter much to me anyway because I liked the pressure of her perfect lips on mine. I wanted to take it deeper, make her toes curl in her cowgirl boots, but I held out a little longer. I knew it was just a matter of time. She wasn't necessarily a girl that got around, but I also knew she was experienced. I'd learned that she'd had a lot of boyfriends … A LOT. Word travels quickly in equine circles, especially when it involves one of the finest cowgirls I'd ever laid my eyes on. This woman was a pro. She knew her way around men.

"OK," she whispered into my kiss. "You've played my way so far, been a perfect gentleman, on this second date of ours. I sense that you'll respect my body and maybe my mind."

I narrowed my eyes considering her comment.

"Actually, it's our first date," I reminded her, breaking from our kiss. "And I'll do more than just respect you, miss. If I have it my way, I plan to worship this body and learn that mind of yours," I said, gliding a hand down her back and kissing the nape of her neck. I littered her with little kisses, moving my lips up to just below her ear. She groaned in return, slipping her fingers between the top two buttons of my shirt, popping them open. I tipped my head back and bit my lip.

"Tonight, I want to do fantasy," she murmured.

"Fantasy?" I questioned, pulse accelerating through my veins at her touch on my bare skin.

"I don't usually come on so strong, but something about that ride of yours has me all giddy," she said breathily. "It's just that it's our second – I mean, first date and all, so I don't want you to think poorly of me."

"What are you babbling about?" I chuckled softly into her hair. She smelled so pretty. It was intoxicating. I really liked touching this girl.

Madison moved her mouth to mine and absorbed me in her kiss. She was the one to take us farther. Her tongue danced with mine, rhythmically and with abandon. We became one. It wasn't awkward or fast. Our kiss was deliberate and slow. I wanted her with every fiber of my being.

Where had this woman been all my life?

It was as if she had been designed for me. Madison fit like a perfect pair of designer boots, supple and broken in, just right and just for me.

Madison loosened my shirt from my waistline. Once it was untucked, her hands traveled up my bare back. Her touch, delicate and soft, brought a chill to my skin. Electricity jolted through my veins, and I crushed her body to mine.

"Ken ... I want you to take me like one of your buckle bunnies," she murmured into my lips. "I want fantasy. Do with me what you did on rodeo. I want to feel dominated."

I pulled back and blinked at her. This offer was too good to be true. Madison was so beautiful and sexy leaning against my truck. She was obviously feeling sultry. I couldn't let her down, so I figured I'd steal a page from my own self-serving days just this once.

"Are you sure?" I asked, looking at her sideways and pushing her soft blond hair over her shoulder.

"Yes," she exhaled, pulling me to her again by the belt buckle hung at the front of my pants, breath warm on my lips.

Considering her icy eyes, I saw the want settled there. It was more intense, but similar to the desire I saw earlier for the necklace now hanging around her neck.

"Just be sure to use this," she added. The wrapper crinkled as Madison slipped a foil packet into my shirt pocket. She began moving her hands along the leather circling my waist. "Take me, Ken."

Accepting the proposition, I nodded to her and offered a sinister grin. Her eyes went wide and then wild. A smile tugged at the corners of her mouth. I leaned in and kissed her cheek.

"I figured a rodeo boy wouldn't object," she said, pressing her full bosom to my chest.

I told myself that I'd do this, but certainly not like I used to. This wasn't for me. It was for her. A fantasy. I'd only known her for a short time, but I knew I was different. Changed ... because of her, because of the love for her that I could feel coming. Sallie Mae always told me 'love comes like lightning,' and now I finally knew what she meant. I was certain that intimacy would never be the same for me, but I'd play along tonight because she asked me to. I'd be the guy I'd always been. I took a step back and took her in with my eyes. Her skirt fluttered about her tanned knees.

Oh, how I love sundresses above cowgirl boots.

"Don't know what it is … I just like the look of you – and I love all of you," I said as I lowered the tailgate of my truck. She eyed it all wide-eyed and beautiful, hesitating. Reaching out, I turned her by the waist and gently bent her over the dropped down tailgate. To my surprise, she obliged. Her backside was so glorious. I lifted the hem of her skirt and thought about shifting her lacy under things to the side.

I can't believe she's mine.

I leaned over Madison, pressing my clothed body to hers. She twisted her face to me and met my lips, my tongue breaking through, meeting hers then tangling and twisting until I felt like something inside me might burst. Slow down, cowboy, I reminded myself.

Pulling from her mouth, I kissed her earlobe, traced my tongue down her neck, and pressed my lips between her bare shoulder blades exposed between the thin straps of her dress. I let my hands travel to her waist, and I maneuvered her glorious rear toward me tenderly, a move that was familiar no matter how unfamiliar the body beneath me.

"My daddy's not gonna like it when he gets word of this … of us," Madison breathed, writhing sensually at my touch. When she uttered those words it felt like a dagger entered my heart. I abruptly stopped.

"No," I said, removing my hands from her body. "I'm sorry. Not with you. Not like this. You're different."

"What? What's wrong, Ken?"

"I can't do this with you … not like this," I uttered, backing away from my truck.

"Why? We were having fun."

"This thing between us. It's more to me than havin' a little fun, tryin' to piss off your daddy, or me gettin' another notch on my belt. I've got plenty of those. You're not just some conquest to me."

"Oh," she said dejectedly, turning to face me. I watched her smooth her skirt, the one I'd just lifted up over her back, desire for her still burning deeply in me.

"It seems love makes the wildest spirit tame and tamest spirit wild. I want, but I'm not gonna, Madison."

"Is that what makes you a real cowboy, Ken?" she asked with a smirk.

"You have no idea how much I want to have my way with you, Miss McCall. Nothing would have stopped me in the past … with anyone … until you. It matters to me now. I want to wait, Madison. Let's train that horse of yours and see where this thing goes. Take our time." I cleared my throat and crossed my hands over my chest. "And … I'll be needing to meet that father of yours, too."

Her eyes darkened. "Ken …"

Even though Sallie Mae had given me a good inkling as to her history, I had to hear it from the horse's mouth. I wanted Madison's version. I interrupted her, "I'll be needin' to know exactly why he won't be likin' the likes of me. You still haven't enlightened me there."

"It's a long story."

"I've got all the time in the world for you, Madison McCall. I'm a pretty good listener."

"OK, cowboy. Have it your way. We'll start working with Lyric tomorrow. Maybe I'll enlighten you then. Do you remember the drill?" she asked with an eyebrow raised. I watched her adjust her shoulder straps so her dress hung properly over her perfect breasts. I momentarily wondered what I had done.

Shaking the thought from my mind, I answered, "Yes, I remember. Sterling holds early morning sales calls on Mondays and Thursdays with his staff. He'll be out the door by 6 a.m., and I'll be there when he's gone," I answered, closing the tailgate of my truck with a bang, both of our eyes lingering on it for a moment contemplating what almost happened there.

"Good memory. Now take me home," Madison demanded with a smile, a lifted chin and an index finger pointed at the cab of my jalopy.

I addressed her with a tip of my Stetson. "Yes … *Boss.*"

"That's right, cowboy. The lady leads in this partnership," she said, sauntering past me. As she went by, I swatted her rear with an open palm. It made a popping sound, and we both laughed. I opened her door, and she climbed in. We made the short drive to the McCall place in relative silence, but certain electricity lingered between us in the cab of my truck.

"I'll get out here, cowboy," she cued. I pulled my truck into the gravel at the side of the road, put it in park, and leaned toward Madison to steal a last kiss. When she let me, I scooted a little closer until her warm slender shoulder pressed to mine. I didn't want this first date with Madison to ever end.

"I'll walk the rest of the way up the drive. Don't want to piss off the old man. You be here tomorrow, Ken?"

"With bells on," I promised, meeting her stare. I caught her hand and gave it one last kiss before she slipped off the bench seat.

"You remember now that Mondays and Thursdays are our days for working with Lyric," she said, swinging the truck door shut.

"I'll remember," I confirmed. She nodded and started toward her home. Her home for now anyway; I was going to take this cowgirl away. I waited to watch her disappear down the dirt drive, that lovely sundress billowing about her knees. I palmed my face thinking about her earlier offer.

My eyes traveled the length of her long, lean legs rising out of those cowgirl boots before she was swallowed by the night and out of sight. I dragged a hand over my mouth, rubbed my stubble-ridden chin, and let out a groan.

What had I done?

CHAPTER 19

M adison was the best damn thing I'd ever lucked into. I'd turned a new leaf. I felt giddy about this girl, and I couldn't wait to get out to the McCall's place the next day. It was easy to bounce out of bed. My rodeo-worn body didn't even feel broken, all full of aches and pains like it usually did. I pulled in the drive just seconds after 6 a.m. Sterling would be gone, and my cowgirl would be waiting for me down in the barn. As I meandered up the long drive, I went tense when I saw another, much nicer truck approaching mine.

Could Sterling be running late for his meeting this morning?

I slowed my speed as the other vehicle approached. When we passed each other, I looked out my rolled down window and was met by her brother's angry glare. I gave JD a curt nod and pressed the gas. He certainly didn't look too happy to see me on the premises, and I wasn't interested in any confrontations today.

I parked my beater outside the barn and jogged into the aisle. I couldn't wait to see her again. Contentment spread across her lovely face, Madison had Cash out in the cross ties and was grooming his dark coat quietly. Taking notice of me, she looked up.

"Morning, cowboy," she said flatly. "You're late."

"I … uh … I wasn't sure if I was too close to six. Didn't want to get 'cha in trouble on day one," I stuttered.

"I'm just teasin', Ken. Relax," she said as a big smile met her bright, blue eyes. I still wasn't sure that I much cared for being called Ken, but let it slide *again*.

"Saw your brother on the way in. I'm guessin' he don't much like guys around you or the ranch either. The look he gave just about put me to death."

"Oh, never mind JD," Madison said with a wave of her hand. "If he isn't working over a woman or riding his bulls, he's always got some sort of bug up his butt. I have a feelin' he struck out on one or the other last night. He was heading off to put some hours in at the dealership. That's something he doesn't do when he's winning or when he's got a warm body in his bed. When he works for Dad he gets to drive one of the dealership rigs instead of his junker. Pretty sure that's why he does it. A nice truck helps him in the sacking girls department."

"Will he tell your father that I'm here?"

"Nope. JD and I have a deal. I don't tell about the women he sneaks into the house. He keeps out of my business and my barn," she said over her shoulder, returning Cash to his stall. "You wouldn't believe the kind of things I kept coming across out here. I had to put my foot down. I was sick of finding him in the barn all tangled up with his women. I'll spare you the dirty details, but they certainly were not the sort of sights I wanted to see first thing in the morning."

"No, guessin' that wouldn't be a sight I'd want to see either. Where do you want to start today, miss?" I asked, changing the subject.

"Thought I'd let you lead today, cowboy," Madison said, hanging Cash's halter on his stall.

"OK, then."

I was happy to take the reins and show this cowgirl what I could do.

"I reckon we should just continue where we left off with Lyric," I said, extending my hand to Madison. I smiled when she placed hers in mine without hesitation. "Just bein' with her, that is. When she offers that little muzzle to us, we'll know we can take her further."

I led Madison to Lyric's stall and opened the door. The little filly took flight at the sight of us. I shook my head as she scurried between her mother and the back wall of the stall.

"This might take a while. Ladies first," I said, gesturing inside. "I recommend sitting on opposite sides this time to give Lyric more to get used to. Now she'll have to deal with one of us on each side of her box stall."

"Oh, OK," Madison said. I liked how she reluctantly released my hand and found her position in the stall.

I didn't want to send her away, but it was the right approach for the filly. Settling into my own spot in the sawdust, I longed to be next to Madison, to press my lips to hers, to admire the curves of her body with my hands, but I didn't know where we had left it last night or if I could still call her mine today.

For most of the morning, we just sat there in the stall. It was agony for all of us. For Lyric, we were invading her safe place. For me, I longed to be near Madison. Then there was that special something in Madison's gaze indicating to me that she was suffering our separation, too. Over the dark coat of the frustrated filly, our eyes gravitated toward each other's. We were like magnets. I'd feel her eyes on me and catch her looking. Then she'd feel me on her and catch me looking at her. The energy hung heavy in the space between us. I'd sit in the fearful filly's stall with this woman forever just to keep feeling this feeling. For now, I settled with letting her future show horse be the force driving us together, but I knew I had to find a way to be in this woman's life … permanently.

"Ever thought about having a partner in that business you fantasize about startin'?" I asked her across the distance, searching for my way in.

"I'm thinkin' so," she said with a faraway look in her eyes. The soft smile that drove me wild was pasted on her plush lips. It was all she offered on the subject as we leaned against our separate walls to simply be with the horse and longingly look at each other.

After several hours passed, my pulse sped up when Lyric left the safety of her mother's side and cautiously crossed the stall. She was finally exploring, finding her confidence, realizing that the humans hanging out with her weren't a threat. She took one calculated step, then another with her long adolescent legs. Lyric snuffled the air, and then shifted some shavings around with her little lips. She wandered a little farther toward Madison's position in the stall. I bit my lip.

Go to her. Please go to her, little horse.

Hovering in front of Madison, Lyric outstretched her lean neck to sniff one of Madison's upturned palms resting atop her knee. In disbelief, I knuckled the corners of my eyes. The filly had come around quickly. My sight refocused just in time to catch Lyric place her petite charcoal muzzle into Madison's open hand. Madison held her breath and pressed her lips together, clearly afraid to frighten the filly away. My heart grew when our eyes met. She was pleased. It looked like a light flipped on inside her when Lyric let her in. Madison just beamed at the breakthrough, a thumb slowly gliding over the filly's velveteen nose.

That little horse and I had something in common. We had both taken to Madison McCall, and fast. The cowgirls I'd been around on the rodeo circuit knew their mounts and were energized by their horses' speed, but that seemed to be where it stopped. Madison was different than them. She had a similar intuition about horses as I did, although hers was perhaps stronger. I recognized this difference in her immediately. I could tell she loved all things equine and not just the winning. She appreciated them for their natural way of being, whether they were earning her a prize or not. Horses seemed to sense it and warmed to her easily. Being in her presence, you could almost feel her gratitude for them swelling around you. I'd never met a girl so tuned into horses.

Madison and I got our start spending time in that stall. It was working with the little horse that we really fell in love with each other. Lyric was a sleek filly with good breeding, but a fearful disposition – one we were working to overcome. She was bright and curious, but skittish. She had traits that could become dangerous as she grew larger if not addressed early. Madison's biggest dreams were pinned to the pretty foal. She had handpicked Lyric's dam and sire in hopes of proving to her daddy that she had talent for selecting bloodlines.

And she wanted my help. Mine.

So I decided Madison's dreams were mine now, too. I wanted to be the partner she dreamily thought of when I asked if she'd considered one for her business. I wanted to see her start it up. I'd make sure that her business would become a reality. That is, if she'd have me.

So I had Lyric in a halter and leading pretty for Madison a few short weeks later.

CHAPTER 20

"Ken?" Madison called.

"Yes?" I answered, peeking out from Lyric's stall. Madison was expertly crouched in front of a tack box, avoiding the spurs attached to her boots as she rummaged through it. My eyes wandered hungrily over the woman. She looked alluring with her hair swept up in a ponytail, wearing an ordinary tank top and worn-in blue jeans, balancing on her broken-in boot tips. I'd made progress with the filly. Madison not so much. Lyric was letting me lead her in small circles around the stall and use a body brush to manage her fuzzy baby fur, but I hadn't gotten my hands on Madison for a while now.

"I need to speak with you, Ken," she said, pulling a hoof pick from the bottom of the box and standing.

"OK," I said, stepping out from the stall and sliding its door shut. Madison set the hoof pick on a bale of hay near Lyric's stall front.

"I want to try and pick out Lyric's feet today, but first, will you walk with me?" she asked, starting down the aisle.

"Of course," I said as she passed me by. I took a deep breath in the shadows of the barn. I wasn't sure what I was about to hear. I turned and followed the woman out into the sunlight.

"I think I'm ready to tell you about my daddy now," she said apprehensively once I caught up to her. I'd been waiting for this day to come, hoping that she would open up to me.

"I know I've been a little distant," Madison continued. "I've been wrestling with my past, but I'm going to tell you everything now. There are a few things you need to know about Sterling McCall before he learns that I've fallen in love with you, Ken."

"Madison, I ..." I began as a rush of emotion hit me. I needed to tell her I loved her, too. I'd been holding on to the words all this time. I wanted to let them out so she would know. I patted the pocket of my jeans. There was a surprise waiting for this moment in there. I lurched toward her, picked her up and spun her around. "I ... I'm in ..."

"Ken. Shh. Please put me down. I need to tell you this first and right now. It's hard for me. I haven't told anyone this, so just let me talk before I reconsider. My family's been trained to hold our last name up high in this community. We keep our secrets to ourselves. My daddy won't have me or my brother tarnishing our reputation."

"I'm sorry. Please, continue. I'm listening," I assured her, giving her a squeeze before I set her down. I didn't lead on that I knew anything. I would hold my conversation with Sallie Mae and my love for Madison McCall close to the vest ... for now.

"So there are some things you need to know about my father before you meet him," she began again.

"OK. What are they, Madison," I asked, tightening my fists. I didn't like the sound of this.

"Goes something like this. Always leave what you think you know at the door because my daddy knows it all. Don't walk too proud around him. Definitely don't talk too loud. He hates the rodeo. AND ... he can get really mean," she said sadly.

I clenched my jaw, but held my tongue. I didn't like how this was going already.

"I learned how to manage it though," she continued, flashing me a hesitant smile. "First, I figured out that I shouldn't bring boys around, especially not ones like you. That seemed to help some, but I don't want to do that anymore now that I've met you. I want you around all the time, Ken. It's just that the strangest things can set him off, so rather than try and figure him out, I just stay as cool as a cucumber. I don't respond when he gets angry and starts his raging. You still with me?"

"I'm listening, but I don't like it," I said through gritted teeth.

"I'm just going to keep going or else I'm not going to say it all. So like I said, he's got a temper. He only had to raise a hand to me once for me to learn that standing up for myself wasn't going to work with him. I can't fight him, and he won't hear what I have to say. So now I just take it, sort of anyway. I know now that his cruel words are meant for my momma and not me. They still hurt me emotionally though, so that's why I've been saving, planning for the right time to leave. It'll be my turn to go soon."

"So your mother left, is that it?" I asked even though I knew the answer.

"Kinda, but there's more to it than just that. It all started when my uncle …" Madison was starting to break. Her voice quivered as she continued, "My uncle … he was killed on the rodeo circuit."

I took her in my arms, and she held on to me, wiping a sniffling nose on my shoulder.

"Come, let's sit," I said, leading her beneath a big oak tree. I positioned myself against its trunk and pulled Madison down to me. She slipped between my legs, and I wrapped my arms across her chest. She clunked my boot with hers.

"It's just such a sad story. My family is a mess," she whimpered.

"Just tell it, Madison. I ain't judgin'. This might be therapeutic even," I whispered near her ear and smoothed the stray pieces of hair at her temple that had come loose from her ponytail.

"OK," she breathed. "I'll put on my big girl boots."

"That's a good cowgirl," I cooed playfully, trying to take a little edge off the situation. She swatted me lightly on the thigh with her palm.

"I loved being a McCall kid. That is, before everything happened. Everyone knew who we were, and I got to be around horses all the time. Daddy ... well ... he was fun back then. I was his girl. I had the best barrel pony, and I loved that I got to go on tour with my whole family. We lived in a luxury RV with huge living quarters out on different fairgrounds all year long. The whole family got to do what each of us really loved doing. I got to be around horses. JD was learning the bull riding ropes from our uncle. Daddy raised the winning bucking bulls that my brother wanted to ride. Mama loved to cook and made us all wonderful spreads of food that we'd feast on after our events. In the evenings, everyone would gather around a bonfire, and my uncle would play his guitar. We were happy then," Madison said, wistfully. "Then the accident happened."

"Take a breath, Madison," I encouraged. I quietly examined her while she paused to gather herself. She was beautiful even when she was distressed. Everything in me yearned to take her pain away.

"I'd never seen so much blood," Madison said, sitting up and turning to face me. She crossed her legs, folding them up between my outstretched ones. "JD and I were just kids back then. We were so excited to see our uncle take on one of our daddy's bulls. They'd been razzing each other about who would win – man or bull – for days. People were taking bets, so the crowd was thick. As people passed bills between them, JD and I squeezed our way to the railing to see their go. When that gate opened, I felt like I was staring right into the devil's eyes. I couldn't believe it because the bull was so friendly at home. We called him Jake. He'd even let me pet him. I'd never been afraid of him before, but on that day, Jake became a writhing, twisted scary thing in the rodeo ring.

My uncle didn't stand a chance. He flailed around like a ragdoll on Jake's back, lost his balance and the grip on his bull rope. He was off in the blink of an eye. He wasn't wearing a vest … no one did back then. Jake slammed him to the ground straight out of the chute." Madison stopped to let out a sob.

"It's OK. I'm right here. I've got you." I pressed my lips to her cheek.

"The crowd watched in horror as Jake ignored the bull fighters waving frantically, trying to distract him from my unconscious uncle," she continued. "Their efforts were no help. With one vicious leap into the air, all 2,000 pounds of that animal came crashing down on my uncle's chest. Split him right open in front of everyone. Then my daddy, he just walked into the ring and shot Jake over and over again in the head until he was sure he was dead. Left him there in the dirt next to my uncle. I remember JD hollering for my uncle and for Jake. He loved them both. Jake was the one JD wanted to ride one day. His dream was always to ride bulls, just like our uncle did. His passion for the event today is a tribute to my uncle. JD was just a boy when he lost the family member he felt closest to. I think he still carries a crumpled newspaper clipping of our uncle's big break into the rodeo scene in his wallet."

"Kind explains why your brother always seems so angry. I guess," I added. Madison nodded her agreement.

"Then my mama left. I was just a girl, but I could feel it coming. I could hear Daddy yelling and knocking her around through my bedroom walls at night. She ran away with some rodeo guy because my daddy was such a dick. I don't really remember if my father was ever nice after the accident happened. It felt like a storm was always brewing in our house. All the love had blown away and was replaced with constant thunder. My mom was smart though. I get why she did what she did. She knew if she left him properly through a divorce, it wouldn't matter. He'd see to it that she wouldn't get a dime of his money because of her affair. She knew if she took us kids, he'd hunt her down until someone got hurt, so she left JD and me behind. All I have left of my mother is a note telling me all of this. She wanted us to know that she'd at least considered taking us with her," Madison said, wiping a tear from her eye and handing me the note she had in her pocket.

I glanced over the pretty cursive, wondering if Madison always carried it with her or if she had put it in her pocket for this conversation.

"Madison, this is a lot for a person to deal with," I said, handing the note back to her. "How did you manage? How do you manage? Why do you stay here?" I asked. I knew my concern had touched my brow.

"I may not engage with my father, but I certainly act out in other ways. I do things that I know he won't like. I do things just waiting to get caught. Like the night I almost gave myself to you."

I tried not to look hurt hearing that I was only a means to upset her daddy, but I knew the expression already forming on my face had given me away. Noticing me, Madison put a cool palm to my forearm.

"Ken, I am glad you stopped us. You should probably know that your interruption is the reason I've fallen for you. I would have loved you and left you then. It's just what I used to do. I never would have gotten to know you if you hadn't stopped us. These last weeks have been the happiest ones I've had in ages. That's because of you, cowboy," she said, taking my hand and giving it a squeeze. My face instantly brightened. I caressed Madison's sad cheek.

"I've always looked for opportunities to antagonize my father in my own secret ways. It's how I still feel powerful. JD gets the worst of it, probably because he's a man. Rumor is men don't bruise as easily as women, inside or out. I'm pretty sure that's a lie, but JD stays fairly loyal to our daddy. Not sure why, probably for the money. He really just wants to ride bulls and women. JD is pretty simple, single-minded."

"It's easier for us guys to act tough is all, but deep down, I'm sure JD is hurtin', too," I said.

"Well, my father's never gotten right with it all either. Playing tough, he threw himself into his businesses, just cared about making money and controlling us. I can't even count how many times he said to me, 'I won't have you turn out like your momma, all horses and whorin' around with cowboys.' He tried to control JD, too, putting money in people's pockets to put him on an easy bull so he wouldn't end up like our uncle. He'd even stoop so low as to have someone spy on me while I was on a date or out researching horses. That's why I want to do it on my own. Just gotta save so I can get out. I hate tending bar, but it's good money. I gotta get out from under him, Ken."

"Yes, I reckon you do," I said, burying the fury I was feeling toward her father for the moment.

"He wouldn't even let me run barrels anymore. He said it was too much like a rodeo sport. After momma left, he sold my barrel pony and put me in Western events on a Quarter Horse. He said he preferred me buttoned up in bling and riding slow on Cash. Cash became everything to me when everything else was falling apart. I was grateful that I still had a horse. Cash and I have been through a lot together."

"What about the shows now? I've seen you turning barrels. How do you get away with it?" I asked.

"I enter on Penny's barrel horses whenever he isn't looking. Sometimes when my friend Trish is in town, she'll lend me one of hers. She's a good barrel horse trainer, even has a couple qualified for the finals in Vegas this year."

I couldn't help but chuckle. Her comment turned me on. I liked that fire, independence and defiance of authority. I never once liked her for her money or for her daddy's business. I'd be happy to defy him with her.

"So what about you, cowboy? Where do you come from?" Madison looked at me expectantly.

"Uh ..."

"Come on, Ken. I need to think about something else. Please tell me about you."

"All right. Not much to tell really. Don't know a whole lot about my parents. My mother died young. My father was a drifter so I've been told."

"Who raised you then, Ken?" Madison questioned, worry evident in the crease between her eyebrows.

"Spent my life on the road. Got took in by a rodeoin' uncle. He taught me most of what I know about horses and bronc bustin'. Don't have much by way of roots to speak of. Not sure where my uncle is these days. We went our separate ways when I turned 18. Strange that we both have rodeo uncles in our blood."

"Seems we have sad stories in common, too. Everyone's got a sad story, I suppose," Madison said sweetly, before pecking me on the lips. "Come on, cowboy. How's about we get back to writing a story of our own. Let's make it a happy one. We have a horse to train back in that barn."

"Thinkin' we've got a business to discuss, too, miss," I added. I knew she loved me now. I was in. I wasn't scared of her past or her father.

"Yes, I suppose we do, Ken," Madison said, slipping her hand in mine.

"I love you, Madison," I said as we re-entered the barn hand-in-hand. "You know I love you, right?"

"Yes. I know, Ken," Madison whispered, squeezing my hand and meeting my eyes. It felt like a weight had been lifted from between us now that Madison's secrets were out in the open. She suddenly seemed lighter in her boots.

CHAPTER 21

"I'm glad I told you about all that, Ken," Madison said, smiling at me, leaning against Lyric's stall. "It was a relief to finally share it with someone. I'm glad it was with someone I love."

I blinked several times, and my heart set to racing. There it was again. Madison McCall loved me. I stretched an arm out over her shoulder and braced myself against the wall. With my other hand, I touched her cheek. I wanted all of her right then, right there. Madison removed my cowboy hat, hung it on a hook and ran her fingers through my hair. I leaned in and kissed her mouth hard. She returned my move with equal force. My fingers tangled in her tresses as her hands lifted my T-shirt up my back. I released her for a moment as she raised the shirt over my head. Her hands trailed my bare chest, fingertips grazing my pectoral muscles, over my belly button, down my happy trail to the button at the front of my jeans. She popped it open and made a happy humming sound as she wrapped a leg around my waist and then the other. I boosted Madison's body up onto my hips, and her breasts pushed against me in her tank top as she slung her arms around my neck. She squeezed my sides, hanging on with those long, strong equestrian legs of hers. I opened Lyric's stall and stumbled in backwards.

Together we fell over in a heap into the deep sawdust. Lyric scrambled for the safety of her mother as we laughed.

"She might be too young to see this, Ken," Madison giggled as she fumbled for the zipper of my pants.

"Don't quite care, miss," I said, moving toward her mouth again and pulling her to me. She allowed my hand to travel up the inside of her top and over her bra. Madison moaned at my touch and pulled the elastic from her ponytail, letting her long blonde hair loose. The sawdust was prickly on my skin, but it was nothing compared to the uncomfortable tug coming from the front of my jeans.

"What's going on here?" a voice boomed.

Startled, we both shot up and out of the shavings.

"What's he doing here?" Madison exclaimed, panic in her eyes. There wasn't anywhere to hide. There was no way to get out of that stall fast enough to escape him. She furiously tried to brush the shavings from her clothing. "He should still be in meetings. I checked his calendar this morning to be sure. Seems there's nothing we can do now. I guess it's time you met my daddy, Ken."

My eyes grew wide. I zipped up and buttoned my jeans fast. The heavy footsteps approached then stopped in front of the stall. Madison turned white as a ghost. I grimaced at the enormous amount shavings in her hair.

Sterling peered into the stall, eyes widening at the sight of us. "Madison McCall! What the hell is going on here! Look at you, Madison," he hollered, banging his fist on the stall door spooking Lyric and her mother. Madison and I had to scurry not to be trampled by their fearful hooves. I could see the purple veins pulsing on his forehead. "I come home for a file I'd forgotten to find a battered old truck in my driveway and my daughter slutting around in a stall with a random cowboy? This is not the way for a McCall to behave, young lady. I'm disgusted." He furiously rattled the door between us before he turned and spat on the aisle.

"Daddy, I –" Madison peeped.

"Madison, get your whorin' ass out of there … NOW!" Sterling demanded, thrusting the stall door open.

I knew this particular situation wouldn't look good to any father. I had to do something before things got too ugly.

"Sir, I'm McKennon … McKennon Kelly," I said, sheepishly stepping out of the stall. I retrieved my hat from the hook next to Lyric's halter and placed it on my head. I was shirtless, but at least I still had my Wranglers on. I extended my hand to him.

"Take your hat off when you're talking to me, boy," Sterling barked.

"Apologies, Mr. McCall," I said, removing my Stetson and holding it to my bare chest while scanning the aisle for my rogue T-shirt.

"Rodeo man, huh?" Sterling snarled, eyeballing my belt buckle.

"Used to be, sir," I replied, hustling over to the stall front where Madison had tucked my white T-shirt between the bars. I pulled it over my head, hung my cowboy hat back on the hook and held my hand out to Sterling again in an effort to make a proper introduction to the man. I wanted him to know I was different, that I wasn't on the circuit anymore. More than anything, I wanted to keep Madison out of trouble. He just shook his head rejecting my peace offering.

"Ah, I see. You're the one then," he said, slivering his eyes. "Had a good ride recently, did ya? I read all about that ride of yours. Hasty Pete? Nice score."

"Sir?" I asked, looking to Madison. She furled her brow and shook her head.

"So, I finally meet the person who's been influencing my silly daughter. Don't think I didn't know you've been up to something, Madison," Sterling growled, giving his daughter a stern eye.

"Influencing? How's that, sir?" I asked.

"She thinks she's in love. She thinks you're the man of her dreams. She thinks you're a man that believes in her dreams.

Well, you're filling her head with nonsense, son. Lettin' her believe you'll stick around. Lettin' her think she's got talent for selecting horses. She's never gonna get that horse training business going. Oh yes, Madison, I've read your little pink journal. It's fascinating," he fluttered his eyes and sneered at her.

"You didn't," Madison said, betrayed.

"You can't hide anything from me! Those pages are filled with ludicrous dreams. Love just isn't your thing, Madison. And horse training is no place for a woman. You're much better at just circling that show pen, looking pretty and prancing around with good-for-nothin' rodeo boys."

Madison caught my hand, gripping it tightly. She knew I was ready to jump to her defense. I clenched my teeth, flexed my jaw. It was work to remain composed, but I promised myself I would not brawl with her father. Not the first time I met him, at least.

"He's no horse trainer either," Sterling grunted to Madison. I didn't like how he looked me up and down.

"I beg to differ, Daddy. He's quite talented with horses. He's been helping me with Lyric here, and I'm very pleased with the progress."

"I can see the progress you've been making, Madison. You're just like your mother – bringing men on my premises behind my back and letting them have their way with you. You behave like a tramp, not a McCall." Sterling turned his angry eyes on me. "And you. You aren't the first rodeo man I've found Madison with. You're one of many, and I'm sure there will be many more. None of them have stuck around. What makes you any different?"

"Daddy, it's not like that," Madison pleaded.

"I'll not have you be with the likes of him and have my empire ruined," Sterling bellowed, pointing a finger at me. The horses were becoming restless inside the barn at the commotion. Lyric pawed nervously in the corner of her stall while others nickered to each other. Sterling's voice continued to rise. "He's nobody from nowhere and not good enough for this family or for my daughter. He's a drifter just like the rest of your cowboys, Madison. I'll bet he gets bored with you and is back on the road in under a year. Believe me, I know the rodeo boys. They can't be trusted with a woman's heart because they don't care about their own."

"I've had enough of this, Daddy," Madison said, stepping in front of me and putting her hands on her hips. "I'm sorry, but Ken is my guy." She turned her back on her father and faced me. "I've fallen for you in a big way, cowboy. I want to go with you, be where you are."

"Is that so?" Sterling replied, closing the distance between us, shoving Madison to the side. "I know your kind," he growled.

He was so close to my face, I could feel the heat of his breath. I took a step back to create some needed space between us.

"What? Don't look so surprised, son! It's almost laughable that you'd be offended by my comments. Do you really think that you're the first broke cowboy fresh off the rodeo circuit to waltz through my door and try to get at my money by using my daughter?"

"Daddy ... please. Don't do this," Madison begged, stepping between us. She grabbed my hand again and held it firmly.

"You won't ever have a place in my empire, cowboy! You may have pulled the wool over Madison's eyes now that you've gotten between her thighs, but I'm no idiot," Sterling yelled as he put a finger in my chest.

That was it. This man didn't know a thing about me.

"I'm sorry," I said through clenched teeth. I let go of Madison's hand. Sterling's eyes were like darts as he watched me replace my cowboy hat on my head. I tipped it to Madison and started to back away from both of them. I knew the McCalls would be trouble. The whole lot of them had their fair share of crazy, and things were turning out exactly as I predicted they would.

I have to end it ... end it now ... before the situation gets any worse. He'll never let me love her.

"Ken. No! It doesn't have to be like this," Madison implored as her eyes welled with tears. She reached out, grabbing my hand again. "Please don't go."

"I can't do this," I said, peeling her palm from mine. A sinister smile grew across Sterling's lips. I kept backing down the aisle, watching Madison. I didn't know what I was doing, just that I needed to get out of there. I didn't belong.

"Ken …" Madison called out and started toward me.

"Where do you think you're going?" Sterling demanded, catching Madison by the crook of her arm and jerking her backwards.

"After him," Madison stated firmly.

"Oh no, you're not," Sterling scolded as he dragged her into the tack room and kicked the door shut with the tip of his boot.

"Listen to your father!" I yelled down the aisle. I was furious. My pride was bruised. I raced to my truck, slammed the door and peeled out of the McCall's manicured drive, surely leaving some tire tread behind.

I had to straighten out my mind.

CHAPTER 22

Trying to cool my temper, I drove around aimlessly for a long while. I didn't want to go back to the little room I was sharing with Brody out at the training stables. I needed to be alone. The day was beginning to fade, sun streaking the sky spectacularly in orange and pink. Leaving Madison behind certainly wasn't the most chivalrous move, but I'd rather be holding the handle than lying at the sharp end of the knife. During the confrontation with Sterling, I felt more like an animal belly up waiting to be gutted than the man I wanted to be for her. Getting out of there was the only way to put the handle in my possession again.

As my rage started to subside, it was replaced by an overwhelming depression at the realization that I just ruined the good thing that had begun to bloom between Madison and me. I needed to think about what to do now. I drove to Sterling's auto dealership. I parked my car in front of the building, got out and swung the door shut. I peered into the window, taking in all the plaques engraved with Sterling's name nailed to the wall of the lobby. I'd never be like him, the good or the bad parts. I sat down on the bench outside where the mechanics likely took their cigarette breaks and looked out over row upon row of his big, beautiful trucks. I looked out over what I could never give Madison. I dropped my head in my hands, recollecting it all.

"Hey," a soft voice unexpectedly called out in the night.

It spooked me. I jumped to my feet, scooting the bench and knocking over the metal ashtray next to it, causing a dang ruckus. My heart leapt from my chest into my throat.

"He wouldn't let me leave," Madison whispered, stepping into the light. Her eyes were red and mascara streaked her face. "He dragged me back to the house, but I snuck out my bedroom window after I was sure he fell asleep."

"How'd you know I'd be here?" I asked.

"Didn't." She shrugged her shoulders. "Been driving around town, hoping I'd find you somewhere. Don't know why I came here. Just did."

"You heard what your father said, Madison," I muttered. I wasn't able to look her in the eyes. "I can't give you any of this."

"Let's talk. Come on, Ken," Madison said, producing a key ring with the McCall tag on it. She slid it into the lock and opened the front door.

"I don't want all this," she said, waving her hand around as I followed her inside. "I don't want deep pockets. I don't need money to burn. I want a man who knows who he is, but doesn't make a habit of pushing it around. I want you. Just you."

"You sure about that, Madison?"

"Tell me, Ken, which of these is your favorite?" she asked, wiping her face to clear the smudged makeup.

I gave her a disheartened look and shook my head, but still idled over to one of her daddy's trucks parked in the showroom. It was my dream truck. I put a hand to the tinted window and peered in on the plush leather seats. I pulled the door handle.

Locked.

"That one?"

I nodded. Fresh faced again, Madison hovered in the doorway of one of the offices lining the showroom floor. I looked at the nameplate on the glass beside her. It was her father's.

"I knew that would be the one. It's my favorite, too. You've got nice taste, cowboy," she said, jingling a set of keys that she just pulled off a board containing the whole lot of dealership truck keys.

"What 'cha got there, cowgirl?" I asked.

"Why don't you come see?" she teased.

I smiled and rapped on the hood of my dream truck before jogging toward my dream girl. As I chased her around Sterling's office, she laughed from the other side of his desk, careful to keep the keys out of my reach. Madison held the keys to the truck I coveted and to my heart. Finally, she stopped running and tossed them to me. I caught the keys and rubbed a thumb over them in the palm of my hand. I pretended they were actually mine for a moment.

"You said you wanted to talk, miss?" I asked, extending my hand to Madison.

"Yes, I do," she said, a little breathless from our chase. She accepted my hand, and I led her to the black quad cab, three-quarter ton, chromed out dually with the full tow package, unlocked the door and nodded to the backseat. Madison stepped into the truck, and I climbed in after her. With the door shut, we were overcome with newness, new leather, new truck, hopefully a new us.

"You are the man I want, Ken. I've been around enough to know that now. I love you," she said, her fingers fumbling to the buckle at my waist. She slipped in front of me and straddled my lap right there in the back of Sterling's quad cab.

"I'm sorry I left like I did," I blurted, grabbing her hand from my waist. "The way he was talkin' about you, about me, about us … well … I was afraid he was right, and that I'm not good enough for you. I shouldn't have left you there."

"I know you didn't mean to do that," Madison said, nuzzling my neck. "I'm in love with you, Ken. I can't take it back. So from now on, will you promise to do the best you can?"

I pulled back and looked at her. "I promise, Madison."

"Good," she purred.

"Do you know that no one's ever called me Ken before?" I asked, narrowing my eyes at her. She just smiled in response. There was a glint in her eye. She liked being the first. If I had it my way, she would be the only.

"Are you in love with me because your father doesn't like me, or do you actually like me for me?" I inquired.

Madison's eyes softened, and she clutched the hem of her top. She pulled it over her head, tossed it behind her shoulder and shook her blond hair out of its ponytail. There was a thumb-print sized bruise on the inside of her thin upper arm. She touched my cheek as I ran my finger over the purple mark Sterling left on her perfect body.

"Madison ... I ..."

"How about a little less talkin', Ken? Let's do something else with our mouths like kissin'. Or perhaps a little bit more?" She raised an eyebrow and smiled down on me in her lacy bra. I quivered as she ran her hands through the hair at the base of my neck. She locked her fingertips there and gave a slight tug. "I'd like to get back to where we left off in that stall," she added. The building pressure was pulsating below my waist.

"OK, but I want to ask you somethin' first," I said, sucking in breath trying to restrain myself. "Lift your hips for a second."

Madison obliged by shifting onto her knees, and I dug into the front pocket of my jeans. Producing a ring, I held it up to Madison with my index finger and thumb. It wasn't much, but it was a start. I'd had it for a while and was waiting for the right time.

"I want to marry you, Madison McCall. I was aiming to do this by the book, but it doesn't seem like anything about you and me is going to be by the book, so I'm making up the rules now. Making things up as we go, and you coming after me tonight … well, that just confirmed it all for me. Madison, I want to marry you. Do you want to marry me?"

"Yes," she said breathlessly, placing her right hand to the exposed skin of her chest. I took the other and slipped the simple gold band on her left finger. "Oh, McKennon," she whispered. It was the first time she'd said my birth name. It was the prettiest sound I'd ever heard.

Still is to this day.

It was then that she loosened my belt from its loops, unfastened the button on my jeans and dragged down the zipper. I was a man ripe for the taking. Still straddling me, Madison reached up beneath her skirt. She lifted a long lean leg, then the other and slid her panties off over her cowgirl boots without a hitch. Balling them in her hand, she tossed them into the front seat of the truck with a giggle. Knees on either side of me, arms draped around my neck, she lifted her body again so I could wiggle my pants down and free myself. Madison moaned into my kiss as she softly lowered herself, gliding my manhood inside of her. Finding her stride, she rode me gently, smoothly, lovingly. And just like that, on display in his showroom, Madison McCall had her way with me in the backseat of one of her daddy's trucks.

CHAPTER 23

That was the first time we made love.
Yes, love.

It wasn't sex to me. Never was with her. It was the longest I'd ever waited for a woman. It was worth it.

"Let's do it, Ken. Let's run off and get married," Madison said, leaning over the front seat to retrieve her undergarments. "Let's get out of this town for a while."

"When?" I asked, pulling my jeans up from around my knees.

"Is right now too soon?" she inquired, hooking the clasp of her bra. That was all she needed to say. I was in.

"Where do you want to go?"

"Let's go to Vegas," she whispered over her shoulder. "It would be so scandalous." I liked the naughty look that spread across her pretty face.

"What about your horses?" I asked.

"Our neighbor's daughter is always happy to look after the horses when we go out of town. I just have to make a call. What about yours, Ken?"

"I'll make arrangements with Brody," I said, sealing the deal.

I had a few training paychecks saved up and what was left from my big win on Hasty Pete. I could make ends meet, especially in Las Vegas, so we decided right then and there to make the drive. I knew my trusted old truck would get us there. It sure didn't look like much, but it was reliable. I did all its maintenance myself to keep it purring along like a kitten. It never let me down.

I was exhilarated by the abruptness of our decision. Madison called her neighbor, and then she called into work to let them know she would need her upcoming shifts covered. I made similar arrangements. We took off with just the clothes on our backs and picked things up along the way as we needed them. The whole 17 hours and 27 minutes of our trip were spent in complete bliss. We took our time stopping at roadside diners and peeking in small town windows until we found a wedding band that would fit my finger. Madison even found a wedding dress.

"Can I have a minute?" she asked, stopping short in front of a woman's clothing store in some town in the middle of somewhere. "Why don't you go get us some more coffee?"

"Latte?"

"That would be dreamy," she replied, one hand on the door to the store. "Vanilla, please."

"One vanilla latte coming up, pretty lady," I said, touching the tip of my hat.

When I returned with two cups, Madison was sitting on a bench waiting for me. She held a box on her lap. Handing the drink to her, I poked a finger into the corner, trying to lift the lid.

"Hey! No peeking," she giggled, swatting my hand away. "You can't see this until our wedding day."

I smiled, taking a sip of my black coffee to fuel up for the remainder of the drive. We both loved road trips. They were a part of the rodeo and horse showing lifestyle. To us, Las Vegas was just a short jaunt. After all, we both had toured around the country a time or two. Madison had been seasoned to the road while hunting points across state lines for her Quarter Horse Queen title and me while repeatedly chasing after my next bronc bustin' paycheck.

The timing couldn't have been more perfect for a couple of horse lovers to head to Vegas for an impromptu wedding. The rodeo finals were in town. As fate would have it, we had an automatic best man and maid of honor waiting for us there. JD had already headed that way with a bunch of pro bull riders. Trish, a fellow horse trainer and one of Madison's closest friends, had a couple clients qualify their horses on barrels for the rodeo finals. Madison made the calls from the road, and they both agreed to attend our ceremony, although JD standing in as my best man took some coercing. In the end, he caved for his sister, and then we both promptly powered down our phones. We felt right at home when we arrived. As we cruised down the strip for the first time together, there were cowboys and cowgirls dressed to the nines everywhere. The rodeo lifestyle invaded Vegas this time of year.

We settled on a ceremony package from a place called the Little Chapel of the West, complete with a cowboy minister who would marry us in front of a hitching post for $650. They even offered a Western soloist who would sing one of Madison's favorite Johnny Cash tunes while we lit the unity candle. Looking back on it now, it all seemed a little hokey, but Madison was in wedding bliss, and we just wanted to seal the deal. I can still hear her giggling as she picked the place out of a big blue binder the size of a telephone book when we checked into our very Vegas hotel room.

Not long after we settled in, Trish banged on the door.

"Outta my way, cowboy," she said, combing the fingers of her free hand through her black pixie cut in frustration. "I've got work to do," she exclaimed, barging past me and tossing several totes on the dresser. I put both my palms up in surrender.

"Madison is all yours, Trish, but not for long," I said, winking at Madison as she popped the cork on some bubbles.

"Champs?" she asked Trish.

"Indeed," Trish nodded. "Thought you don't like drinking, young lady?"

"Stop teasing. This is a special occasion," Madison giggled, holding a very expensive bottle of champagne in the air so Trish could read the label.

Another knock came to the door.

"I'll leave you cowgirls to it then," I said, heading back to the door to welcome Madison's brother.

"McKennon," JD said, stepping into our room, taking in the hideous décor. "Nice place. I dig the shag carpeting." I couldn't help but chuckle at his comment. With the rodeo in town, the pickings were slim. After being turned away by several places sporting no vacancy signs, we just happened to luck across an establishment with a cancellation.

"Only the best. We've even got a kitchen," I said, motioning toward the tiny kitchenette.

"I'm going to have my way with you in here after the ceremony, cowboy," Madison hollered, pointing at a mini hot tub in the corner of our three-star hotel room. Glass of bubbly in hand, she was perched on the edge of our king-sized bed covered in a terribly tacky lime green bedspread.

"I'll hold you to that, miss," I said, nodding to her from the kitchenette counter. I smiled watching a giddy Madison bounce on our soon-to-be wedding night bed. I could hardly wait to have her all to myself again and as my wife.

As Trish started in on Madison's nails, makeup and hair, JD and I cracked open a couple of beers. My heart was full watching the ladies happily sipping on their champagne. Trish's laughter filled the room as they whispered to each other.

"Cheers, man," JD said, lifting his bottle and clinking it with mine. Like Madison said, it was a special occasion, so I'd bend my own rules just a little today. The beer tasted good on my lips. It'd been ages since I'd had any alcohol.

"I reckon they will be feeling a little light in their cowgirl boots right soon. I bought them a bottle of the good stuff," I replied.

"Seems so," JD said, taking a swig of his ale.

"So did you pick up that package for me?" I asked quietly.

"Yep. Slip me a key, and I'll put it on the bed after the girls leave the room."

"Thanks, JD," I said, sliding the extra key across the counter.

"Sure. Least I could do now that we are going to be brothers."

"You OK with me marrying Madison, JD?"

"Yeah. I've been thinking on it since Madison's call. I've never seen anyone look at her the way you do. I noticed it right away. I keep an eye on her you know."

I nodded my head in agreement.

"Not to mention she wouldn't shut the hell up about what a good guy you are when she was working on gettin' me to stand up for you. Guessin' you two make a good fit. Word is you're pretty wise with horses. Madison's got big dreams, so that'll come in handy."

"Good. I'm glad to hear that. I wasn't able to ask your father for her hand, so I'm asking you as her family member now. Feels like the right thing to do. Can I have your sister's hand in marriage, JD?" I held my breath and held out my hand. JD took it and slapped me on the arm.

"Welcome to the family, brother. It's a hell of a messy party." JD shook his head clearly pondering it all. "Here's to you and Madison. Bottoms up," JD shouted, slamming the contents of his bottle.

"Bottoms up," the girls chimed in and drained their glasses.

"OK, you two! Now shoo," Trish barked, waving JD and me away. "We've got finishing touches to do, and a man can't see his future wife in her wedding dress until the moment she walks down the aisle."

"All right. All right. We'll be leaving now," I assured her. I walked across the room to Madison and planted a kiss on her pink lips. I lingered on her mouth a moment. When I pulled away, I fixed my eyes on her icy blue ones and held her gaze. "I'll be seeing you in less than an hour, miss. You should know that I can't wait to make you my wife."

"I can't either," she said breathily.

"Enough of this love bird stuff! Out," Trish demanded, grabbing my chin and interrupting our moment. "There will be plenty of time for that tonight."

"Out!" Trish said again, looping an arm in mine and dragging me toward the door. JD held it open. He looked like he was ready to get out of there.

"Here's your hat, cowboy," Trish said, handing me my black Stetson. I put the hat on my head, took one last look at Madison and mouthed 'I love you,' just before Trish shoved me into the hall.

"Drink?" JD asked, handing me the blazer I'd acquired on the road and starting toward the elevator.

"That'll do," I said, shrugging the coat on over my new white dress shirt.

CHAPTER 24

After fueling up, I pull my truck back on the road. This stretch from the Lone Star State to the Heartland is a main thoroughfare connecting the important horse states. I know it like the back of my hand. I've driven it many times before with horses in tow – first when I was a regular on the rodeo scene, then later when Madison and I took our business on the road.

I surf the radio, readying to make the long drive north. I can drive this route with blinders on, but I need something to drown out the recent memories of my life with Madison. Since I've stopped soaking myself in whiskey, they come all too often and are far too vivid. Reliving our wedding in my mind is especially painful. Settling on a country station, I focus on the lyrics of the current tune. It's about a city girl gone country, and just like that, thoughts of Devon come spiraling back to me. I feel a little happier even.

A small smile tugs at my lips as I reflect on Devon's early days at Green Briar. I liked the look of her from the start — lean and athletic with auburn hair always tucked under a ball cap. I rather enjoyed the blush that crept up beneath that hat when I spoke to her.

I got a kick out of watching her walk down the barn aisle. There was something childlike about her gait. She always moved at a quick pace, her ponytail pulled through the back of her cap and swinging across her shoulder blades. I couldn't help but watch the pockets of her blue jeans as she went by, ignoring the little spark of guilt that crept in as I did, because there was nothing youthful whatsoever about the sway of her curvy hips. The way they moved were all grown up.

I often tried to catch Devon in action when she thought no one was looking – during a tender moment with Faith, when she was deep in thought hammering away at that laptop, when she was just daydreaming under the big oak on the hilltop, and especially when she wasn't trying so dang hard. That's when I like her most. Her zest for the horse life made me feel light inside after being so dark for so long.

Devon and Madison couldn't be more different, and that makes me happy. If I am going to move on, I certainly don't want anything about them to seem the same, not their minds, not their expressions, especially not their bodies.

Madison was a force. She was extraordinarily beautiful, and she knew it. Not to mention, the woman was seasoned in the horse industry *and* with men when I met her. I always felt like she was out of my league, even after she became my wife. I wish I had even a little bit of her confidence. She knew what she wanted out of life. Devon, on the other hand, is softer. She's beautiful, too, but in a different sort of way. It's as though she doesn't have any idea just how beautiful she actually is. She's a head-turner for sure, but more manageable than a red racecar like Madison. Devon is more like a silver beamer, a quiet luxury.

With Devon, I feel like the teacher, at least when it comes to the horses. I am the seasoned one this time around, and I like that. Devon looks to me with those doe eyes and wants to know more. I love those big brown eyes of hers. They're almost mahogany, the color of a horse's dark bay coat. There is innocence behind them, and they soften when I speak, especially about Faith. It's as if my knowledge is her drug. She is hungry for me to share more information all the time.

As I ponder the two women of my life, it occurs to me that Devon has everything and also nothing when it comes to me. She has my heart, but doesn't even know it. I keep driving her away. When I did let her in, it was just a little, only to leave again. I behave so terribly toward her.

Am I ready to fix all of that, to love her, to actually start living again, to shed this shell of the man that I've become? Am I ready to put some actual skin in the game for the first time in a very long while?

Thinking of Devon, I feel something besides sadness stir inside of me. I could give her a quick call just to let her know I am all right.

I check the face of my phone. It's just about dead. I dig around in my truck's console, searching for its charger. It's a small step, but at least in a direction other than backwards. Just when I am readying to plug it in and reconnect with Devon, I feel something soft. I lift the item to my gaze, and my chest clenches. It's one of the promotional koozies Madison had made for our new business. When we were prospecting, we passed them around at horse shows. As I squeeze it with my fingertips, a fresh wave of guilt washes over me. I toss the phone onto the seat next to me. I don't care if I lose the charge. I turn the radio off and drive for the next four hours in silence, aching for something I can't have.

Madison.

Having done enough driving for the day, I stop at a familiar hotel and settle in for the night. I'm disappointed to learn that room 323 is already occupied, but at least I passed up the last liquor store I saw. I bring the damn koozie in with me and just sit there on the edge of the tiny double bed looking at our logo. A dull pain in my chest, I rub my finger over the raised font and shake my head at all of it.

The longing I harbor for Madison is debilitating. Memories of her are everywhere. I know the emptiness from losing a spouse isn't supposed to just go away, but I imagined that it would get easier with time. I have to right the thing that went terribly wrong in my past, and then maybe freedom will be feasible.

Putting the koozie to the side, I reach for my wallet, the bed groans with the shift of my weight. I take out the bent, faded picture of Madison and me on our wedding day. We were so happy then, the future bright and full of possibility, so I let the memories come again.

CHAPTER 25

S tanding at the end of the aisle in my new blazer, best Stetson,
blue jeans and boots with JD at my side, I felt calm, complete
and madly in love. When the doors to the tiny chapel opened
revealing Madison, it was like something supernatural swooped
into the room and took my breath away. She looked stunning in
a simple white dress. Its chiffon skimmed her calves and floated
above her new, white cowgirl boots as she walked toward the front
of the chapel. She carried a bouquet of daisies that reminded me
of the ones I'd brought her the first time I set foot on the McCall
property. Her hair was piled on top of her head, a few pieces cas-
cading around her face in loose curls. Her eyes were bright and
clear. Madison positively glowed. Trish followed behind, holding
a bouquet of her own in a simple black dress.

The ceremony took all of 20 minutes, and we sealed the deal
with a kiss in front of our cowboy minister. Madison got a big hug
from her friend, and I got a slap on the back from JD in the parking lot of the Little Chapel of the West.

"Take care of her, bro," JD said. "Now that your wedding's out
of the way, I'm off to find the action since you're not having a reception. Plenty of willing cowgirls in this town right now, and I

won't be missing out on that." Madison rolled her eyes and Trish slugged him in the shoulder.

"I still can't believe you two are forgoin' a reception! Here in Vegas of all places," Trish said, shaking her head. "You certainly make a unique couple. I'm going check on my horses and their riders now. My phone has been blowing up. Everyone's getting a case of the nerves. We run tomorrow. I'm so happy for you both."

Madison and I watched our maid of honor and best man head off in different directions. Trish stepped up and into her rig. JD hailed a cab. I found our room's window on the building across the street and looked up at it longingly. Madison would find a surprise waiting for her there.

"You sure you don't want to have a reception, Madison?" I asked.

"Yes. I've had enough drinking for one day, husband of mine. All I want now is to be alone with you and do what newly-married people do," she said, wrapping her arms around me and kissing me deeply.

"Well then, off we go," I said, sweeping Madison off her feet and marching toward our hotel. I carried my bride all the way to our room, over its threshold and put her down lovingly on the bed. I was bursting with happiness, envisioning our future of training and loving horses together.

"There's one more thing. Look," I said, pointing to a package wrapped in silver paper and tied with a turquoise bow. I removed my cowboy hat and set it on a table.

"Oh, Ken," Madison said, lifting the box into her lap.

"A wedding gift for you, cowgirl," I whispered near her ear before kissing her cheek.

"But, how did you get it in our room?"

"I had an accomplice. Think your brother and I are gonna get along just fine after all. Go on now. Open it," I said, sliding off my cowboy boots and standing them in the corner of the room before strutting over to sit next to her on the bed.

Madison tore through the paper, and it fluttered to the floor around our feet.

"Oh my, Ken. They are exquisite," she said, lifting a pair of very beautiful, very expensive, square-toed, black designer cowgirl boots from beneath the tissue in the box.

"I'll have you know that I don't miss a thing. I saw you looking at them in that store window while we were on the road. You looked at those boots the same way you looked at the necklace at the rodeo."

"They are so expensive," she said, kneading the supple leather before hugging the boots to her chest. "I love them. What a lovely wedding gift. Thank you."

"Only the best for you, Madison Kelly," I said, nodding to the corner of the room where I had removed my own of a very similar design. "I vow from now on and forever only the best for you. Whatever you want will be yours so long as I'm around."

"Thank you, husband," she murmured, pulling me to her. I was immediately absorbed in her kiss and lost myself in the heat of the moment. I couldn't wait to take her as my wife for the first time. Thoughtlessly, I started to go at her like I did with all my previous conquests. I was taken aback when she gripped my forearm.

"No. Not like that," she said, stopping me in my tracks. The moment stretched, and she gave me a stern look before she spoke again.

"Let me show you what I like. This is our wedding night. We only get one of these. I want to make it special. Give me a second, would you?" she asked as a softer expression crossed her face. When I nodded, she scooted out from under me and scurried away from the bed.

I dragged a hand across my face at what I had just done. Madison was no rodeo conquest. I wiggled out of my sport coat, hung it on a chair, and then pushed myself back in the stack of oversized pillows on the bed. I let out a sigh and folded my arms behind my head. Madison McCall was my wife. That meant some things about me would have to change. I clearly had some work to do in that department. It all had happened so suddenly, but I couldn't have been a happier man. I wanted to be the best version of me for her. Since we'd met, thoughts of what it would be like to call her my own had been constantly running through my mind. Now it was a reality.

"What do you think, Ken?" Madison called from the doorway of the bathroom, giving me a little shimmy.

She had changed into a nightie and was wearing the designer boots I had just given her. It was the prettiest satin, silky thing I'd ever seen. I'd never had a woman wearing something like that. Oh, I'd fantasized about it, but never actually had it. Pretty sure buckle bunnies don't own such things. She strutted across the room and joined me on the bed, nestling into the deep pillows beside me.

"How'd I get so lucky?" I whispered, kissing her shoulder and placing my palm to her stomach so I could feel the soft nightdress she was wearing.

"Ken, when are you gonna stop talkin' so we can start kissin'?" she giggled. I shifted toward her.

"So kissin' is what you want miss?" I pressed my lips to hers and kissed her with everything I had until she released a soft moan.

"McKennon," Madison sighed as my hand gently grazed her body still covered by the nightgown. This was only the second time I'd heard Madison say my real name. I cherished the fact that the first time was when I asked her to be my wife, and the second was after she'd become my wife.

"You can take this off, but leave those on," she coached, pinching the material of her lingerie then pointing to her new boots. "I want to look at them while you make love to me."

That was just about the hottest thing my new wife could say to me. Eyes fixed on mine, Madison raised her arms and I lifted the negligee up over her head. She smiled while my gaze hungrily roamed her curves, drinking all of her in. The moonlight was beautiful on her naked body as she knelt before me on the bed. Madison opened the buttons at the front of my dress shirt and peeled it from my shoulders. I could hardly contain myself standing there. My skin was smoldering beneath her touch. She leaned back and wiggled those boots for me. I loosened my belt and hastily stripped out of my jeans. Once free of my clothing, we made love, differently than we had the first time, but no less passionately, giving ourselves to each other completely.

During my marriage to Madison, I learned to be a good lover, not just a good lay. She taught me how to really please a woman fully and how to make the lovemaking last. My old style had been to just grab a woman by the hips and take her from behind. I was always in a rush, but with Madison, I slowed everything down. I learned how to move, how to touch, how to enjoy, how to appreciate a *woman*, not a girl, not a buckle bunny. Madison was a prize and expected to be treated as such. She wasn't disposable. Madison was the whole package – secure, confident, in control and aware. At first, I often felt klutzy, awkward and amateur when I touched her. I never knew intimacy could be like that. She was a patient and kind teacher though. I still don't know how I lucked into being her husband.

Madison made me feel like a man – every time, but especially this time, our wedding night was indeed special – a gift and I relive it often in love. We stayed in bed for a week, all tangled up in our newlywed sheets. We only rose to satisfy our hunger for each other or food. Our week of bliss came to a roaring halt when Madison turned her phone back on to find 37 missed messages from her father. Then JD called.

CHAPTER 26

"Hello?" Madison said, eyeing me as she hit the speaker button.

"You best be calling Dad, Madison," JD said. "He's heard about what you've done."

"I figured this was coming. Thanks for the heads up, JD."

"Sure, sis. Good luck. Here if you need me."

"Bye, JD."

"Bye."

I took Madison's hand and pressed my lips to her knuckles.

"Better start packing, I suppose," she said, squeezing my hand before shifting the sheets and sitting up. "Just one thing to get out of the way first," Madison added, waving her phone.

"You're actually calling your father?" I asked, raising a brow and rising from the bed we had spent the whole week in.

"Ken, I have to. My horses are still there. No telling what he'll do if he doesn't hear from me soon."

"I don't know if that's a good idea, Madison," I said, pulling my boxer briefs on.

"Trust me, Ken. I have to do this."

I nodded and gave her a weak smile. I wasn't ready for reality to set in or our week of laying low to come to an end. My heart started to pound as I watched her hold the phone to her ear. This wasn't going to go well.

"Daddy," Madison whispered into the receiver. Sterling's voice thundered from the other end. The phone didn't need to have the speaker on. I could hear his yell loud and clear.

"How dare you not return my calls, Madison? I've heard about your little escapade to Las Vegas. You're a traitor just like your mother!" Sterling spat.

"Daddy, I just –" Madison started in protest.

"Don't say another word! I have a few things to say, and then I'll have you know you are dead to me! You and your lover boy best be getting those horses out of my barn and your belongings off my property quickly. When I first got word of this treason, I had half a mind to put a bullet in each one of their heads. Consider their lives and my generosity a wedding gift! You're dead to me, girl! Y'hear?"

"Yes, Daddy," Madison answered meekly before hanging up the phone. She looked ill. I could see her throat working, trying to hold back a sob as the tears began to well in her eyes. I rushed to her side and held her.

"Come on. Let's pack up and go. It's gonna be OK, Madison. This is the kick-start we needed. I'm so sorry to see you hurt like this, but you've wanted to start that business of yours, so let's go do it. We'll get your horses out of there. Trust me."

She nodded, wiped her nose and pulled out the dresser drawers, aimlessly stuffing what little we had picked up on our way to Vegas in a plastic shopping bag.

We left Las Vegas in the direction we had come. We weren't so sure where home would be once we got back. Madison clutched my hand, but said little during the drive. All we knew is that we had each other, our horses and a business to get off the ground and fast.

Upon our return, Madison learned that she had been fired from her job while we were away. It didn't bother me any. I didn't want her tending bar anyway. We shacked up in my bunk for a few nights. It wasn't ideal sharing a room with Brody, but it provided a roof over our heads. It pained me to see Madison anguishing over getting her horses out of Sterling's barn while we figured out our next move.

I knew we needed a quiet place, off the beaten trail, almost a sanctuary, where we would have a chance to get our business in order and our marriage started off right. I needed to be free of the scrutiny of other trainers, riders and gossipers who claimed to be horse lovers at any training facility we might share. Renting a shared space wasn't an option.

Deep down, I wanted – *no*, needed – to get dirty, earth dirty, hard work dirty. I think Madison wanted that, too. We wanted to enjoy the fruit of our efforts, sit down at the end of the day feeling the work we had done, the callouses on our hands our labor would surely create, mattered.

We wanted to care for our horses ourselves. It was important to us to know how much water our clients' horses drank during the day, how to ration feed in order to keep weight on from rigorous training schedules, and the nutritional content of the hay the horses would receive. We wanted to clean stalls and have the satisfaction of sweat running down our backs. We knew we wouldn't be able to afford staff to do those chores for us in the beginning. It was of no matter though because we didn't want anyone else to know our business better than we did.

I wanted to give Madison everything, and Madison wanted to try on a life that was truly not fed by her father's silver spoon. I had to affirm that I was good enough for Sterling McCall's daughter. I had something to prove and was dead set on proving it.

We needed our own place. It defeated me that I couldn't afford to buy us one. Not right then anyway, so we banged on every door with fences and a barn, determined not to give up until we found what we were looking for. We had to move fast before our little town's rumor mill started churning. It was only a matter of time before Sterling found out what we were up to. I'd never forgive myself if something happened to the horses we had left at his place.

CHAPTER 27

The sun creeps into my motel room through a slit in the cheap plastic shades like a laser in my eye and drags me back to reality. I eye the koozie and our wedding photo on the nightstand, toss an arm over my eyes, and groan. I don't know what's worse – waking up every morning whiskey-soaked or waking up sober, wishing I was whiskey-soaked. Both feel pretty awful.

Dragging a hand across my stubble-ridden face, I fling the comforter to the side, and my feet find the floor. It's evident just how much I've abused my body over the last few weeks. I'm still trying to recover and clearly suffer a multi-day hangover. I can't remember the last time I've actually eaten anything substantial.

I need a shower and ... eggs.

I dig through my small black duffle bag and produce the last clean white T-shirt, pair of underwear and socks. I'll keep wearing the same jeans I've been wearing. I hate driving in stiff, just washed jeans. I need them good and worn to do any serious driving. I never ceased to battle with Madison over washing my jeans. She always wanted me in clean, pressed ones when we went to horse shows. She told me they presented better to clients. I told her that they crushed my balls when I was driving the truck and trailer. A cowboy with crushed nuts is never a happy one, so she let me have my way most of the time.

I didn't anticipate taking this journey or being away from Green Briar for an extended period of time. I don't much look forward to going to a laundry mat. I wander into the bathroom, hold the clean shirt to my nose, and take a deep breath of it in. It still smells of Green Briar. My thoughts drift back there, and Devon's soft lips flit through my mind. I shake thoughts of home and the woman waiting on me there from my head as I pull back the plastic shower curtain. I turn the water hot, peel off my day-old tee, and step out of my boxer briefs. I stand in the mirror and look over my lean frame. My muscles appear more pronounced than they had just weeks ago. I haven't been eating much. I'm surely dehydrated. I put a hand over my heart and trail the fingers of my other hand over each of my abs, letting my thumb dip into the grooves between them. I follow the 'V' of my hips and think about Devon again. That time with her in the motel room was so erotic. The urgency of her mouth. The brilliance of her exposed body. That red bra.

Damn that red bra and those forsaken boots.

I feel my manhood stir, and it surprises me. During all this time, it has just been hanging unused in front of me like some long lost appendage that had stopped working many moons ago. I can't remember the last time I'd even satisfied myself. The whiskey sure rendered that part of me useless, but so does the depression I am trying to keep at bay. I'm a shell of the cowboy I once was. I reach out and put both my hands on the dingy bathroom counter. I stare at my wedding band. Dropping my head, I just shake it at the thought of trying intimacy again. I'm coming undone caught between a future and the past. Madison is always in my head with me.

Can this body ever be with another? Am I capable of loving anyone again?

I just don't know. That sort of satisfaction feels like a distant memory now. I wonder if I still have what it takes to really be with a woman. Overwrought with guilt, I put my hand on my heart and point at the ceiling. I step into the shower and hope the hot blast will wash all of these thoughts away.

Still edgy, but feeling semi-refreshed from my shower, I trot across the street to the truck stop with breakfast on my mind. I pull open the glass door, and the bell chimes.

CHAPTER 28

Memories flood my mind as I slide into a booth. This is the sort of place Madison and I would come to figure out what we wanted to do to move our business forward. She thought the best business conversations happened over breakfast no matter what time of day it was.

After we eloped, everything between Madison and me started to take shape. It came easily. On our drive back from Vegas, we made a pact to go slow and be deliberate. The agreement between us stuck, from the way we made love, to the way we started and eventually ran our business. We were thoughtful, precise and paid attention to our reactions – most of the time anyway until that damn stallion came into our lives and turned everything upside down.

We were in a booth just like this at a very similar restaurant the day I found Green Briar. Madison and I just happened to split up that particular day. JD lent Madison his junker while he put in time at the dealership, and we stealthily picked it up from the edge of Sterling's property in the middle of the night. We were starting to get desperate and thought we could cover more ground driving the backcountry dirt roads individually. In our search for the isolated space we craved, we hadn't been able to turn up a single lead. We were faced with rejection every time – either the places had a bad taste in their mouths from leasing to trainers in the past due to unpaid debts, were full or really meant the word 'private' when it was printed on their sign. Our fresh start seemed out of reach.

When I turned up Green Briar, I cautiously looked side to side as I inched down the dirt drive. No signs of life anywhere. I knew immediately that it was different from the places where I grew up and rode horses. My youth around horses involved listening for the roar of an engine from the guy who worked as a mechanic out of his garage next door to my uncle's small homestead. I was always waiting for my horse to spook as I navigated his path, trying to avoid discarded tires and rusted tractor parts that littered the trails. Then there was this other gent on his motorcycle. He would give it extra gas when he passed our place just because I was on horseback. I'd watch him go by as my horse skittered at the bike's sound. I'm pretty sure he always mouthed an inappropriate word to me as he passed by. It was a pretty poor environment, but at least I had access to horses as a kid.

Green Briar wasn't like Madison's perfectly manicured space on Sterling's land either. This was no plotted out hobby farm architected just for horses – the place was beautiful and sprawling.

I remember feeling nervous, yet hopeful, surveying the landscape when I pulled in its driveway. My eyes swept the grounds, looking for any signs of movement … nothing. I spied a horse trailer capable of transporting eight horses parked alongside the stable. I looked at it longingly. It was the type of trailer I needed to get all of Madison's horses out of Sterling's place at once. Putting the fact that I only had a two-horse trailer out of my mind, I continued to look around. The lush pastures were uninhabited, not a horse or human in sight. It made me curious.

Why was such a beautiful ranch not being used?

The barn looked ghostly. From what I could tell sitting behind my wheel, it was empty, maybe a little rundown, but looked to have good bones. I could fix her up for sure.

Pulling in and parking, I walked sheepishly from my truck toward the main barn. I remember my feet feeling connected to the dirt of the place. Once I crossed the threshold of the barn doors and moved into the cool shadows, I had to adjust my eyes, the transition from the bright sunlight threw me off. I rubbed my eyes, squeezed them tight and then looked up again. I couldn't believe what I saw: the grand 20-stall barn was empty. The stalls were built from expensive hardwood and lined either side of the long aisle. They were in need of a good varnishing and the hardware on the stalls a polishing, but everything seemed in working order. I pushed on down the cement corridor, peering between the iron bars. Not a single living thing was rustling inside the box stalls. They were all stripped of bedding, and thick cobwebs hung in their corners. It seemed nothing had lived in this barn for a long while. All was quiet and lonely. It was exactly what Madison and I needed.

Starting to leave, I turned and glanced around the stable again. The space gave me the lingering sense that something good had happened here, but was since long gone. If I could bring Madison and our horses here, maybe we could make it great again.

I took a deep, steadying breath in the shadows of the barn, turned to the sunlight and walked toward the farmhouse. I looked for any sign of life around me.

Nothing.

My only companion was the quiet billowing of overgrown grounds for as far as I could see, an ocean of grasses, excellent for grazing. As I approached, I noticed the front door was open a foot or so. I took the steps quickly and peered in the screen door.

"Hello?" I called.

No response.

"Hello? Is anyone in there?" I called out again. Something didn't set right with me. Taking a deep breath, I opened the screen with a squeak and pushed the slightly ajar door open further with my fingertips. I quickly dropped back onto the porch as the screen snapped into place.

"Hello?" I called again through the screen door. "Is everything OK in there?"

Nothing.

I pressed my face to the mesh and squinted into the dark house. That's when I saw her, just inside. I saw small bare feet attached to a body laid out in the long hall. The other half of her appeared to be face down in the adjacent room. I rushed in, afraid whoever was in there might be hurt or, even worse, dead. I gazed around the place and lifted a crocheted blanket off a davenport in the parlor. I knelt on the cool linoleum beside the slight body motionless on the floor and covered her. Willing myself to move, I shook her just the slightest.

"Ma'am, are you OK?" I asked. I leaned close to her face and felt a puff of breath.

Not dead.

"Ma'am," I said again, gently cupping her shoulder.

I was relieved when she released a little murmur. It was undecipherable, but at least it was a sound. She tipped her head and met my eyes. Hers were cloudy blue, sad sapphires cloaked by soft wrinkles. I suddenly felt compelled to take care of her. She was delicate and light as a feather when I picked her up. Boney. Her skin was paper thin, peach and luminescent, almost transparent. I could see that there was still blue blood working through the veins in her hands. I couldn't help but think that I might break her if I squeezed too tightly.

CHAPTER 29

"Eggs?" I jump at the waitress's inquiry.

"Uh ... yes ... eggs," I respond, not fully present. I am still with the memory.

"So ... you want those cooked, or should I just bring over the carton?" she asks with an eyebrow raise and a small smile spreading across her very pretty lips. For a moment, I wonder why such a lovely lady is waiting tables at a truck stop, then I come back to reality.

Not my business.

"Pardon me. Just lost in a thought, miss. I'll have three of 'em scrambled ... and some rye toast, too. Please. That'll be it." I'm not really hungry, but I know I need to eat.

"You got it, cowboy. Want coffee?" she asks, giving me a once over and a real smile.

I nod. I feel bashful at the thought of her finding me attractive when I despise myself so. I take my cowboy hat off, set it next to me in the booth, and rake my fingers through my hair. It's still damp from the shower.

A bus boy drops a brown mug of coffee in front of me. I spin it around and gaze into it. I've been in a haze, and I can't seem to shake this days old hangover. I spoon in some sugar and take a big sip.

Need caffeine.

What seems like seconds later, the lovely waitress scoots a plate of eggs and toast in front of me. My mouth waters, but my stomach turns.

Hungry. Not hungry.

"Here you are. Had 'em put some cheese on those eggs for you, handsome." She winks at me as she pulls bottles of ketchup and hot sauce from her apron pockets and sets them on the table. I pick up my fork and turn it over in my fingers contemplating the first bite.

"You let me know if you need anything else now," she hums suggestively as she tops off my coffee and slips me the bill. This makes me sad. She's far too young to speak to a man fresh off the road like that.

"I will. Thank you, miss." I pull out my wallet and lay several bills on top of the paper check. I down my breakfast in seconds, but it doesn't do anything to settle my stomach. I don't want to admit it to myself, but the ache I feel isn't hunger. I am homesick for the farm, for Star, for Sophia, for my routine; beyond all that, I am really homesick for Devon.

Finishing my coffee, I pat my shirt pocket and the pockets of my jeans, realizing I've left my cell in the motel room. Afraid I'll lose my impulse to call again, I spot a payphone in the lobby of the restaurant and jog toward it. I dig into my front pocket for the change I got in return for my breakfast. I lift the phone from the receiver and put it to my ear. It feels foreign using the thing. Dropping in the coins, I dial the number I know by heart.

I think of riding Star with Devon on Faith next to me, gliding across the acres at Green Briar. Guilt twists in my stomach recalling the way I'd left her. I left for the mere betrayal that being with her would mean. I shame myself for my thoughts this morning when things are still so incomplete with my wife, my life. I clench my teeth and wait for the pick-up.

"Hello?" Her voice is like heaven, angelic.

"Hi," I breathe.

"McKennon! Is that you?"

"Yes."

"Are you OK?"

I pause, mulling over that question.

Am I OK? No. Not really. I am pretty much having a meltdown.

"Yes. I'm fine," I lie.

"I am so glad to hear from you, dear."

"Sophia, it is so nice to hear your voice. You sound just like an angel."

"Oh, stop your flattery, dear. I know you aren't calling just to say hello. What do you need, McKennon? Just say the word."

This is what I love about Sophia. She never tries to fix the situation or me. She never asks where I am, what I'm doing, or when I'll be back; she always just asks if I'm OK. Sophia is a special human. She gives me enough line to figure things out for myself, but has me hooked at the same time because I know I can count on her. Sophia has gotten good at handling my disappearances, just like JD has. I always come back to them. I owe those two quite a debt for their understanding. They've been the only consistent people in my life since Madison. Swallowing my longing for the comforts of Green Briar, I look out to the expressway, and it comes to me.

"I'll be needin' the address book from the trainin' business. I need to find Sallie Mae. It's in the desk drawer in Mad ... er ... in my office at Green Briar."

I never trust plugging my personal contacts into my cell phone. I feel if I do that, my information is just waiting to go bye-bye. I'm not keen on waiting for some electronic mishap. One thing I love about the horse business is that it's one of the last industries on earth that hasn't been completely digitized. I keep everything handwritten in a single address book.

"I understand. Is that all, dear?" Sophia asks softly.

The address book will be helpful, and I'm glad to have remembered it. There might be some sort of clue in it, not to mention Sallie Mae's contact information. She will know how to find him. I know Sallie Mae has been working in the offices of Quarter Horse shows across the nation since she retired from barrel racing.

"McKennon? Are you there, dear?" Sophia inquires, bringing me out of my trance.

The real truth is I've only just remembered that there might be information in my address book. When I dropped those coins into the payphone, what I really searched my mind for was an excuse to call home, to at least let them all know I am all right. I know this second request is going to show up crazy lazy on my part, but there isn't a store for miles, and I really hate doing laundry.

"I'll need some clean clothes from my place, too. Think you can send me a week's worth of clothes for changing? I'm hopin' to steer clear of any laundry mats. Just my white T-shirts, some underwear, socks and a couple pair of jeans?"

Sophia doesn't even hesitate. "Where will I be sending them, McKennon? I can have them overnighted. I've got a pen and paper right here, dear." I look around the bleak landscape, nothing but dirt, blacktop, a crappy motel, a bar and this diner.

"Suppose I can stay here another night." I dig my room key and its paper keeper from my jeans to read her the address. I need to come up with a plan anyway. I've been driving blind since I'd left. That address book will really help. It has all the names, numbers and places we'd been. It lists the places we'd stay hauling from show to show, the people we know in the business. With it, I'll be able to pinpoint Sallie Mae's whereabouts. I only wonder if I'll be able to open it and see Madison's handwriting again without reaction. I'm doing my very best to avoid anything that might make me want to reach for the first whiskey bottle I encounter. "I'm at the White Horse Inn in Tulsa. Please send them to me here. I'll let the front desk know that I'll be expecting an overnight."

"Consider it done."

"Thank you, Sophia."

"And McKennon …"

"Yes, Sophia?"

"You are missed here at Green Briar, and it isn't just me doing the missing."

"Yes, ma'am." I lower my head and trace a finger over the edge of the payphone.

"We'll see you when you come back, McKennon. Adieu." With that, Sophia hung up. Her words weigh heavy on my heart.

CHAPTER 30

DEVON

Sitting at my favorite Green Briar writing perch, my hands feel leaden on the keyboard. Nothing is coming. I've grown bored with my recent article for *Organic Living* magazine on the evolution of the redskin potato. Even the title, 'From Reject to Delicacy,' annoys me.

My editor is needling me for more articles, and she wants them faster. The money is really rolling in. My professional writing life is taking off, but my heart just isn't in it right now. Poems are coming more easily to me these days. In a strange turn of events, a journal full of private thoughts now provides solace and replaces my laptop.

I power down my computer and slap the top shut. I ferret around in my oversized bag, and I rummage up my notebook.

Is it time for me to move on, stop the waiting and find something new?

I *am* in the position to do so. As I write articles, my bank account grows. I have enough tucked away to make a small stake for Faith and myself. I have to face the fact that McKennon might never stay for good. He's left too many times.

Maybe I'll find another trainer. Maybe I'll move Faith to a new barn. Maybe I'll buy my own place.

Tapping my pen against pursed lips, I look out on Faith from my favorite spot on the farm. I open my journal and the words start to flow ...

I'll find a place to take you
A place of our own
Big green meadows laced in lavender
Great, grand trees for lingering in the shade
We will live in safety
I will have peace of mind
And you will be in sweet harmony
We will race the wind across our acres, heads held high
We will stop where the daisies grow
You can graze
I'll just watch you finally have what for years you've deserved
Under a sky of blue and puffs of white with warm rays on our bodies
We will erase our yesterdays

I tuck my journal and laptop back in my bag. I leave the hilltop in hope of finding some peace on Faith's back. I can't help but crack a smile as I open the gate to Faith's pasture to retrieve her. She welcomes me with her muzzle and immediately starts nosing for kisses. I reward her with an apple slice from the baggie in my pocket, and she happily accepts it. Back in the barn, I occupy myself with a long grooming session, then saddle her, readying for a languid walk over Sophia's acres.

Twisting the leathers, I step into the stirrup and swing myself into the saddle. I need to clear my head. It is clouded with thoughts of leaving Green Briar, a certain handsome cowboy, and the haunting memory of the embarrassing scene at the Tumbleweed Inn. I plan to take a ride through Green Briar's pastures to get away from life for a while, just Faith and me with the wind tussling the soft grasses around us. Sadly, I quickly realize my mind isn't interested in complying with my plan.

What was I thinking going to that hotel in a freaking trench coat?

I tip my head to the sun and relish the breeze as it slips over my cheeks. Faith's hoof beats are rhythmic in my ears, but it isn't enough to stop my mind from spinning.

Am I a fool to think that I really belong here or with him?

McKennon and I definitely aren't cut from the same cloth. Yet … even though we are different, McKennon brings out the best in me. McKennon's packaging is simple, but contains a keen intellect within it. From him, I've learned that it is experience that teaches us, especially when it comes to horses. I understand now that not everything I need to know can be learned from a book. I'm not a horse trainer. I don't feel compelled to research anymore. I don't want to mess her up after his help got us this far. Faith's training is stalled, and so am I.

Do I really want to find a new trainer?

Trying to put my wandering thoughts out of mind, Faith and I clip-clop toward JD. I watch him turn Star out to pasture. McKennon has left behind one of his chicken-scratched notes outlining Star's care in his absence. In it, he said that Star has earned the right to rest. Like clockwork, JD secures the gate, then gives me a wave, and Faith whinnies to them as she does every morning.

I feel turned out to pasture by the man, too, but not to recuperate from a job well done. I am the loser left to my own devices like an elder show horse cast away, not wanted anymore.

I can't fathom how McKennon could leave Star behind, especially after his dream-achieving win on the stallion's back. I'd never be able to separate from Faith like that. At least seeing Star every morning feels like a piece of McKennon is still at Green Briar, perhaps a promise that he will return. I look up to the sky from my saddle as McKennon often did.

Where are you, McKennon? Are you coming back to us?

Star begins pacing his fence line as we approach. I give Faith a little bump with my spurs to keep her moving. She's tuned in to her surroundings, to the situation.

"Come on, Faith," I groan as she resists going forward. Finally, I manage to guide her by.

Is her behavior evidence that she misses our rides with McKennon and Star, too?

Against my better judgment, I desperately want to hold on to what is left of McKennon here. I guide Faith onto the path that leads to the lower pastures where the herd is out to graze. I often ride by to say 'hi' to the pretty little Palomino-Paint when I need a good dose of innocence.

I'm fond of McKennon's favorite little filly, the one I met during our first ride together. I loved how she'd put her tiny muzzle in the palm of his gloved hand that day. It feels like just yesterday that McKennon had appraised her show pen promise. I gave her a nickname in his absence. I call her Willa, for short. I named her after the weepy willow tree she favors in the pasture. If I ride Faith up to the pasture's edge quietly enough, I can sometimes catch Willa frolicking in the shade of the big tree. She prances beneath it, hiding and seeking, with the other foals. I love to watch her pull the elastic branches with her mouth before letting them snap back into place to startle those brave enough to play with her. Willa's behavior often displeases the mother mares. I get a giggle out of it when they pin their ears and swish their tails in irritation at the filly's antics.

When Willa spots us, she releases a shrill whinny and streaks across the pasture like a blaze of sunshine. She lopes up to the gate to greet us with a tiny nicker, then sniffs noses with Faith. Even though they can't tell me so, I am confident they've become friends.

A visit to Willa always makes me feel better, but then I ride by McKennon's house, hoping he'll be there. When he isn't, I lose the slight glee the Palomino-Paint gave me. I miss the sight of him, the jingle of his spurs.

Where has my cowboy gone?

I pull Faith up and survey the land, recollecting our early horse-back jaunts through Green Briar's acres. Faith's white mane shimmers in the sunlight. I stroke beneath it and lose myself in memories of when we were first discovering each other. With McKennon, I had cast my instincts to the wind. I cringe thinking about how reckless I'd been with Faith. I think of galloping Faith full out, the alarm on McKennon's handsome face when I pushed my horse and myself too far, and then the first time his body held mine.

Did I do those things to impress him?

Thinking back on it, I really didn't know any better. All my falls, going to a horse show when I wasn't ready, my forgetfulness at tightening her girth ... my near-death experience. That's the sort of equine knowledge one can only learn from time spent in the saddle and under the guidance of a good trainer. No research could ever teach me what McKennon or those experiences did. I certainly grew as a cowgirl because of them. I filed each one away in my brain's "do not attempt again" file. Experience is the best teacher when it comes to Faith, and the lessons are often harsh ones. I still grimace though. I know I probably would have thought better about at least some of it if I hadn't been so cowboy obsessed. And then, there is the evening of the Tumbleweed Inn.

What a terrible idea that was!

I shudder as I think about standing before him in that wretched motel room with my body exposed, trench coat around my ankles, lusting after something I couldn't have. I wanted to make love to him. I wanted to bring him home to Green Briar. I thought I could make him remember us. I never thought he would turn me away in my fire-engine red bra. Things did not go the way I expected.

What do I really know about this man after all?

Contemplating my mixed emotions, I wish I'd just steered clear of him and minded my p's and q's like they warned me to. Sophia and JD are right. I can't compete with the life he had before with his wife.

Do I even want to?

As we approach the hillcrest that leads to McKennon's house, I stop Faith and take a deep breath. It pains me every time I see the curtains pulled tight, the dust covering the rockers on his porch, everything untouched for some time now.

Can I handle the sight of his house empty again?

I look back over my shoulder at the Palomino-Paint tucked beneath her willow tree. Willa. At least she is a reminder of the good days with McKennon. I miss him. I hate him for leaving us.

Would I be happier if I'd never come to Green Briar? If I had never met McKennon?

Realizing that doesn't much matter now, I cue Faith forward. When my eyes see activity at his residence, my heart starts to hammer. From a distance, I watch her float to his front door, turn the key in its lock and disappear inside. I ride Faith up to McKennon's house for a closer look and will myself to wait patiently at the front steps. Sophia will have to come out eventually.

CHAPTER 31

The groan and slam of an aged screen door snaps me back to reality. Sophia, angelic and thin, stands on McKennon's stoop. I eye his belongings cradled in her arms. The hem of her skirt flutters on the breeze as her gaze settles on me.

"Is he coming back, Sophia?" I ask from the saddle. Her blue eyes are penetrating.

"I don't know, dear," she admits, raising her shoulders and the small stack of his stuff. "He's asked me to send some clothes and his address book."

"Do you know where he is now?" I ask and immediately wish I'd held my tongue.

"Yes, but only because he's asked me to send these things. I don't ask those sorts of questions of him, Devon. If McKennon wants someone to know where he is, he will tell them."

"Oh." It's all I can muster. It's evident that McKennon hasn't inquired about me.

"I know you miss him, honey. I can only imagine how difficult this situation must be for you, but you've done the right thing by turning him loose. McKennon is a smart man. When he gets himself straightened out, I think he'll come to terms with the intelligent choice. I think that choice is you." She smiles up at me with her light eyes, and just like that my thoughts of finding another trainer or leaving Green Briar evaporate. There is certain magic to Sophia. Her words always bring me peace.

"Would you come sit with me, dear?" she asks, setting down the goods she gathered from McKennon's house on a small table. Sophia hastily dusts off two seats with her handkerchief, settles into one of the rocking chairs and nods toward the other. She retrieves McKennon's items and places them on her lap.

I dismount Faith and tie her to the hitch out front. I approach the little house and take the steps slowly. I lower myself into the same rocker I sat in the first night I spent with McKennon Kelly. My mind wanders back to just how uneventful that first evening was. My cheeks heat at the memory of McKennon's omelet garnished with fresh strawberries.

"You just go in and out of his place?" I ask.

"I never had children, Devon. McKennon is the closest thing to a son I'll ever have. We trust each other." Sophia takes pause and smooths his T-shirts folded on her legs. "We are tied together, not by blood, but by something bigger, by circumstance. I lost my will to live when my husband died. Then that cowboy came knocking at my door. He and his pretty young wife nursed me back to health. I saw promise in those two, recently married, and seeking to start their business. They gave Green Briar and me a second chance. We created a new family. It was wonderful here until –" her voice travels off.

"I always knew something special and tragic happened at Green Briar," I offer, reaching out and touching her thin shoulder. It is the truth, but also an attempt to keep her talking.

"Life can be tricky, my dear. A person can have it all in their lifetime, but there's a hitch ... no one can have it all right now.

Be patient with him and yourself, Devon. Patience will prevail. McKennon has dragons he needs to slay, and until he does, their fire will keep driving him away."

I sigh and nod. My body feels heavy, sad, tired.

"Did you know he told me I could tell you what happened before you left for the show? Sometimes I wonder if I did you a disservice by not telling you the whole story. I didn't tell you because I wanted McKennon to disclose the truth in his own way. I gather you know some, but are rather in the dark about most of it, dear. Is this true?"

I nod. A sense of relief washes over me. I want to know. *Finally.*

"What do you know, dear?" Sophia asks.

"I know that McKennon's wife passed away. I know her name was Madison."

"Is that all?"

"Yes," I whisper.

"It's time you knew what happened."

"That would mean a lot to me, Sophia. It's been difficult to be in the dark."

"Now Devon, I don't know all the intricate details. I wasn't there, and no one would make much mention of the accident when they returned. I can give you the generalities though."

"Please tell me what you know, Sophia," I implore.

"Madison and McKennon started a horse training business – M&M Kelly Quarter Horse Training and Services."

My eyes go wide when she says the name. I remember analyzing the koozie McKennon slipped over the beer we shared at the horse show.

"Did he tell you about the business, dear?" Sophia asks, observing my reaction.

"Not really. I saw one of their koozies once."

146

"Oh yes, Madison was very good at marketing that business of theirs. Anyhow, life led them to me, and they started it up here at Green Briar."

"Do you believe it was fate, Sophia?"

"Yes, dear. Call it fate. Let's settle there."

There it is again ... fate.

"Are you ready for me to continue, dear?" Sophia asks.

"Yes," I answer, swallowing hard. Fate led me to Faith and to Green Briar. It helps some to hear from Sophia that fate links all of us here somehow — even Madison.

"You see, McKennon was so taken with his young wife that he would do anything for her. He would also do anything to convince her father that he was good enough to be her man. That's what set the whole thing in motion. McKennon wanted to give Madison the world, so he bought a horse that she wanted. He did so against his better judgment. The horse had excellent breeding, but was damaged. It was likely the young stallion had been abused at the hands of his previous handlers. Still, they pinned the future of their business on the horse's show pen success. Madison named him Charming. McKennon called him by a different nickname. The goal was to make a champion out of him that they could then stand at stud. It was planned to have him father the offspring of the breeding arm of their business. So, determined to prove himself, McKennon rushed the poor horse's training and skipped healing him. He only broke his own rules once. It was the biggest lesson that man has ever learned. It cost him his wife."

"Oh my," I gasp. "What happened, Sophia?"

Keep going! Don't stop. Not now. Not when I am on the brink of understanding everything!

"I'm sorry, dear. Memories can be difficult to relive. It was wonderful having them all here at Green Briar. Like I said before, we became a family ... that is, until the winning got in the way.

It's why McKennon refused to train you. He saw the talent in that horse of yours … and you. It worried him when his feelings started to bloom. He was afraid he would repeat the past and go over the edge again."

"Over the edge? I don't understand. How?"

"I'm sorry. Let me start all the way at the beginning. It begins with my marriage. My husband was much older than me. I was just a wisp of a thing when I met him. He reeked of class. I was immediately taken with him. I remember the first time I laid eyes on him. He was leaning on the rail of a pen, watching his horses make their practice rounds, smoking a fancy cigar. He had a scotch in hand and looked dapper in his suit coat. My heart skipped a beat when he took notice of me noticing him." Sophia sighs that pretty sigh of hers and shifts the big diamond on her left hand.

"He sounds handsome."

Sophia nods enthusiastically with a faraway look in her eyes. It is clear that she understands McKennon's lament because she's experienced the loss of a beloved spouse, too. It is a part of their bond and something I can't even pretend to comprehend.

"My parents died when I was very young. They were immigrants fresh from overseas. We had no family to speak of in America. That's what everyone told me anyway when I was old enough to ask questions," she continues. "As a child, I was moved from orphanage to temporary home to foster home after foster home and back to the orphanage again. I was so unwanted. The only emotion I can remember feeling during that time was loneliness. That is, except when I read books. I read books about horses mostly. Those stories took me away and made the lonesomeness bearable. Books made me fall in love with horses even though I'd never seen one before. I prayed for one. I dreamed of them – big, beautiful Warmblooded ones. I wanted to soar over jumps on horseback. I clung to the television during the Olympics when my foster parents would let me. Ha! Foster *parents*," Sophia spits the word. "What a vile definition. None of them were parents to me."

"Oh, Sophia. I had no idea."

"When I was finally on my own, I rented a small room. Just turned 18, I worked as a waitress for what seemed like ages to pay my rent and save up enough money to attend The National Horse Show, a competition for hunters, equitation and show jumpers. I bought a one-way bus ticket to New York City, gave up the small room I rented and took myself to where the horses were. I didn't know what I would do after I attended the horse show, but I didn't care. All I had was a tiny suitcase of belongings. Seeing a horse for the first time made me feel so alive. Standing ringside, I felt happy for the first time in my life. My heart leapt when they leapt over the jumps.

That's when I met Andrew Clark. He was a business tycoon. Oil. He was Southern and charming with just the slightest drawl. His accent was new to my East Coast ears and made my heart go all giddy. He was in his 40s. I was much younger, nearly half his age, but it was no matter to me. I inquired after him from another patron of the show and learned that he invested in horses for pleasure. Thoroughbreds and Warmbloods mostly for track and field. I don't know what he saw in me, but he caught me staring at him that day and just strutted right up to me. 'Do you like horses, miss?' he asked. When I nodded, he simply took me by the hand and said, 'You haven't seen horses until you've met mine. Come.' Then he walked me behind the scenes of the show.

The moment was electric. I could barely breathe there was so much to take in: the grand stables, the beautiful horses, the smell of the hay, and the shavings, then there was his cologne. It made me weak in the knees. He introduced me to his horses one-by-one. He had a whole stable full there. I shook hands with their trainer. One of his steeds had made the jump-off round, and there was excitement in the air. I felt so fancy, regal roaming around with him."

"I can only imagine, Sophia." I leaned forward. This story had me on the edge of my rocker.

"'This one here is Titan. He's going to win us this competition today,' Andrew told me proudly. 'He's been bred to exhibit calmness and style. This sport requires equine boldness, power, accuracy and control. Speed also is a factor, and Titan's got it. He's designed for winning jump-off courses. Sophia, I would be honored if you would accompany me in my box for the final round of the competition.'"

"You must have been on cloud nine, Sophia!"

"I was! How could a girl say no? Together, we watched Titan jump big, bravely and fast. There was something careful and accurate about the horse's movements. He avoided any knockdowns of the jumping poles and was balanced as he galloped beneath his rider. Andrew whispered the details of a clean ride near my ear. 'The rider must choose the best line to each fence, saving ground with well-planned turns and lines, adjusting the horse's stride for each fence and distance. In a jump-off, a rider must balance the need to go as fast as possible and turn as tightly as possible against the horse's ability to jump cleanly with good height. As you can see, Titan makes that easy for Bruce.' Andrew smiled and slapped his knee as all four of his horse's hooves cleared the last jump. 'By golly! He's done it,' Andrew shouted, springing from his seat. 'I'll be back to collect you.' He kissed me on the cheek and rushed to the arena floor. I watched from the stands as the team retrieved the engraved silver platter and a very large paycheck during the awards ceremony. It was the best day of my life."

"It sounds like a perfect romance, Sophia." I want her to elaborate. I want all the details. Sophia is always cryptic. The fact that she's divulging this much information about the past is rare. She's never said more than a few words about her husband to me.

"Oh, it was. After we spent the day together, he folded me into his arms in the stables next to Titan's stall, and I let him. Can you believe it? I'd never been with a man before my husband. It feels like yesterday that Andrew said, 'If you come with me, I will give you all of this and all of the horses your heart desires.' I remember clutching the handle of my small case, holding my only worldly belongings, and saying, 'I'll go with you.' My answer sent his smile dazzling. He kissed my breath and my lipstick away. Taking my bag, then my hand, Andrew led me right into a tack shop on site at the show. 'Sit,' he said, pointing at a chair and instructing the manager of the shop to fit me to my first pair of paddock boots. As he paid for them from a wallet with more bills than I'd ever seen, he winked at me and whispered, 'You'll need those where I'm taking you.' He brought me here to Green Briar."

"It's like a fairytale."

"It certainly felt like one to me," Sophia murmurs. "Our love was instant, real. My husband provided stability for the first time in my life. He was the only real family I ever had. After we married, I was terrified to have children. I thought we might die and leave them like my parents had left me, so we had horses instead. Lots of them. We filled this place with horses. I learned to ride here. He bought me the best mounts and had me work with the best trainers. I'll have you know that I even qualified for the Olympic team." Sophia shifts her shoulders back, raises her elegant chin and gives a determined, proud smile.

"Sophia! That's amazing," I exclaim.

"I was well on my way until my horse came up lame. I was working on qualifying again when my husband became ill. It was a battle we fought for many years. When he died, part of me died, too. I sold all our horses. I couldn't bear to see them anymore, but I couldn't leave Green Briar. I was waiting to die here when McKennon found me."

I remain quiet as Sophia confesses her tragedy. I don't dare ask why or how her husband died. I don't need to. It is enough to know she loved and lost something more important to her than living. It makes me wonder back to McKennon and what he might be going through.

"So that's how McKennon came to be part of Green Briar. It wasn't long after McKennon and Madison settled onto the farm that McKennon went off to apprentice with some of the best horse trainers of the time. He was already plenty talented, but he had this need to substantiate himself. Poor cowboy has never known that he is good enough just the way he is. I suppose growing up on the rodeo circuit without knowing a mother or father could do that to a man. I set him up with some of the protégés of the trainers Andrew and I worked with in our heyday. Still, even having the experience of working with top trainers, McKennon rushed things with Charming. He didn't take the time to create a connection with him. He wanted to show Madison's father so badly. He abandoned everything he had learned."

"What did Madison's father have that McKennon didn't?" I ask.

"Oh, Sterling McCall has it all. He is the richest man in the county. Has an auto dealership with the nicest trucks on its lot and owns an outrageously successful Western apparel company. Ever heard of Sterling Ranch Wear and Tack?"

"Everyone knows that brand!" I respond in disbelief.

"I figured you've heard of it. Another thing about Sterling McCall is he detests the rodeo scene, which made McKennon an instant enemy. McKennon didn't think he could compete with the riches Madison was accustomed to. He did know, though, that if he set his mind to it, he could win her heart with a good horse. He knew he could bring in money that way and validate he deserved to be in Madison's life. Everyone except McKennon knew Madison loved him for who he was, not what he could buy her."

"I see." I am wringing my hands, hopeful she'll keep going. I am afraid to say too much or maybe too little. Sophia shifts in her seat and gazes upon me. An angelic expression relaxes across her face.

"Dear, I want to be clear. I am sharing this with you because I want you to know that with McKennon ... well ... it's going to be a waiting game."

I look down at my hands and bite my lip.

"I guess I kind of figured that, Sophia." I shrug my shoulders. "I'm still here, aren't I?" I give her a half-hearted smile.

"Indeed. Shall I continue?" she asks.

I nod.

"Did you know that JD is McKennon's brother-in-law?"

"Uh. I just recently learned that one." I grimace, thinking back my conversation with JD the morning before I visited McKennon's motel room in my stupid trench coat.

"I see. Well, it was JD who helped me find McKennon wasting away in a seedy motel. McKennon was really in a bad way after Madison passed away. We begged him to come back. He eventually agreed, but had me get rid of all of their horses before he'd set foot on Green Briar again. They were such brilliant animals hand-selected by Madison. It pained me so to sell them off, but I had done the same thing when I lost Andrew. I knew the man couldn't bear to see anything that reminded him of her. He stayed away while I found every last one a good home."

"What happened to the horse? Charming. The one that caused the accident?"

"McKennon had JD take him away straight from the show. He was sold at an auction, and that's all I know. A sales slip and a check made out to Green Briar arrived from the place. I returned the certificate to the American Quarter Horse Association along with a completed transfer form showing the date of sale and the very little contact information I received for the buyer."

"Then what happened?" I ask, scooting to the end of my seat again. I desperately want to know exactly how that horse killed McKennon's wife, but this is not the time to inquire. I have to just listen right now.

"I kept all of his music, books, belt buckles and trophies. I held on to the things I thought he could still celebrate or connect with. I had cabinets and shelves built to hold everything, but I made sure that there wasn't a trace of Madison except for her handwritten business records. I figured he would need them one day. I figured right."

"He asked for them?" Sophia nods and fingers the worn address book in her lap.

"Anyway, McKennon had done a good job clearing her out on his own after the accident. The man was like a bull in a china cabinet. He set everything that reminded him of Madison ablaze in the fireplace and outside on Green Briar's lawn. While he was hiding away in that dank motel, I had the guesthouse freshly painted. I knew peace would be difficult for him to achieve. The weight of the world came down on him when he lost Madison, so I made certain his home was a blank canvas. He eventually moved back in, but it was on one condition. He asked for the freedom to leave if he wanted and whenever he wanted with no questions asked. I agreed.

He was slow to heal, but he started to come back to us. The man you know now is half as vibrant as he once was. It has pained me so to watch McKennon suffer. I knew he still had talent. Instinct told me being with horses again could help free him, so I asked him to raise horses again. For me. I asked him to train them. For me. At first, he resisted. The rumor mill had not been kind to him.

A lot of folks blamed him for what happened to Madison. I told him, 'You don't have to train people. You don't have to deal with people. I'll do the buying and selling. I'll do the negotiating, but I can't go back to having Green Brian empty of people or horses. Not after you all made it so full for me again. You are my family, McKennon.' All he said was 'OK,' so I brought in some stock, and he started our small herd. I know you've been out to meet them. I see you spending time with the foals. Those horses are the reason McKennon is still standing."

I can't believe the enormity of it all. My heart aches for Sophia and McKennon.

"McKennon saved my life. It's a life I am grateful to have now, so I wanted to do what I could for him in return. I gave him the only things I had to offer, and that is this ranch, these horses. And he is good at it. Every glimmering enhancement to this facility has been of his doing. He is an excellent horseman. I was afraid, though, that he had lost his purpose. That is, until he met you."

"Me? I didn't do anything. He's left me, too." I scuff my boot on the porch.

"Life isn't convenient, Devon. It's rather messy. It's a series of emotions tied together on this tightrope we walk with others. People don't always have the same thoughts or paths or shared aspirations. Sometimes the best things we can do are to just wait … or listen … or look for the signs. Wait for him. He will return." Sophia stands from her rocker, touches me on the shoulder and offers a slight smile.

"Thank you for telling me all of this, Sophia." It is killing me to hold my tongue right now. My journalistic side had been line-listing questions in my mind the whole time. Sophia's book of life is BIG, and she only shared a few chapters with me. Her words were the cliff notes at best. But at least I have a loose summary of what happened here at Green Briar. That is good enough for now.

"You're welcome, dear," she says, gliding down the front steps with McKennon's things and leaving me alone with my thoughts.

CHAPTER 32

Gently rocking myself, I watch Sophia make her way toward the big house, parting the green grasses of her stead like the sea. I am grateful for her guidance.

I'll wait while he works it out. However long it takes. I will wait for McKennon.

I've never felt something so animalistic, so primal, so crazed as the desire I harbor for McKennon. I like it, *and* it scares me. It feels somehow destined though. I knew the emotions were different from the start, part making me feel like a woman obsessed and part making me feel my wholeness, all of my female sensuousness. My reaction to him is real, alive, wild. I've never had that sort of attraction to a man or experienced this kind of desire before. At the time, I treated it like a gift.

Now ... now I wonder. Can I really have the man or the horse life I imagine for myself?

With McKennon gone – my cowboy away – it seems impossible. Still, Sophia's talk helped me realize that I don't want to give up on my horse, find a different trainer, go to a new barn or buy a place of my own. I have my dream horse in Faith. McKennon feels like my match. Green Briar is home. All I really want is for everything to go back to the way it was before I knew too much or anything at all. Back then, my cowgirl lifestyle was pristine. Perhaps, it is better in my mind and fantasies than in reality. Maybe it's just a work of fiction. Maybe I made it all up.

Why does all this real world stuff keep getting in the way of my fantasy fictional one?

I leave the porch, retrieve my journal from Faith's saddlebag and plunk down in the grass beside her tied to the rail. I cross my legs and open to a fresh page. My quill is sharp, and it needs paper.

Winter of my heart
Tonight could we just forget?
And gallop beneath the moonlight
And ride until our horses sprout wings, their hooves touching the stars
Can we dismount in the heavens and taste the frost on each other's lips?
Would you hold my hand then while we are alone
And look into my eyes
And watch me exhale in a cloud of breath
And let me put my cold nose on your cheek
So I can believe I've found something beautiful
And would you pretend to try a little harder to make amends with the past?
You don't know where you are going
And neither do I
I'm starting to wonder ...
Was that kiss we shared a dream, or was it real?

I slap my journal shut and let my movie reel mind kick into action. A soundtrack stirs in my head. I recall one of my favorite country songs. In the tune, the songstress croons about a cowboy taking her away from buildings standing tall to a place where she can crush dirt in her hand and grow something wild. I had that feeling for a fleeting moment with McKennon. I want to feel like that again.

CHAPTER 33

MCKENNON

Since I'm staying on at the motel one more night waiting for my address book and fresh clothes, I decide to work on my plan. The room is making me depressed. I've just been lying on the bed, flipping the channels, not for the watching, but for the noise. I step out into the parking lot and scan the area. There isn't much to see, just a bar and the diner. I need to keep my head straight and steer away from any alcohol, so the diner it is. I open the door and step back into the restaurant. I eye the payphone I called Green Briar from this morning then look around the joint. No sign of the pretty waitress.

Thank heaven.

I don't want her thinking I came back in for her. I consider the booth I sat in earlier, but it reminds me yet again of the ones I had shared with my wife so many moons ago. I walk past it. I take up residence at the counter in front of the kitchen and settle onto a vinyl-topped stool with a tear in it. I am proud I avoided the local bar. My mind is finally feeling clear rather than foggy, but the memories are still as painful as ever.

"What'll you be having?" a husky-voiced waitress asks.

"Coffee for now. Thanks."

She silently slides a cup in front of me.

Certainly not as friendly as the morning help.

Stirring a spoonful of sugar into the cup, I watch the brown liquid spin and feel the usual tug at my heart. I wish my wife were here. Madison was meticulous at writing things down. She took notes on everything: feedings, vet visits, contacts. She always carried a notepad, scribbled things or thoughts down, and then organized them later. It's probably why she was such a productive person. Me on the other hand, I feel good if I check off one thing on my to-do list a day. That's what I loved about Madison. She made me better. She made me want to be more. Made me the man I am today. And I hate that she had to die before I could realize just how much she contributed to my life. I don't know if I can give all she taught me to another woman. Madison would probably want me to. She loved me unconditionally like that, but I still wonder why me?

Why do I get to stay? Why do I get to contemplate whether I get to love again? Why do I get a second chance?

I take a swallow of the scalding coffee and force myself to focus. I have to come up with a plan. I spread my map out on the counter in front of me.

Where is that damn horse? Where is Sallie Mae?

I curse myself for not saving any phone numbers except JD's in my dang cell phone. My resistance to technology is really tripping me up on this quest. I have to get to Sallie Mae. She'll know how to find that damn stallion. She always knows how to dig up information or knows someone who can. I need my address book.

I have one shot at this. If I fail, then I've wasted several tanks of gas and a whole lot of days that I could've spent trying to love Devon, but that evil horse calls to me, even though I haven't seen him in years. My mind wanders back to my life at Green Briar. So much for planning ...

CHAPTER 34

Once I had her in my arms, she resisted with what little strength she had. The elderly woman made a noise that probably would have sounded like a shriek were she not so weak. I was a stranger in her home after all. It was to be expected that she would be fearful.

"I'm not going to hurt you, ma'am. I promise you that." I met her eyes and smiled. "I am here to help."

"No hospitals, Andrew," she moaned when I started down the hall ready to carry her out to my truck.

"Uh. Yes, ma'am," I said, wondering who Andrew could be.

It wasn't hard to figure out that Sophia had been starving herself. Why she was doing that was the real question. I didn't know what else to do so I tucked her into bed and made her something to eat. I warmed a can of soup I'd found in her pantry.

"Ma'am, I've made you something to eat," I said, cautiously peering around the door into her bedroom. It was then that she addressed me. It was in a sweet, low, musical voice and a bit strained.

"I can see now that you aren't my husband. You do look quite a lot like Andrew in his younger years though. I'm sorry for the confusion. What I do know is that you are a strange man in my home. A kind man, it seems, but a stranger none-the-less."

I stepped into the room, carrying the soup on a tray I'd found in the kitchen and introduced myself, "I'm McKennon Kelly, ma'am."

"I am Sophia Matilda Washington-Clark. Please just call me Sophia." She reached out with her dainty, crooked fingers and gave my forearm a timid squeeze.

I took note of the caution in her eyes as I set the tray down on her lap and handed her a spoon.

"I'm not going to hurt you, ma'am. I promise you that," I repeated, taking a seat on a chair in the corner of the room.

She nodded then finished the whole bowl of soup before she spoke again.

"I can't quite recall the last time I've had anything to eat," she said, resting the spoon in the bowl. "Now tell me, kind stranger, what brings you here? Why don't you tell me a little about yourself so I feel less inclined to phone the authorities?"

"Well, ma'am, I've just married the love of my life. Her name is Madison. We're looking for a horse property to lease. You see, I am a horse trainer, and my wife has got a wonderful eye for talented horses. She's got the intuition." Rising from my chair, I crossed the room, opened my wallet, removed our wedding snapshot from the Little Chapel of the West and handed it to Sophia.

"What kind of horses, Mr. Kelly?" she asked, taking the photo. She tapped the comforter I'd tucked her into. It was an invitation to sit down.

"Quarter Horses, ma'am," I replied, perching on the corner of the bed. I was careful not to sit too close.

"Hmm. I don't know a thing about Quarter Horses. Your wife is quite beautiful," she said with a smile, handing the picture back to me.

"Yes, yes, she is. I've got to take care of her. Never loved some-thin' so much," I replied, lovingly tucking the photograph back into my worn wallet.

"I appreciate true love, dear. My husband and I always had Thoroughbreds and Warmbloods. I was an aspiring Olympian once. That's what he built this facility for. Our dream was for me to win the gold. Look there," she said, pointing an index finger toward a velvet box on the dresser in her room. "Bring that to me, would you?"

I crossed the floor, retrieved the item, handed it over, and then positioned myself on the edge of the bed again.

"I trust a man who's head over heels in love with his new wife and just made me soup isn't going to rob me now. Am I correct?" she asked, eyeing me.

"No, no, ma'am. Like I said, I'm here to help. Don't mean you no harm," I assured, palms up in surrender. "Just ended up here lookin' for a place to make a name for myself in the horse business. So, what do you have there?" I asked, gesturing toward the box.

She opened the lid and peered in. "This is the medal I re-ceived in the competition that qualified me," Sophia answered, caressing the box. "My horse came up lame before the Games, and an alternate rider had to take my place."

"I'm sorry to hear that, ma'am. I imagine that must have been quite a disappointment."

"Yes, yes, it was. Alas, that is all in the past now," she said, snap-ping the lid shut, setting it down next to her on the comforter. "So tell me, what is it you plan to do with these Quarter Horses?"

"Madison and I are going to start up our own training business."

"How do you plan to start this business, dear?" she probed.

"Well, we just need a place to begin. That's what led me here. We need a facility fit for makin' champions."

"And if you had this place to begin?" she asked, sitting up a little straighter in bed.

"You see, we don't have a lot to offer right now, but we're in it to make some champions, then start breeding them. Your facility would make for the perfect starting place. We'd be willing to make you a partner. May I add that I'm a pretty handy fellow, in case you could use a little elbow grease and some fixin' around here."

Sophia pursed her time-lined lips and cocked her head in thought. She considered me for some time. Finally, she spoke.

"You seem like an honest man, and I'm intrigued by your story. I suppose I could use a partner here at Green Briar. I let it go when I let myself go. After my husband died – rest his soul – I fell into a bad way. I never loved a man the way I loved my Andrew before or since. I just wanted to lie down and die when he left this world, so that's what I did. I couldn't bring myself to leave the house or feed myself. I was desperately lost. Now you've found me, and I just have to think that you ... what was your name again?"

"McKennon ... McKennon Kelly, ma'am."

"McKennon. Yes. I'm sorry. Well, McKennon, I just have to think that maybe your arrival and finding me the way you did is a gift from my husband. I just have to believe he's telling me that I need to go on. He must not be ready to see me yet," she said, smiling at me.

My heart went out to Sophia. I would help her. I'd make her ranch great again.

"Maybe you'll be the one to pull me out of the darkness," she continued, thoughtfully. "When you came knockin' on my door, I don't think I'd eaten in over a week. I just wasn't hungry anymore. Didn't see the point. Then you, a perfect stranger, just picked me up off the floor and made me soup."

"Yes, ma'am. You were in pretty bad shape. Glad I stumbled across you and could help. Madison and me, we'd be willin' to whip you back into shape with our downhome cookin'. If you'll have us over for dinner sometime." I winked at her and squeezed her thin, peach fingers.

"How about more than just dinner, cowboy? There might be some life left in this old woman yet. I might be able to learn some new tricks. Bring me your Quarter Horses, Mr. Kelly. Introduce me to your lovely and talented wife."

"Wha- R-r-really?" I sputtered, not able to contain my excitement. I knew I was grinning from ear to ear.

"Yes, really," she said, through her smile. "I have all this land that I don't know what to do with. It would be nice to have horses and people around again."

"You won't be disappointed with this decision, ma'am. I promise you that."

"Please call me Sophia, partner," she said. "There's a guest house down by the stables. Consider it yours."

"When can we move in?" I asked.

This was too good to be true.

"As soon as you like. We can discuss the financials once you've settled in."

"Sophia?" I cleared my throat.

This was a big ask.

"Go on, McKennon."

"Would it be too much of an inconvenience if I asked to borrow that 8-horse trailer of yours down by the barn? I can leave collateral. I can sign papers. Whatever you need to feel comfortable with such a big request. My wife's got seven horses, and I've got one. With Green Briar's trailer, I could swoop them all up at once."

Sophia looked around the room then her eyes settled on my left hand.

"Your ring. Leave your wedding ring, and you can use my trailer. If you love your wife as much as I think you do, you'll be back for that particular item."

I put my hand out in front of me and examined the band. I didn't want to take it off, but I had to. I took a deep breath, pulled it from my finger and pressed the ring into the palm of Sophia's hand.

"You take care of that for me now, Sophia," I said, standing and my eyes already heading toward the door. "I'll be back for it and for you. Make sure you get some rest now."

"I will. I have a feeling I'll need my strength for what lies ahead. Adieu, McKennon. I'll see you soon," Sophia said, closing her palm around my golden wedding band. She brought her fist to her heart and smiled at me.

With a tip of my hat, I stepped out the door.

CHAPTER 35

I met my wife back at the restaurant as planned.

"Where did you get this trailer? And where is your wedding ring?" Madison asked incredulously, a hand on her hip.

"I've found a place. It's perfect for us. No time for questions right now. Let's go get your horses. I've already picked up mine. I don't want to leave him standing around in there too long. I'll fill you in on the way. C'mon." I opened the door to my truck and motioned for her to get in. Madison gave me one of her looks.

"Trust me," I said. Once she was buckled in the passenger seat, I excitedly filled her in on finding Green Briar, helping Sophia and leaving my ring behind in exchange for the trailer. We headed straight for Sterling's place to retrieve her horses.

"Oh, Ken. It's happening. It's really happening. We are really going to do this. Aren't we?"

"Like I said, Madison. Anything for you." I squeezed her hand.

"I can't wait to see my horses and get them to their new home. I'll finally be out from under my father," she squealed, bouncing in her seat. Her happiness made my heart soar.

When we arrived at the McCall place, Sterling was standing in the little pristine barn that Madison had once loved. From the looks of it, Sterling had gotten a head start on us. The aisle was lined with boxes labeled with Madison's name.

"Heard you were back in town," he growled, glaring at us. Sterling motioned to the cardboard containers. "I took the liberty of having your room boxed up, Madison."

"Sir," I said, tipping my hat to Sterling and not meeting his eyes.

"Not a word from you, homewrecker. I'm only out here to be sure your grubby paws don't take anything Madison hasn't bought with her own money."

I tightened my jaw and my fists.

"We won't be long, Daddy," Madison assured him.

"You're a traitor just like your mama," he spat at her, arms crossed in front of his chest. "Used me and my money to get your start. Now you're taken off with a rodeo slacker, just like she did. You are a disgrace, Madison."

We worked swiftly to gather her belongings. I couldn't stand to be in this place much longer. His words were cutting. I knew Madison was holding back her tears, her tongue and her breath as she haltered Remy, Rosie, Pumpkin, Trey, Lyric and her mother. She led each silently up into the horse trailer. We had some really good stock to start our business off with. Thank heaven none of them gave us any trouble loading. Madison walked toward the stall that contained her favorite, Cash. Sterling stepped in front of her.

"Daddy, what are you doing?"

"You will not touch my property again. My money paid for this horse. He won't be going anywhere with you."

Fury blazed in my veins, I started to move toward him.

"Ken. Don't," she pleaded. Her eyes were glistening.

"Yeah, *Ken. Don't*," Sterling repeated, putting a hand on the pistol at his hip and unfastening the holster.

"I've told you once, and I'm telling you again. I'll not have you be with the likes of him. I will not have my empire ruined. He's not good enough for this family, for my daughter."

"Not your choice, Daddy. He's my husband now," Madison snapped. She tossed Cash's halter and lead at Sterling's feet then sauntered up next to me where I was standing across the aisle. Madison grabbed my arm and tugged me toward her. Those icy eyes of hers were afire when she kissed me hard on the mouth in front of her father. "Let's go home, Ken," she barked, shooting Sterling a defiant last look. "Our future is waiting for us." Madison stomped out of the barn and lifted the ramp of Green Briar's trailer.

"He's a drifter, Madison. I'll bet he gets bored with you and is back on the road in under a year. I know the rodeo boys," he called after her.

"I'm takin' care of her now," I grumbled. It took everything I had to remain in control.

"Yeah, with what? I know you don't have anything to give her. And you know it, too, cowboy."

"I'll prove it. We have a plan," I snarled, exiting the barn.

"I'll bet," Sterling snorted with a roll of his eyes. He slid the stable's doors shut behind us. Cash whinnied from inside.

"There will be a new passcode on the gate the moment you're off my property, Madison. There's no coming back either. Y'hear? You better be clear about the choice you're making," Sterling hollered.

"I'm not coming back, Daddy! Goodbye. Let's go, Ken!" Madison climbed in the passenger side of my truck and slammed the door.

I crossed the drive, hopped into the driver's seat, and put it in gear. I was relieved to get the heck out of there. Madison sat resigned in the front seat. She hadn't thought that she would have to leave Cash behind. Neither had I.

I let out the breath I felt like I'd been holding since we crossed under the McCall's ranch entryway. I pulled off the dirt drive onto the pavement of the street. As we turned, Sterling's bronze sign screamed his name in my side mirror, and Madison finally lost it.

"What am I going to do without Cash?" she cried out. "He is a kindred spirit. The horse I've learned everything on. How can I leave him there? With *him*? Who is going to take care of him, Ken?" She looked to me with glassy eyes, black mascara rivers running down her flawless cheeks.

I knew her heart was breaking, and mine was aching for hers. When I left home, I left my childhood horse behind. It's not really something you ever fully recover from. I believe their spirit is always in the saddle with you every time you ride.

I didn't have the words to console Madison right then, so I just reached across that leather bench seat and took her hand. I gave it a reassuring squeeze, and she returned it. I smiled at the beautiful woman by my side and just knew that everything was going to be all right.

To my surprise at that very moment, she said, "I know that everything is going to be all right, Ken."

The woman could read my mind. It reaffirmed that we were connected to each other and meant to be. Together, we were unstoppable. I just held her hand tight as we made our way back to Green Briar with the horses that would help us create our foundation. Now, all we had to do was find the perfect stallion to cover our mares and hopefully the mares of others willing to pay for the service.

CHAPTER 36

We went to work straight away when we got back to Green Briar. We wanted to show Sophia she had made the right choice. Madison and I worked side by side. That's what I loved most about our early days on the farm. Madison liked the work. She worked as hard as any cowboy I knew. I especially enjoyed watching her clean buckets. No matter the angle, it was always a good view. She'd wear a tank top and blue jeans – both tight. If I was looking down the aisle at her front, I could see her perfect breasts plunging in the 'U' of her neckline. If I was to watch from behind, I could witness her fine backside wiggling behind pockets with each scrub brush stroke. When she'd stop to wipe her brow, I'd make sure she'd catch me admiring her. When she did, I'd always get one of her sexy, sinister smiles. Then I'd know that we'd be having a good night. Our days at Green Briar were filled with love and hard work. My nights with Madison were sweet and laced with heat.

We called our business M&M Kelly Quarter Horse Training and Services. Often, we'd just call it M&M Quarter Horses. It was a simple name, nothing fancy, which suited us just fine. We decided Madison would manage the office, coach the student riders and ride our horses at the shows. She was best suited for keeping the ledger and receipts organized. She was also the master of sitting pretty in the show pen. She knew how present a horse and how to nail a showmanship or horsemanship pattern. The judges couldn't seem to keep their eyes off of her, not to mention she had already created quite a reputation for herself. She was the Quarter Horse Queen after all. At the shows, I was confident we'd be a shoo-in to make the placings with Madison's equitation on an excellent mount.

We determined I'd work the horses, get them going correct and honest so any rider could just get on and hopefully win. Madison was capable of training horses, but she didn't necessarily want to. She told me she preferred watching me doing the training. She said it made her fall in love with me over and over again. I loved how she would saunter up to me while I was lunging a horse, put her arms around me, and whisper in my ear while the dust swirled around us. She said she liked my touch with the horses, that is, until Demon came home with us.

"When are you going to ride?" she would ask, and add that she loved the sway of my hips in the saddle. Her lips would tug just the slightest on my earlobe. "You may be riding horses now, but you're gonna ride me later, cowboy," she would tease. I quivered every time she told me my riding made her have dirty thoughts. When she was being all sexy, it made me feel sexy, too. The woman had me wrapped around her finger. I loved the way she loved me. Madison made me feel special, noticed, and alive when before her, I'd been resigned to be a drifter. I never thought I was capable of loving a woman until Madison taught me how.

Green Briar was the perfect place to process, to think, to practice my new skills and try to let the anger I carried for Madison's father fall away from me. We needed the silence the country horse farm provided. I wanted to experience lack of expectation and judgment as I bonded with my new wife.

We made our home at Green Briar. Sophia and Madison took to each other quickly. We even ended up having our dinners together. Sophia called us family. After tending to what needed fixing around the place, with my wife's blessing and Sophia's help, I went on the road for a few months to apprentice with some of the best horse trainers in the business.

To say Madison had been busy while I was away was an understatement. I couldn't believe all the goodies she had created to promote our business. There were jackets, vests, shirts, hats, pens, notepads and more – all bearing our logo. She even had magnets made for the sides of our truck, and a new sign had been hung in front of the barn. It was the koozies that I liked best. I plucked one out of the box and tucked it in my pocket before she could close the lid on my hungry hand. When I asked her how we could afford them, she pecked me on the cheek and told me Sophia offered to take care of the bill. Sophia was mighty generous to us. Madison had even gone to some horse shows on her own, proudly reporting that she been out racking up points on the circuit for us already. There were clients with horses in need of training lined up for my return, too.

It was on Sophia's land that things really started to bloom. We were building a winning clientele for M&M Kelly Quarter Horse Training & Services by selecting riders of like mind with promising equine prospects. Things were looking up for Madison and me. There wasn't a better feeling than strolling across a fairground knowing that horse training was my profession. I reveled in the fact that I didn't have to report to an office, and no one was telling me how to do my job. I did it all my way. Madison and I were happy. We had a good broodmare in Lyric's mother, and eventually Lyric would grow into one herself, but we still needed the right stud for breeding the future. That's when Madison went looking for a young stallion. What we ended up with was a demon. Not long after we brought the damn horse home, we were sitting down to dinner in Sophia's kitchen, and a knock came to the door. Everyone looked around the table at each other.

"Are we expecting a guest?" I asked.

"No," Sophia replied. Madison shook her head.

"I'll get it," I said, wadding my napkin and setting it next to my plate. "Both of you wait here until I come back."

"OK, Ken," Madison said, putting her palm on Sophia's forearm and giving it a squeeze.

I was surprised to see him on the porch. I opened the screen door.

"Come on in," I said, noting his duffle bag and black eye. I pushed the door wider, and JD stepped inside the house.

"Figured you and Madison oughta know that my dad's talking about lining some of the judge's pockets to keep you out of the ribbons. Heard it myself. Came home early from an event, and he was on his cell. Didn't know I was there."

"What happened to your face?" I asked, concerned.

"When I heard what he was planning for Cash … well, I shoulda known better than to stick up for Madison. He popped me in the eye when I told him I'd overheard his conversation and intended to tell my sister about the payoffs and the horse."

"What's he doing with Cash?"

"He's going so low. He's planning to send Cash back in the show pen to try and unsettle Madison. He offered Cash up to a show ring nemesis from Madison's youth days. She snatched up the opportunity to lease Cash, just like that. I know Madison is going to feel the knife turn in her back when she gets word of the news. I wanted her to hear it from me first. It's going to break her heart. She loves that horse." JD dropped his duffle bag in the hall and hung his head. "He's thrown me out. Told me the code to the gate would be changed as soon as I was off his property. Called me a traitor."

"You'll be needin' a place to stay then. You're welcome here," I said, putting a reassuring hand to JD's broad shoulder. "We were just sitting down to supper. Fix yourself a plate."

"Thanks, brother. I promise to earn my keep, but I'd like to make a few bucks, too. I'm gonna need some cash between bull ridin' events. I'll help at the shows. Go on the road with you guys if you need me to. Always like seducing those show pony cowgirls, so it's no skin off my knee. They don't know what hit 'em when a bull rider enters their turf." JD smirked and shifted his belt buckle. That was more like JD. He obviously wasn't too devastated by the black eye his father had just given him.

"Sure, we can figure somethin' out. We'll be needin' all the help we can get to get this business off the ground." I extended my hand, and JD put his palm in it.

"You want to break it to Madison then?"

"Might be best if I do, McKennon."

"All right then, but be gentle, JD," I said as I escorted him into the kitchen.

Madison was visibly hurt and saddened by JD's black eye, but handled the news of Cash's fate relatively well. We sure owed JD for letting us know that Sterling was up to no good. It figured that it wasn't until our little outfit started winning some respectable shows that Sterling even noticed or cared about what Madison and I were up to. Our horses were beating some of Sterling's top clients of the Western apparel store and his dealership. He didn't like that. Paying people off and rubbing Madison's beloved Cash in our faces was his way to derail us.

Even though we already knew that Sterling made plans to undermine us, it was still uncomfortable when we started seeing Cash and his new rider out at the shows. Madison kept her composure, but I knew Sterling's evil antics were starting to get the best of her. Cash would nicker as he passed Madison and Remy in the practice ring. He would strain toward them, wanting to acknowledge the long lost members of his herd. Every time I watched Madison's enemy snatch Cash by the reins and pull him away from them, his mouth wide at the pressure on his bit, I wanted to pull the wench from her saddle. She was no cowgirl. Her shoulders slouched, and her seat bumped along with Cash's stride. Money could rent her a winning mount, but nothing could help her horsemanship. She looked like a fish out of water on his regal back. A back fit for Madison, my queen. I wondered if I'd ever be able to get him back for her. I could see that Madison's heart ached when she had to face them, so to protect my wife's heart, I decided it would be best if we took to the road and started showing in other counties and other states.

CHAPTER 37

W hen Sterling started to interfere, there was additional pressure on me to finish Demon. Madison didn't say it. She didn't have to. I could sense her anxiousness for me to get a move on. I did my best with the limited free time I had for our own horses while I was home at Green Briar. I was splitting time between horse shows and working with our growing clientele. I tried to pack in as much training time with him as possible. The problem was I just couldn't get anywhere with the young stallion.

For the time being, Remy was earning us enough wins and attention on the road to draw us customers, so to buy a little more time, we decided Demon's big debut would be at the Congress in the fall. Madison dreamed of finding the one that could win M&M Quarter Horses a title there. She believed it would be Demon. She wanted me to make the horse a champion and win a couple big competitions with him, so we could start breeding to the best Quarter Horse mares. He was supposed to be the future of our business. Unfortunately, that damn horse had other plans.

"He is the most dangerous horse I've ever been around in my entire life, Madison," I said, lifting my hat to run my hand through my hair. I was frustrated. "I can't put a finger on what happened to him to make him so dangerous."

"What exactly do you mean by dangerous, Ken?"

"Just about anything sets him off, but I've noticed he is especially sensitive to loud noises and ... me. My physical presence seems to infuriate him just as much as his behavior angers me."

"I can't imagine why. I happen to enjoy your physical presence quite a lot," she teased.

"Come on, Madison. This isn't a joke. I *mean* it! I can't get near him. If I'm lucky to catch him off guard, I can get within range, but then he charges, ears pinned, teeth bared, nostrils flared. He kicks with his back legs. He strikes with his front hooves. If a thunderstorm is coming ... forget it. He goes running like a lunatic. He's better suited for the rodeo circuit than being a show pen pony. He's ranker than the craziest wild horses I've drawn in my bronc bustin' days. He's even tried to jump over the fence on me. He's turned on me so many times I've lost count, a kick here, a bite there. You've seen the bruises, Madison. I'm lucky he hasn't broken any of my bones, *and* I haven't even ridden the bastard yet. He's no good. I'm sorry, Madison. I can't get through to him. Damn horse reminds me of your father."

"My goodness, Ken. Have I been that busy with our business that I haven't noticed this going on? I thought he bumped you around some, but I didn't realize it was this serious."

"Oh, it's serious all right. I think he's hopeless. I've never felt like this about a horse before. I've always been able to find a way in."

"What if we turn him out to pasture for a while, let him grow up and settle down?" she asked, tapping her lip with a finger, trying to be helpful.

"Madison! For heaven's sake! That's what the breeder we bought him from was doing. Remember? You realize if we give him anymore time off, we'll miss his two-year-old eligibility for the

Western Pleasure Futurity at the Congress. He's already entered. Remember? That $30,000 purse is guaranteed to the winner, not to mention the sponsorships that would come with that kind of win. Madison, I have to get him going under saddle. We need to win that money. This is our big chance to prove ourselves, to prove our business has merit, and to show your father. I've already declared you his rider, and I can't change that. Thought he'd go better under you than me. Paired with your show pen swagger, I felt like no one will be able to take their eyes off of you two, but now I'm not so sure I want you in the saddle on him at all, especially not at that show."

"Why don't we take him to a few local horse shows and see how he goes for me then?"

"Won't work," I said, shaking my head. "Horses enrolled in that particular futurity cannot have been shown under saddle before the start of the class at the Congress. That's the rule. It's what we have to do to get us a chance at the big bucks."

"That's right. I forgot about that," Madison sighed. "Ken, I know you can do this. You see something special in Charming, too? Don't you?" she asked, putting her hands on my chest pockets and leaning her head on my shoulder.

"Yeah," I said, wrapping my arm around her waist. "I see somethin' because you do, Madison."

"I'll start paying more attention when you are working with him, Ken. Promise. I picked him after all."

"That'd be nice. I could use a little of that cowgirl magic of yours. I'm gonna tame that wild beast for you. Give me some more time," I said, mulling the horse over in my mind. I had him contained in Green Briar's round pen. I hoped it would still be up when I went back to retrieve him. Madison's cell vibrated in her pocket, and she pulled away from my embrace to answer it.

"Sorry, honey. I have to take this," she said, waving the phone. "I've been waiting for this call from the seamstress. She's been working on the new outfit for me to wear to the big show."

"You are going to look beautiful, wife," I said as she picked up the phone.

"Lots of bling," she mouthed with a little shimmy. She gave me a wink and one of those small mischievous smiles that I loved so much.

"Hello, this is Madison Kelly," she said as she tossed her golden hair over her shoulder, tucked a hand in the back pocket of her jeans, and wandered out into the sunlight heading for the house. Gosh, I loved the look of her and that she took my last name. I had to fix that damn horse for Madison *pronto*.

As I marched toward the fence, lunge whip in hand, I examined him. He really was a beautiful horse, built just right for Western pleasure. When I was in arms reach of him, shockingly, Demon ambled toward me and put his muzzle out.

"What am I gonna do with you, man? Can't you at least give it a little try? I'm willin' to give it a try. So how about you?" I reached up to pet his face. Demon's ears pricked at my new approach, but it was short lived. Before I could touch him, he spun in the soft dirt, and both hind hooves shot over the rail aimed at my head.

I gripped the lunge whip tight. I couldn't let him get away with this behavior. I had to work with him in the pen right now. I opened the door, posturing toward Demon aggressively, using the kind of body language other horses use in the wild to assert their dominance. He pinned his ears and lunged with his teeth bared. I gave my whip a good crack.

At the loud noise, Demon bolted circling, one angry eye on me, ear tipped inward, wildly spinning around, his midnight coat turning even darker with his perspiration.

"Whoa, boy, slow down," I murmured after 30 minutes of his furious galloping. I was trying to woo him to come in to me or quiet down. I didn't want him to over exert himself, but his response was to go even faster. His answer was 'no,' so we kept going and going.

Three hours later, both of us were covered in dirt-caked sweat, but I finally had him listening to me ... a little anyway. He was willingly changing direction, and once Demon almost came halfway to me.

Another hour in, the devil horse just stopped. Demon pivoted toward me, but didn't come to me. His head hung at his knees. He just stood there heaving.

Progress.

CHAPTER 38

I 've always thought women make better riders. After all, they are the better partner in most relationships.

Why should it be any different with horses?

Women give, self-sacrifice, listen and care take. Connect. I envy the connection between a woman and her horse because each is willing to give up ego for the union. They share true partnership, build a relationship of give and take, ebb and flow. When a horse joins up with a woman, it is as graceful as if they are floating – like flying without wings. Even the worst pairs still had a little of that magic, even Madison's archenemy and Cash. That connection gave me hope that my wife paired with the demon horse could win it all and bring our business the success we both desired.

I understand why my wife fell for Demon. While his behavior certainly wasn't charming, he was a real looker – jet black with dark eyes, flowing mane and tail, straight legs, a good hock, solid hooves and the right breeding. Both his sire and his dam had earned recognition in the show pen. He was built for our discipline of choice. If only he had a sound mind and a better attitude.

I hated whoever screwed him up. I worried that I was screwing him up even more.

Madison kept her promise and started attending Demon's training sessions. I'd finally been able to halter, saddle and get him into a snaffle. It wasn't easy, but I'd gotten him there. Today, I was going to attempt to ride him.

We started with the usual. Him racing around the pen in a frenzy, stirrups slapping his sides. After a 45-minute, blood-pumping race going through his gaits, most of it at a gallop, he would stop, drop his head and heave. This was the routine.

"Would you come in here and take hold of him?" I asked as I approached him slowly, the poor sweaty mess. "I'm gonna get on him today." He pinned his ears as I closed the distance between us like he did every time, but at least he had finally stopped trying to bite or kick me. He was resigned.

Madison opened the gate and walked toward us. Demon lifted his head and nickered as she approached, both ears pricked toward her. It was an act of anticipation.

Odd.

"Hi there, Charming," Madison cooed, taking his reins and rubbing beneath his chin. The stallion bumped her with his muzzle playfully. "That a boy. You be good for my Ken now. You hear?"

I looked at them aghast. I'd never seen the horse be playful with another being, human or horse.

"All right," I said, twisting the stirrup, preparing to mount. "Hold him good, Madison. If he starts gettin' nuts, you get yourself out of this round pen. No kidding." She nodded as I grabbed the horn and lifted myself above his back. Slowly settling myself in the saddle's seat, I held my breath. The horse was broke. He'd been ridden before, but not by me, and I didn't know how much time he actually had under saddle. I was ready for anything to happen.

Nothing.

Madison let go of the reins and backed away. Demon kept his attention on her and seemed compliant enough. I fluttered my legs at his side, and he moved forward to the rail of the small circular pen. I smiled to Madison watching us from the center of the enclosure.

"Good boy, Charming! He doesn't seem so bad to me," she called out.

"I think you being in here with us is making a difference," I called back.

I'd made three laps at the walk on Demon when I saw JD hop in his truck and slam the door with a bang. He started his jalopy and pulled out of the parking area. He waved as he passed us in the pen. I lifted my hand to wave back, and that's when it happened. That piece of junk truck backfired. I clenched my teeth and sat deeper in the saddle ready for the eruption. I knew the noise sounded like a sonic boom to Demon. I had just enough time to holler to Madison.

"Get out now!" I bellowed and stuck my spurs in Demon's side, hoping to get his attention. He didn't like that. Madison scurried out of the enclosure and shut the door behind her.

Demon bolted sideways at the sound and whinnied at the top of his lungs when Madison left the pen. It was no use. No amount of spurring or pulling on the bit would help. The horse was locked up in his mind. He went into a bucking rage. I held on for mere minutes. This horse was strong, stronger than the best of the best on the bucking bronc circuit. He bested Hasty Pete that day in the round pen. I came crashing out of the saddle and hit the ground, shoulder first.

Demon had his ears pinned, eyes rolled back and white, as he struck the ground with his front hooves inches from my head. The whoosh of skull-crushing near misses reverberated in my ears. Madison was back inside in seconds. She waved her hands and stood between the devil horse and me.

"No! No, Charming!" she screamed. Then he just stopped raging and stood before her. Ears pricked up and forward again. He was interested in her. She went to him and stroked his damp, slick shoulder then gathered his loose reins.

Madison turned back to me, Demon's reins looped at the crook of her elbow.

"Ken. Are you OK?" she asked, touching my shoulder, concern written across her face.

"Yeah. I think so," I said, righting myself to a sitting position.

"Maybe I should be the one riding him, Ken."

"No! Too dangerous," I growled, retrieving my cowboy hat and placing it back on my head.

My pride was bruised. I didn't want to admit defeat or that Madison might be able to do better. And so the devil horse launched me again and again and again. That's how it went over and over with Demon, with Madison and with me.

CHAPTER 39

I t was clear bringing Demon home to Green Briar had eased the pain of losing Cash for my wife. Madison had immediately taken to him. It was me who struggled with the horse. It was all spurs, battles and pinned ears. All I wanted to do was connect with Demon, but his rejection of me only fueled my distaste for him. He reminded me of Sterling. I hated how he withheld his affection and disapproved of me, tossing his head in the air and flattening his ears when I approached him.

I'd never worked with a horse that could barely tolerate me. On a daily basis, I felt lucky if he'd let me halter him and lead him into the round pen. If I actually got him inside, I'd have to drive him away with my lunge whip and make him work circles around me until he was a frothy mess. It was only then that he would let me get near enough to saddle him. He had to be too exhausted to fight me anymore. Once I finally pulled myself up on to his back, I was near exhausted myself, and then he'd just stand there sour, knees locked. That's when I made the frustrated choice to start using my spurs as more than just an aide. I never considered using my spurs aggressively with a horse before. With that choice,

I abandoned my roots, training beliefs and everything I'd learned from my mentors about natural horsemanship.

I knew Madison was at the rail watching me work with him. I also knew that she frowned upon my decision. I did it anyway. I shifted in the saddle to look at her for a moment and then gave Demon a swift spur to the belly. At impact, he grunted, but stood his ground. I gritted my teeth and gave him the spur again. This time, he took a reluctant step forward, but his ears went flat back and his teeth ground down on the metal bit in his mouth. The horse was as angry as I was, but, at least, he was going forward.

"How long is it going to go like this, Ken? You don't behave like this with any of our other horses," Madison called out.

"Could be months, could be a couple weeks, maybe a few more days. It's up to him really," I replied sarcastically.

"Are the spurs necessary? I just get the feeling he wants to be asked, not told," Madison pleaded.

"Not all horses are kind, Madison. This horse is one of the mean ones. That's the end of it," I responded, dismissing her observation. My clash with him was making me sour toward her, too.

My words visibly pained her. She hung her head, turned and disappeared into the barn. I didn't say or do anything. I just watched her go, and that was the end of Madison attending our training sessions.

Madison was right, of course, but I couldn't let her win. She saw straight through me. She knew my progress with Demon had stalled. I was sore that the horse would respond to her and not me. Not to mention, it drove me crazy the way she pestered about the spurs. I didn't really want to be mean to Madison. I just didn't have anyone else around to take my frustrations out on.

The negative conversations I was having with myself certainly weren't helping the situation either. I worried that I couldn't give Madison enough, that I wouldn't be able to get through to the horse, that I'd sold her a mucked up bill of goods. Sterling's comments haunted me. I just didn't feel good enough. I hadn't earned the right to be her husband. So, I kept trying, and in the trying, I kept getting further away. I was stuck.

The funny thing about the situation was the fact that I was doing all of it for her, to give her the life I thought she deserved, yet I was awful to her while I was doing it. That damn horse conjured up all of my insecurities. The needling fear of failure crept in every time I worked with him. I felt like the devil horse was always doing his best to expose the person I didn't want anyone to see. Demon was revealing the angry, stubborn, scared and mean me. I heard someone say once that horses are a reflection of their handlers. I couldn't agree more. Still, I kept doing what I was doing. I found myself wondering who it was I'd become. I was treating horses wrong, treating my wife wrong, just plain being wrong.

I took to stuffing cotton down his ear canals to muffle loud noises rather than working on desensitizing him to such things, chasing him around the round pen at a gallop until he was dead tired, and then riding him harder until he was even more tired. I held on through the bucking until I exhausted him, and he had nothing more to give. I went off the road, stayed home at Green Briar and worked him like that for 30 days, every day, no breaks for him or me. When he stopped trying to throw me, I felt hopeful. I could still sense his disdain for me, but I didn't care. I was absorbed in the win. I was going to achieve Madison's dream, and no beast was going to keep me from accomplishing it.

Sixty days later, I had him riding relatively quiet, trailer loading and unloading without much fuss, and I even lit a small firecracker outside his stall with all that cotton stuffed in his ears.

Nothing.

I felt like we were going to be OK after all. The next day, Madison, JD and I loaded him up and took off for the big show.

CHAPTER 40

The night before the show, I was jittery over what lay ahead for us, for the horse and for the business. This would be the ride of Madison's life and the pinnacle of my reputation as a horse trainer. That is, if we could pull off the win. What I really wanted was a swig of whiskey to calm me down, but I'd made a promise to my wife long ago. I wasn't going to go back on it now.

To top it off, Madison and I had another fight over how I'd been training Demon. We were trying to get a good night's rest cramped in the living quarters of the Green Briar horse trailer. Sleep was next to impossible lying on the small mattress tucked in the gooseneck, but add in bickering, and I knew I could kiss any sweet dreams goodbye. It was definitely not a great place to have a spat.

"We have to talk about the spurs, Ken. I don't want to wear them tomorrow," Madison said carefully.

"Not this again, Madison. What makes you think you know how to do it any better? You're so righteous! You think you know everything don't you?" I hollered. I just wanted to sleep. I didn't have a lot of patience for much of anything else right then.

"Ken," she whispered. "Come back to me. Please. I am the same person today that I was the day we met. I am afraid it's you who has changed. Not me."

"Oh, get off your high horse!" I barked.

"Do you remember when you said you'd let me be the boss and that you'd help me with this vision for my horse business? I still remember that day. It was one of the best moments of my life. I believed you when you said that. It's one of the reasons I fell in love with you, Ken. Now, it's *our* horse business, and we *have* to communicate about it. Sometimes things are going to be hard to hear."

"And this is all about using spurs?" I asked. I sounded cold. There was an edge to my voice when I talked to her that never used to be there. I couldn't reckon why I kept being so nasty either. Deep down, I felt awful, but I just couldn't stop.

"I'm scared about how that horse has changed you, Ken. It's like in order to feel like you've succeeded, you've got to affirm something to yourself. Don't you see that you are already a success to me?"

"Yeah, right," I sneered. "Let's share that breakthrough with your father." I tried to change the topic and lure her into a fight by dangling Sterling in the mix.

"I'd really like it if we could communicate better about Charming's training, particularly the spurs. I think the spurs are a bad idea," she said, not taking the bait.

"You don't know anything," I growled. Minding the low over-hang of the gooseneck, I sat up and slipped off the small bed. Feet on the floor again, I yanked the comforter off the mattress and her. Turning my back on the conversation, I tried to make the tiny horse trailer couch look like an appealing place to sleep.

"Recall the proverb, Ken. Don't spur a willing horse," she said to me softly.

"He's not willing, Madison. He's a monster! Why can't you understand that?"

"He's willing for me, Ken. I've ridden him several times on my own when you've been out on errands. I know I shouldn't have kept that from you, but I didn't think you'd let me ride him otherwise until the show. He went low and slow. Charming was a perfect gentleman without the spurs ... for me anyway."

Those words made me go quiet.

In the end, it was probably a woman's touch, Madison's touch, that the horse really needed, but I'd denied them both that. If I'd just let her go in and work with him, without the spurs he hated so much, I doubt any of this would have happened. More than once, Madison had said to me, 'Ken, I don't think he likes the spurs. Can't we just use your method without the spurs? Our heels still work, you know.' She was right, but I wasn't going give her the satisfaction.

The thing that bothered me most was that spur training wasn't supposed to be about being aggressive with the horses. It was a tool. It was all about making a rider's cues virtually invisible and creating a willing partner out of the horse. Spurs were used as an aide to encourage them to move off at the slightest touch. Thinking back on it, he probably would have accepted the cues without the spurs, but I had it in my head that not using them would make me look like less of a cowboy.

What kind of horse trainer would I be if I let him go in the show pen being ridden without spurs?

What I realized now is that I was afraid to be different from everyone else, to train a horse differently than the socially-accepted way, to do something that would make people like Sterling talk about me.

I resisted Demon's resistance. That was my biggest mistake, my lesson learned. I didn't listen to the horse. I ignored Madison's instinct. It was this tragic experience that changed the course of my life and haunts me now. Resisting change morphed me into the person I am today. Now, I have compassion in everything I do, but I sure didn't have it back then.

To be honest, I ended up being jealous of the exact thing that attracted me to my wife in the first place. All of our horses seemed to like her just a little bit better, the difficult ones especially. I hated that Demon was easier on her. I started to resent her for it, and act a fool I did.

That night, I didn't end up sleeping on the couch, but I gave Madison the cold shoulder in bed. She still snuggled up to me on that tiny little mattress, her breasts pressed against my back, her knees tucked behind mine as she ran her fingers through my hair.

"What's wrong, Ken?" she whispered, breath sweet and warm on the back of my neck.

"Nothin'," I muttered, shifting away from her under the covers. My goal was to drift to sleep ignoring her.

"I love you," she said, scooting against me again. "No matter how far away you try and make yourself."

Of course, I hate myself now for not holding her tight that night.

CHAPTER 41

We'd been keeping the devil horse under wraps, partly because he was so unpredictable, but also to make a big splash for our little operation. Revealing him here was a risk, but my gut told me it was a good bet. The horse moved like nothing I'd ever seen. When he was going well, his cadence took my breath away. If only we weren't constantly butting heads.

JD held the brim of his baseball cap tightly with one hand as he led Demon, dancing on the end of the lead, across the parking lot with the other. The wind was tossing the horse's tail around behind him and threatened to tear unrestrained hats from people's heads. As I rushed behind them, I instructed JD to give Demon's stud chain a yank. I looked up at the sky. It had turned ominous, almost as dark as our stallion's coat. The look of it made me nervous. Demon always got excitable when it stormed, a symbol of his thunderous personality perhaps. I carried the pail of grooming supplies and Madison's chaps, fringe whipping up with the wind's fury. She rushed along beside us, holding her cowgirl hat on her head by its crown.

"Gosh, I hope it doesn't storm, Ken."

"Me, too," I said through clamped teeth. I was still sour from our fight the night before.

I looked past Madison at the black clouds rolling toward us. I popped my collar against the cold gusts coming in, feeling glad I had jammed an extra heap of cotton into Demon's ears. We hustled into the make-up arena of the coliseum. There were only three classes to go before our own. I just needed to get Madison on, Demon warmed up, show a good face to potential sponsors, and then send them in the ring to perform three gaits each way. That's all they needed to do. I really wanted this win.

"Ken, he's really anxious today," Madison said. I tightened the cinch until I heard Demon grunt. Ignoring her comment, I lifted her into the saddle. "What if we just left the spurs off?" Madison asked again.

I'd been nervous around the horse before, but I'd never seen my wife show any nerves around him. It probably had to do with the fact that I hadn't listened to her or let her express her concerns the night before. Our relationship was based on communicating with each other, and I denied her the opportunity. I refused to wear the guilt on my sleeve today.

"He'll be all right. Don't start," I said, not meeting her eyes while I buffed her boots. "Not today, Madison," I continued, adjusting her spurs.

This was our big moment. I wasn't going to let a little sensitivity to spurs ruin our perfectly-polished show pen look. Madison looked impeccable in her new show attire. Her jacket was ice blue and cream with an enormous amount of crystal adhered in a flame-like pattern design. Her matching cream chaps really stood out against the black sheen of Demon's coat. My eyes assessed all the other riders in the practice pen preparing to enter the arena and not a single rider was sans spurs. I knew how shallow the judges could be, and I didn't know how deep Sterling's pockets were or how far he'd go to rig a show of this stature. I wasn't willing to bruise our reputation over a pair of spurs. I was aiming for flawless today.

There was no room for error. We had a lot riding on this. The future of our business's offspring, the name recognition that comes with a win of this caliber, the clients, and the money this could attract were all on the line. I'd even been having conversations with a couple equine supply companies on the possibility of sponsorships. I learned about securing interested investors while I was out rodeoin'. It's a lot easier to get places when you've got sponsors. I knew this horse was talented enough to take the class if he could just keep his shit together long enough to perform three gaits in each direction. We hadn't had a blow up in weeks, and he had seemed relaxed in our warm ups ... until now.

"Ken," Madison begged. "I know I can do this without them. And I know we made an agreement that I would be the horsemanship specialist, and you'd do the training. You've trained him, so I trust your judgment on this, but I just have this feeling."

At that moment, one of our sponsorship prospects strolled up.

"McKennon," he said, tipping his hat with a smile. I tipped mine in return.

"This is my wife, Madison," I said, taking the man's hand. "Madison, this is Al." I shot Madison a look. I couldn't have a little quibble between us mess up the chance at a sponsorship for our start-up. She straightened in the saddle like the experienced cowgirl she'd always been.

"So, is this the super horse you told me about, McKennon?"

"Yes, sir, Al. This here is Devil's in the Details. We call him De
—err, Charming around the barn. I think he's got a real good shot at winning this next class."

"Well, let me get a look at our winner then," Al said, gripping our horse under the chin and turning his head to look him in the eye. I held my breath. Demon's eyes turned dark. It was obvious he wasn't thrilled about Al touching him, but he didn't react.

Thank heaven.

Relieved that Al hadn't set him off, I let out a quiet sigh. The potential sponsor walked around our stud, nodding to himself and rubbing his chin.

"He's a looker, that's for sure, McKennon. I'm thinking he'll look real nice on the front of our feedbags and perhaps the next catalog. With a win, we could really do something special and add in the title."

I couldn't help but let a smile sneak across my face. My heart pounded at the thought of finally bringing in some big-time cash and proving to Sterling our business wasn't a fluke. I was the man making Madison's dream a reality.

Me. McKennon Kelly. I was her hero.

Al started to circle Demon a second time. The microphone clicked on, and the announcer called for Madison's class. As he rounded our horse's rear, Al's hand came down on Demon's rump with a *pop*! That was the end of our calm super horse. Startled by the unexpected touch and noise of the slap, Demon reared and struck out at the closest competitor's horse with his front hooves. Madison kept her seat and did her best to quiet him. I ran to her side and grabbed a rein. I pulled him toward me and away from the other rider's horse.

"Did I do that?" the sponsor asked, adding a whistle to complete his question.

"It could've been anything, Al. Really, this is a big moment. A lot of strong energy in here right now. It affects the horses, makes them jumpy," Madison said before she smiled sweetly.

I looked up to my wife, thankful. My smile was returned with an icy glare. A man with a clipboard stepped up and checked off the number attached to Madison's saddle pad. JD had been watching the whole scenario from the corner of the practice pen. He unfolded his arms from in front of his chest and rushed over with the grooming supplies to give Demon a last once over. JD polished his coat until he gleamed, wiped Madison's boots a second time and gave her a reassuring squeeze of the knee before turning a scowl on me.

"OK, miss," the in-gate manager said. "Let's get on up closer to the entrance now. We gotta keep this show moving. We're running behind, so they've tasked me with putting a stop to the dillydallying at the gate." Demon pawed the ground in annoyance. He was ready to go, to move, to do anything other than just stand there near our loudmouthed prospective sponsor.

The horses and riders started their procession into the coliseum's large oval arena. The stands were already bustling with onlookers. This was one of the more popular classes at the show. The best of the best were going to be out there, all pros and their horses. This was the type of class that could make or break a career. Have a bad go, and the rumor mill was already churning the moment your horse left the pen. Have a superior ride, and you were solicited by sponsors, blinded by the flash of blubs, presented with a huge check and able to charge exorbitant breeding fees.

My chest felt tight, and my gut was in twists. I wished I'd had a few shots of whiskey to calm the nerves. We really needed this to happen. It was our time to make a mark. If we could start breeding him, we wouldn't be in this type of position again. We wouldn't have to discuss spurs or showing because all Demon would be doing is screwing.

If he could just win us this class.

"Let's go, you're next," the ring steward ordered, impatiently rapping on his clipboard, eager to get my horse and rider moving. Demon's ears swiveled back and forth anxiously.

This is it.

My pulse was racing, and so was my mind with the weight of possibility this ride held for our little outfit, for me, for Madison, for Sophia, even for JD. We were a family now, and I wasn't going to let them down. This ride would put Sterling in his place and cement ours in the horse world. If only Demon could keep it together for the tick of the clock. I could never predict when one of his explosions was going to happen, unless, of course, it decided to storm.

"Ken." Madison's blue eyes big as saucers flashed to me. "Can't we just lose the spurs?" Demon's sides heaved as he breathed raggedly. He was clearly agitated. He mouthed his bit repetitively. His neck was slick with nervous sweat, and his skin tweaked like a thousand flies were landing on him. Yet, there wasn't a single fly in the arena.

I ignored the plea in her eyes. My hatred for the horse was blinding me. In that moment, I was powerless, and I gave in to my attachment to success. I let my ego take control and put the thing I loved the most in danger.

"Shut up about the spurs, Madison. Just get out there and freakin' ride," I said, my voice low enough so only she could hear. "Everything that is important to us depends on this ride."

CHAPTER 42

As Madison directed Demon into the arena, I scurried for a perch in the stands. I needed a good view of her class. Madison took an excellent position on the rail. She had plenty of space, no one too close in front or behind her. I sighed with relief, but still felt that tiny pang of fear in the pit of my stomach. I couldn't see what the weather was doing outside the coliseum.

Blasted indoor arena. No windows.

The discomfort in my gut started to fade after Madison guided Demon beautifully through his gaits to the left. I felt a smile settle on my face. I had to admit Madison sure could pick 'em. The two made a beautiful pair. It was impossible not to watch them cruise the arena together. At the lope, Demon's front legs were firing straight and perfect through to his pointed toe. At the jog, he was silly slow and clean. At the walk, Madison kept him moving with forward propulsion, but maintained control of their rail position by speeding him up or slowing him down based on what was in her peripheral view. The woman knew how to show a horse. They both seemed calm, collected and happy.

Squinting my eyes, I shook my head in disbelief. Madison was only using her calves to cue him. She kept the spurs out of his belly. It figured she would find a way around them and me. I actually felt a little proud. The woman always amazed me. It was a given that Madison would do as she darn well pleased, regardless of what I said. I was actually fine with the spurs being just for show as long as she wore them for their looks, and they had a clean ride. I wanted to get a closer look at how she was cueing him without using her spurs.

Maybe I'd take a page from her book this time and incorporate what she was doing into Demon's future training sessions.

The horse was a terror under saddle with just the slightest touch of my spurs; whether a light touch or a swift kick, he resisted them. I don't know if he was abused with spurs before we bought him, or he just didn't like the feel of the metal to his sides. It was a relief to realize I might not need to use them anymore.

Still, it was the popular way to show these days. A horse had to be spur trained to receive top marks. Spur training allowed the rider's movements to be just about invisible. I had learned the method apprenticing with Sophia's dressage contacts. Every cue came from a shift of weight and an undetectable touch from the spurs on a rider's boot. It didn't have to be an aggressive cue. The spurs created a button to press in different places on the horse's belly to ask them to perform a certain movement. A gentle flapping of spurs at a horse's side would encourage the horse to trot. A single spur pressed behind the girth would ask for the lope. Both spurs pressed firmly to each side at the same time would signal a stop. It was called a spur stop. I believed spur training made for a more beautiful ride, an effortless ride. It wasn't meant to hurt the animal.

Moving down from the stands, I leaned on the ledge of the arena and set my sights on them. I was very aware that the five judges in the center of the ring were watching Demon and Madison, too. I usually didn't stand near the rail like the other trainers did. I figured if I had done my job right, my horse and rider wouldn't need any additional coaching from me once they were in the show pen. This time, I had a change of heart. I wanted to be close to Madison … to our success … to Demon. I felt an overwhelming pride in how far we'd taken M&M Quarter Horses. How far I'd actually gotten with our devil horse. How much I loved my wife for the way she accepted all of me. I was starting to feel like we'd actually made it when JD idled up to join me.

"They're lookin' really good, Ken," JD said, slapping me on the back. "The judges can't take their eyes off of them."

"I know," I said, flashing my brother-in-law a smile. "Don't jinx it, OK?"

"All right, I'll hush up," JD replied, flashing his own rock star smile. He was happy for Madison. I could tell by the way he held our things close to his chest. He swept his eyes over her appreciatively as she approached astride Demon.

Madison was just a horse length from where JD and I stood at the rail. She smiled down on us from the saddle. She knew she was having the ride of a lifetime, too. We beamed back at her. As Demon became parallel with me, I locked eyes with the animal. He pinned his ears flat and gritted his teeth. Madison bit her lip and squeezed Demon past me with her calves. The loud speaker clicked on.

"OK, folks. Please reverse and walk. Reverse and walk."

"It's OK, Charming," I heard her whisper as she changed directions away from me at the rail.

Then it happened. A thunderous crack boomed from outside the arena, but echoed within. Demon lurched forward, rearing high and hard. He lashed his polished front hooves out, thrashing them through the air like daggers. I gritted my teeth. I thought I had packed enough cotton in his damn ears to render him utterly deaf. I was wrong.

"Hold on, Madison!" JD shouted, dropping everything he was holding.

The weather had shifted. My heart bolted in my chest. I'd been through this with Demon. I knew what came next. I was off at a mad dash, trying to reach the entrance to the arena before the second boom came. When it did, I wasn't yet within reach. The thunder sent Demon hurling around the ring like a freight train. He was no longer a Western pleasure mount. He turned into one of the broncos I used to make a living on. The minute his front feet would meet the ground, he would crow hop, bouncing and arching his back, trying to throw Madison from the saddle. She stayed on, and when he couldn't unseat her, he shifted gears, delivering an explosive kick into the air. His rear hooves were so high, he was nearly vertical to the horizon of the arena. Still, Madison kept her seat, gripping the saddle horn and hollering 'whoa!' while squeezing him hard in hopes he'd slow. It wasn't enough. Demon was out of control. He sideswiped Madison into the arena wall, smashing her calf. I heard her cry out.

"Madison!" I screamed. "Try a spur stop! Please, Madison!" I was hauling ass running into the arena now. I watched my wife put the spurs in our devil horse's gut to no avail. It only infuriated him more. "God, what have I done? Hold on, Madison! I'm coming!"

Another crash of thunder. I was close enough now to see the horse's eyes. They were white around the edges. His mouth was gapping against Madison's attempts to restrain his gallop. She was giving it everything she had, tugging the reins in her hands. He just kept running. The judges scrambled out of the way, and a spectator swung open the exit gate so Madison's competitors could quickly usher their horses out of the arena. I ran as fast as I could across the deep footing, but my legs felt leaden.

Then suddenly Demon stopped. I took deep breaths in and out. I put my hands on my knees for a flick of time to catch my breath. I looked to Madison. She was soothing Demon. Stroking his neck. Telling him it was OK. She had stayed on him. My wife could've been a rodeo queen. Our eyes met, and she grimaced.

"Take ahold of him, Ken. I need to get off. NOW!" Madison demanded, breathlessly. I shook my head and started to close the distance between us.

"Hell of a ride, cowgirl," I said, up to her. I motioned to grab Demon's reins, still swinging from his rampage. Madison offered a weak smile and started to dismount before I could grip the leathers.

Another clash of thunder exploded from outside the indoor arena. Demon shot straight up with Madison hovering at his side. Her leg already swung over to get off of him. The thunder reverberated in the coliseum again. I lunged for Demon, his eyes wide, the inside of his nostrils pink, his hooves off the ground, his breathing erratic. I moved fast, but not fast enough. In an effort to stop him, Madison grabbed ahold of a rein before I could reach them and pulled his head around. She tugged until Demon's head was bent, his muzzle nearly touching the empty stirrup leather banging on the other side of his belly.

It was an amateur mistake for a horsewoman of Madison's caliber to make. She should have known better than to pull him in that direction, but I'd seen plenty of experienced horsemen have accidents, making similar errors in panicked situations. I couldn't do anything to prevent what I knew would happen next.

Demon lost his balance. All I could do was watch as he toppled over sideways onto Madison.

"Charming!" Madison shrieked, clinging to him helplessly hanging from one side. When I couldn't see her anymore beneath his hulking black barrel, I knew it. I knew he had crushed her.

Immediately, I dropped in the dirt beside her. Demon had already found his way back up on all fours and had cantered away to the exit gate. An onlooker held him by the reins as he pranced about, trying to get out of the arena and away from the racket of the thunderstorm. The coliseum buzzed with the hushed gasps and whispers from the crowd.

"Is she all right?"

"What happened?"

"Is she dead?"

Is she dead?

"Madison," I croaked. I reached out and stroked her hair. "What have I done? What have I done?" My eyes began to blur, hot tears building, ready for rupture as I looked at my wife's crumpled body. I could hear JD shrieking for an ambulance. Madison reached for my hand.

"Just hold on. Please hold on, Madison. I'll fix this. I promise," I pleaded.

"Ken," she wheezed.

No words would come. My eyes streamed tears. I was silent, but inside I was screaming. I took hold of her hand, palm clammy and cold, in mine. I leaned in and kissed her forehead.

"Ken, I love you," she whispered then closed her eyes.

"No!" I yelled, pressing her hand to my heart. "What have I done? What have I done?" I scooped Madison up.

Lifeless.

There wasn't any breath from her lips when I held her near my face. She was limp in my arms. Her body felt broken in so many places. Blood trickled from her nose. I sobbed silently clutching her body. Her life was over in an instant, a flash of time forever embossed in my mind.

Her golden ponytail swung to and fro as I carried her past the familiar faces from the horse show scene, all of them dead to me now. Deafened by the siren blaring and blinded by its lights flashing, I approached the ambulance. The medics opened and slammed doors, shouted things I couldn't hear, and rushed her from my arms. I knew they wouldn't be able to save her. She was already gone.

CHAPTER 43

I f I'd only pulled them out, pulled her off of him, scratched the class. If only I'd cared more about her feelings than what the judges and other trainers thought. If only I hadn't been so damn preoccupied with impressing her father and that sponsor. If only I believed that she could have executed his gaits without the spurs. If only that storm hadn't rolled in.

If only.

I let my relationship with the horse get in the way. I had forgotten that, just like humans, not all horses are made the same.

He and me ... we just didn't get along.

That night, I tore our home apart. I raged.

I left Madison's body with the medics. I left JD with the devil horse. I left Green Briar's truck and trailer keys in the tack stall. I left all of M&M Quarter Horses' equipment behind ... the tack, the grooming supplies and her rhinestone covered show clothes. I didn't care about any of it anymore.

My mind was a whirl. I vaguely remembered telling JD to dump Demon. I didn't care where. The first auction where they sold horses for slaughter would have been fine with me. I was angry, delusional. It all felt like a dream ... everything ... from meeting

Madison to marrying her to finding Sophia to building our business to acquiring the damn horse to losing my wife to the state my life ended up in. I went home in a cab. I didn't care that the ride back to Green Briar cost me a small fortune.

I barged in, the front door swinging open, knob through drywall. I took to dismantling the home that Madison and I lived in, had created together. I savagely ripped things from the walls as I went. I smashed frames. I tore the contents of her closet from the hangers. I formed a pile in the center of the living room.

I stoked a fire. I shoveled it all in, every last bit of her. I burned our pictures then her clothes. I burned everything in that fireplace. I didn't want to catch even a scent of Madison, let alone see something that reminded me of her. While I was tearing apart my home, I could see Sophia standing by the window, her soft shadow hovering there, watching me destroy everything we had created. A momentary pulse of guilt washed through me because it was her place, too. I ignored it and her. I burst into our bedroom to get out of Sophia's view.

I started to strip our bed and flipped the mattress. Irate, I dragged it outside, things crashing over in its wake. I passed Sophia standing on my doorstep, her mouth gapping open. I waved her away.

Not NOW!

I doused our bedding with gasoline, struck a match and set it ablaze. I trounced across the drive, yanked the M&M Kelly Quarter Horse Training and Services sign from the front of the barn, marched it to the fire and tossed it in. I stood watching flames light the night sky. I destroyed what I hoped was every memory of our life together. I was in need of a mind numbing. It took all of the will I had left in me not to burn the place to the ground.

I had to prevent myself from doing any further destruction to Green Briar. I took another cab to a liquor store then to a dumpy motel with what was left of my cash. I didn't get far. I rented a room with the M&M Kelly Quarter Horses' purchasing card and proceeded to drink whiskey. I hadn't had a sip of alcohol since the day we married. It was a lot of time spent sober to throw away, but I didn't care. The promise didn't matter anymore. I just wanted to wash Madison away.

Days passed; I am not sure how many. I'd made sure everything went black.

Blank.

Yet, I could hear a knock to the door. I was weak and still drunk. I closed one eye and made out the slowly whirling ceiling fan above me. Everything else was a blur. I couldn't remember the last time I'd eaten or even been coherent. The only reason I was slightly present now is it seems I'd blacked out finishing the last of my whiskey.

Knock. Knock. Knock.

I pulled the covers over my head and cursed that there wasn't anything left in this room to make me disappear again.

Ignore it. You are nobody to anybody anymore.

I wanted to fade away, slip into darkness and join Madison wherever she was. I didn't care about anything or anyone. My life was over.

The knock came again, only louder this time. Frustrated, I pushed the scratchy motel sheets off of me and tossed the crappy red velour comforter to the side. The room spun as I tried to rise to my feet. Blackout curtains pulled tight, I knocked around empty bottles on the floor as I wandered blindly to the door. The racket made my head scream. I needed some aspirin or another drink fast. I put a hand to my forehead and opened the door.

"Sir, I am the motel manager. Martin McVay." He held out his plump hand for me to shake. I didn't take it.

"What do you want?" I growled.

"Well, sir," he said nervously. He stepped aside, an open palm up. "This young man tells me he is your brother. Seems he's a bit worried about you."

I looked around the heavyset man, squinting at the person behind him.

"He's my – was my brother-in-law," I slurred to Martin. "How the hell did you find me, JD?"

"It wasn't easy, bro."

"I'm not your bro anymore, JD," I grumbled. "She's dead."

"Sir, why don't you step outside, get some fresh air and talk to your brother for a minute," Martin chimed in politely. "You've been in this room for some time. It's not been cleaned. Let my staff service it for you. We appreciate the credit card you left on file and the request to respect your privacy, but when the police showed up with your brother-in-law here saying something about a missing person, sir, I ... I had to ..."

"Had to what?" I hollered. Martin took a step back and wrung his fat hands.

"Easy, Ken," JD said, taking a step forward and placing a hand on the motel manager's shoulder.

"Don't call me Ken, JD!" I put my fist through the wall next to the open door.

"Sir –" the now distressed motel manager began. I shut him up with an angry stare. He gulped and put his hands in his oversized dress pant pockets.

"Easy, McKennon. It's been four weeks since Madi — I mean, since the night you tore everything to hell at Green Briar. Sophia got concerned. She filed a missing persons report. The police found out you were here when the motel ran your card for the month. You missed the service for Madison ..."

"Stop talkin', JD," I spat. "That was the intention." Hearing her name was like an arrow through my heart. The motel manager shifted his weight back and forth uncomfortably, and then took a step back so JD could move between us.

"Sophia. She ... well, I wanted to let you know that she gave my sister a real nice goodbye. Everyone from both the show circuit and the rodeo were there. Even Dad came. Seemed sincerely sad for us and for you. He even tracked down my mom." He paused then cautiously continued, "There's somethin' else. I hate tellin' you this right now, but I'm not sure what's gonna happen next or if you're comin' back, so here it goes. The clients ... they've all gone. They've taken their horses out of Green Briar. The rumor mill is churnin'. They're sayin' you're to blame for Madison's ... well ... you know."

"Figured as much. I'm done anyway, JD. I'm finished training. I don't want to anymore. I deserve this. I deserve all of it."

"What about Sophia?" JD asked.

"Not sure about anything anymore." I rubbed the bridge of my nose and swallowed hard. I needed to numb this knowledge. "Give me a second, will ya?" I mustered, pushing back the tears that wanted to come.

"McKennon. Wait. Will you at least take this? Sophia asked me to give it to you. Go and plug it in, so we can at least get ahold of you." I grimaced at the box in JD's hand.

"All right," I said, accepting the cell phone and charger.

For heaven's sake, now I was a cowboy with a cell phone?

It really didn't matter to me anymore. I was done training. Who would want to call me anyway besides Sophia or JD, I couldn't be sure.

"Thanks, bro. Your phone number is written on the box." JD sounded relieved.

I stepped back into my musty motel room, leaving the door ajar. My head was pounding. I plugged in the phone as requested and left it to charge. I shook a bottle on the nightstand, barely a sip, and put it to my lips.

Nothing but a drop.

I fished my boots out from beneath the bed. I was still wearing the same shirt and jeans as the day it happened. I didn't care if I stunk. I sat on the edge of the mattress to pull the boots on. I rose, returned to the door, and stepped out into the blinding sunshine.

"You ... Martin, you say? Go ahead clean up the room," I instructed, looking the motel manager up and down. His clothes were disheveled and too tight for his portly form. I took note of a ketchup stain near his groin as if he'd just downed a fast food burger. "Charge the damages to my card," I said, addressing the hole I'd just punched in the wall with a nod. I opened and closed my fist, examining the bruising that had sprung up on my knuckles.

"Yes, sir. Right away," he replied. His manners were impeccable for a sleazy motel manager. I watched Martin scurry off across the trash-littered parking lot of the Tumbleweed Inn. I turned back to JD once Martin was out of sight.

"Can you take me to get some whiskey?"

CHAPTER 44

I put my key in the ignition and rest my head on the steering wheel from the weight of all the memories. Waiting around for Sophia's package to arrive gave me nothing to do but think and remember. I'm tired of doing that. Now that I have the address book, I need blurred freeway lines and to find that wretched horse. He is responsible for all of this misery. Sadly, I haven't even gotten that far from Green Briar, never even got close to settin' off on that stretch from Texas to the Heartland I knew so well. As I sit staring out at the potholed parking lot and the freeway full of automobiles speeding past, I reflect on the fact that I have no idea where the horse actually is.

My truck is gassed up, and I'm ready to drive, but to where?

I am running blind. Even if he'd been sold in the North, it doesn't mean he's still up there. The dark reality dawns on me that he could be anywhere, overseas even. He's likely still alive, even though the evil part of me wishes he had gone for meat. Slaughter is pretty unlikely given the U.S. had banned the practice long ago. Demon is surely just in a new home ... somewhere. I slam the dash with the frustration of it all.

Why wasn't I content back then?

I drag a hand across my face, pull my cell phone out of the compartment in the center armrest and retrieve Sophia's package from the passenger seat. I produce my worn address book and remove the thick rubber band holding it together. I swallow hard. Madison's perfect penmanship is scrawled inside. It isn't easy to see her handwriting again, but I still thumb through it.

"That's it!" I exclaim, slapping the page with the back of my hand. I finally have a reason to smile. "Thank heaven for Sophia," I utter, pointing upward.

I dial Sallie Mae. She'll know where to start. A flood of relief washes over me when she picks up on the first ring.

"Sallie Mae. It's McKennon," I bark into the phone.

"Why hello, stranger," Sallie Mae purrs into the phone. "To what do I owe the honor of a phone call from the handsomest cowboy I know? Wait, this isn't a butt dial, is it?" She starts laughing at her own joke.

"No. Sallie Mae, I've got a problem."

"Those seem to follow you around, don't they, cowboy? Is it girl trouble? Need me to bail you out again?"

"It –" I clear my throat. The words feel stuck. "It has to do with my wife, Sallie Mae."

"Oh. Well. Pardon my jokes." Sallie Mae's pep disintegrates instantly. "This sounds serious. How can I help, McKennon?"

"I'm sure you remember that horse of ours. I called him Demon."

"Yes, I remember. Go on."

"I need to track him down, Sallie Mae."

"I see. You tried researching the Quarter Horse Records yet?"

"Where's that? You have an address?"

"Yeah, cowboy. It starts with www and ends with dot com."

"What do you mean?"

"It's an online database, McKennon. It's the official data resource for all registered Quarter Horses. I reckon that's the easiest way to find him."

"You mean the internet?"

"Yes, the internet, McKennon."

"I don't do the internet, Sallie Mae. Madison or Sophia always handled that sort of thing. Computers and me are kinda a no-go. Don't know how to type and all. This cell phone I'm speaking to you on is the closest thing to technology I've got. I only have one number saved in it. Only have the thing because Sophia asked me to carry it."

"I see. Kinda like to hear you are still an old-fashioned type. Most everyone is plugged into those damn things these days. Happy to help, McKennon," she assures, sounding upbeat once more. "What was his registered name again? I'll check the database for you and see what I can turn up."

"Devil's in the Details. That's the bastard's name."

"If you don't me mind asking, what is it that you plan to do when you find him?"

"I'd rather not say, Sallie Mae. Don't want to incriminate you in any way."

"I don't like the sound of this, McKennon."

"You don't have to help me, Sallie Mae, but one way or another, I'm finding that stallion."

"I'll help you, McKennon. When have I ever let you down? I trust you'll do what's right when the time comes. Give me an hour to do a little research, and I'll be back in touch."

"Thank you, Sallie Mae. Always could count on you."

CHAPTER 45

I've been reclined in the driver's seat for a long while trying to catch a catnap, but I am too anxious to sleep. If Sallie Mae comes through, I'll be close to being hot on the trail of that awful animal. I keep checking my phone to make sure the ringer is on and loud enough for me to hear just in case I do nod off. I almost jump out of my skin when it comes to life in my pocket. I fumble with it and answer the phone.

"Hello."

"Howdy, cowboy. Think I've got something for you."

"What did you find, Sallie Mae?"

"Let me explain a little about what I was able to uncover. I'm looking at the website now. It says here that whenever a horse is sold, no matter where the horse is sold, the seller is required to return the certificate to the association along with a completed transfer form showing the date of sale, name and contact information for the buyer. The American Quarter Horse Association then records the change of ownership on the certificate and in their records, and mails the certificate directly to the new owner. Green Briar Farms and M&M Kelly Quarter Horse Training and Services were both listed as the owner on his registration papers, right?"

"That's right."

"Tell me. What you know about his sale?"

"Don't know much. Had JD load him up and drive him to the first livestock auction he could find. Asked 'em to send a cashier's check and the sales receipt to Sophia."

"Right, so if he had them send the sales receipt to Sophia, then as the owner of Green Briar Farms, she would have been legally able to represent M&M Quarter Horses as his seller. She had access to his registration papers at the farm, right?"

"That's all correct. Go on."

"Well, from what I was able to find, it seems Sophia did as the rules state and completed the transfer form showing the date of sale, name and contact info for the buyer."

"So, you know where Demon is then?" I ask, clutching the phone, pressing it closer to my ear.

"Well, sort of. Since I had his full registered name, it was pretty darn easy to find out who the recorded owner is. I just called the records department, and they actually gave me the name and address of the last owner on record over the phone."

"Cough it up, Sallie Mae. Who has him?" I'm impatient.

"It's not that easy, McKennon. They gave me initials and a P.O. Box. That's it."

"What? How can that be?"

"It looks like Sophia followed the rules and sent in all the information, but you said you told JD to take him to auction, right?"

"Yes, that's right."

"Those sort of places don't exactly dot their 'i's and cross their 't's, McKennon. It seems whoever bought him from that place wrote down whatever they felt like and as long as that auction got their cut of the check, they didn't care what was written on the sales certificate. It looks like Sophia used what little information she got in the mail from his sale to complete his transfer to the new owner. Bless her heart. I'm sure she didn't want to see you getting in trouble. If a seller fails to record the transfer of owner-ship of a horse, their membership can be suspended. If she hadn't taken care to follow the rules by submitting that transfer form and sending in his papers, you might not be able to show in AQHA events. Your business wouldn't be able to transfer any more horses into ownership either. Not to mention, you wouldn't be able to stand a stallion, breed a mare, register a foal and worse. You want to breed Star don't you?"

"Yes, I reckon I do. I sure am lucky that Sophia has always been so good to me."

"You sure owe her one for doing the right thing by that horse and his new owner, McKennon."

"I get your point, Sallie Mae, but never mind that now. What did the association say?"

"They gave me the initials S.M. and a P.O. Box. Hold on a minute. Let me gather up my reading glasses. Can't even read my own handwriting without those things." I can hear Sallie Mae shuffling around, and my patience is growing thin. "You there, McKennon?"

"I'm here," I grunt.

"Let's see the zip code is 76258."

I hold the phone away from my ear and just stare at it.

"That's a local zip code, Sallie Mae. Local to Green Briar. How did he go from a crumby livestock auction up north and end up back in our small town? That's odd."

"What about the S.M., McKennon? Who could that be?"

I think on it for a second, then it hits me like a tidal wave.

S.M. Sterling McCall. Who else can it be?

"Sallie Mae. It's gotta be Sterling McCall. Our town is too little for it not to be."

"Madison's father? Why that son of a gun." I can hear her fin-gers flying across the keyboard of her computer. She is quiet for a moment as she browses. "I hate to say this, McKennon, but it looks like that man is almost as invisible online as you are. All I've got here is a short bio and headshot on the dealership website, same with the Western apparel chain. There are a couple old articles – one about his brother's death and another about his dealership donating to a kid's ball league, but not much else."

I pound my fist on the steering wheel.

"McKennon? You all right?"

"Sallie Mae, I've gotta go."

"Be careful, McKennon … and good luck."

"Thank you, Sallie Mae, but I think I ran outta luck a long time ago."

CHAPTER 46

My gut tells me that Sterling has Demon, but I need to be sure. I tip my Stetson low over my eyes, tuck the small empty box under my arm and open the post office door. I don't come here often, but I'm still nervous someone might spot me. I'm not much in the mood for answering questions. I'm happy to see the joint empty when I step inside.

"Can I help you, sir?" the clerk asks when I approach the counter. It irritates me when he tries to meet my eyes under the brim of my hat.

"Just interested in a P.O. Box," I mutter, keeping my head down.

"Happy to help. There are various sizes available," he quips, spreading a brochure out on the counter. He points to the different boxes with the tip of his ballpoint pen.

"OK, I suppose I'll need to think about what size I'll be needin'. How do I know if I've gotten any mail in it anyway? I don't plan on coming 'round the post office every day."

"Oh well, you're in luck," the clerk exclaims. "We are so hip now! We can either send you an email or simply text your phone when you receive mail. Really, it is whichever you prefer. It's an automated thing."

"Huh. Not sure I am ready to make a decision today. Can I keep this flier?"

"Sure, sure. We'll be here when you're ready!"

"I'd like to mail this package, too," I say, placing the tangerine-colored box on the counter. "You do next day delivery?"

"Well, let me see here. What's the address?" he asks, running a finger over the address I scribbled on the box. "Why, this address is here! We can certainly do next day."

"Mark it priority and include a notification that signature is required for receipt," I instruct.

Happily, I watch him deposit my empty, brightly-colored box into the outgoing mail bin. I'm pleased that this trusting post person isn't onto my scheme. After handing over money for the postage, I thank the overly-jubilant mail clerk and head for my truck with a smirk firmly pasted on my lips.

CHAPTER 47

A s day breaks, I groan, drag a hand over my significant stub-ble and stretch the best I can in the confines of my truck. I spent the night in the post office parking lot. I know now that the owner of the P.O. Box will get a text message or email alert that a package, requiring signature, is being held for them at the post office. I figure that will pique anyone's curiosity, and if my gut is right, I'll soon see the owner come to collect the package.

Near noon, I shrink down in my driver's seat watching the fa-miliar face of Sterling McCall stroll across the parking lot and into the post office. Moments later, he pushes open the doors with my orange box under one arm. I hold my breath until he climbs into one of his dealership's luxurious trucks and drives away. I imme-diately snatch up my phone and hit speed dial.

"Hello? McKennon?" JD answers.

"I found him, JD. I found the damn horse." My chest feels heavy.

"What? How? Where?" JD sputters into the receiver.

"Sallie Mae. She helped me. Looked him up in the Quarter Horse database."

"Well ... where is he, bro?"

I take a moment to gather my rage, my guilt. I'm not sure I want to say the words, but I have to end this once and for all.

"Sterling," I spit. "Sterling has had him the whole time."

"Dad? What?"

"You mean to tell me that you didn't know this, JD?" I ask, trying to remain calm. I don't want to blow a gasket … yet. "Do you really expect me to believe that you haven't been keeping this bit of information from me?"

"No, man. I swear I haven't been back there since he popped me in the eye. Remember that, McKennon? He changed the gate code on me. I spend my time at Green Briar or in my trailer gettin' ready to ride a bull or a babe. Every now and then, I'll swing by the dealership to just to check in. We've sorta been working on things, but I swear I don't know anything about the horse. Is it really true? Dad's had him all this time?"

"That's right. He's been at your father's place and right under our noses. The damn beast is right here in our small town when I thought he was up north where you dumped him. He's in Green Briar's freakin' backyard, JD!" I lost what little composure I'd managed to muster.

"McKennon, what're you gonna do?" JD asks hesitantly.

"Headin' to Sterling's place."

"And then?"

"And then maybe I'll come back to Green Briar." I pause, thinking of Sophia and JD. They are all that's left of my family. Then I think of Devon, Faith and Star; they are possibly my future. My heart clenches, and I continue, "At least for my things, that is."

"McKennon, where are you?"

I touch the cool metal of my pistol and roll a bullet between my forefinger and thumb.

"Not far. I'll be making myself known at nightfall, JD. I'm finally going to end it all." I don't wait for his response. I hang up the phone.

CHAPTER 48

DEVON

I am sitting on my tack box, putting another poem to paper, when the call comes in. I tiptoe to the doorway and hover there, straining to hear JD on the phone. I can tell by his tone that it's probably McKennon. He ends the phone call without a goodbye, and I scurry back into the depths of the tack room just before he rounds the corner. Swiping a rag off of a hook next to my bridle, I kneel next to my saddle rack.

"What's up?" I ask, nonchalantly when JD stomps up next to me. I polish the silver plates mounted to the leather, acting as if I'd been cleaning my tack the whole time.

"You need to come with me *now*," he orders, brow furrowed.

Is McKennon OK? Has something happened to him?

"What's going on, JD?" I ask, standing up and dusting off the knees of my jeans. My heart is hammering in my chest.

"I'm not sure yet, but I'm certain it's not going to be pretty. Might need your help, Devon. I don't know what's going to happen or what we'll find when we get where we're going, but I think your presence will help. I don't know though, it might be too dangerous."

"Is it McKennon?" I already know the answer.

"Yes," JD confirms.

"I'm coming then," I respond, ditching the rag I was pretending to use. I retrieve my journal and tuck it in the back pocket of my jeans.

"Where are we going?" I ask as we head toward his truck.

"My father's place. McKennon is getting ready to wage a war," JD says, opening the passenger door and assisting me inside.

I swallow hard and clasp my hands together in my lap. A nervous wave washes over me.

I'd better cowgirl up. I am about to see McKennon again.

"My father and McKennon are like oil and water. Get ready for some fireworks, Devon," JD mutters, jamming his key in the ignition, putting the gear in reverse, and hitting the gas.

CHAPTER 49

MCKENNON

N ight has fallen, and I stand on the dark edge of her family's homestead.

How could Sterling have purchased Demon?

My hand is trembling on my pistol. I'm readying to fire on the stallion that took my wife, stole my life and wrecked my future.

Has he been breeding him all this time?

My stomach turns at the thought. How dare he put those evil genes into the world over and over again? The idea of hundreds of horses as nasty as Demon being bred into existence by Sterling McCall makes me sick. It disgraces Madison's memory.

Fighting back my rage, I make my way through the night. I follow the familiar path leading to the sight of my first date with Madison McCall. I pull back the heavy barn doors and step inside. There is something soothing about being in a stable at night. There's a certain kind of calm after the tack has been put up for the day. My ears tune in to the low hum of a country song playing on a radio plugged in somewhere to the quiet rustling of the horses in their stalls. The warm, moist air scented by hay and pine shavings lingers in my nostrils. For a moment, I feel almost peaceful as I amble down the aisle until I remember what I came for. A pain pricks in my stomach as I pass Lyric's old stall. The memories of the time I spent with Madison in there are so cemented in my mind. I pass Cash and meet his muzzle with my hand. His warm breath on my palm makes my heart swell. Moving deeper into the barn, I grind my teeth.

How can he put the beast that killed Madison in there?

Of course, he's in the end stall. It's the one reserved for Sterling's prized horse. I reach out and open Demon's door. His dark silhouette shifts into view. I touch the pistol at my hip, remove it from its holster and contemplate entering the stallion's enclosure. I curve my index finger against the trigger. My thumb silently disengages the safety. To pay for the murder of Madison, Demon will take a single bullet to his head. I'll be the one to drop the hammer.

CHAPTER 50

DEVON

It doesn't take long for us to make the drive. JD kills the headlights and pulls his truck off into the gravel at the side of the road.

"This is as far as we go. My old man changed the gate code on me when he gave me the boot. We'll have to sneak the rest of the way in."

We climb out of the truck, careful to close the doors quietly behind us.

"What are we going to do, JD?" I whisper in the dark.

"Not sure yet, Devon. Just got a feelin' we need to get down to the barn and fast. Watch the hot wire now." I follow JD and climb between the fence rails of his father's property.

We creep down the gravel driveway on foot, and he leads me toward a dark barn.

"This is where Madison kept and trained her horses when we were younger. It's kinda where she and McKennon started." JD eyes me cautiously. It's obvious that he isn't sure if he should have said it. "Figured I better warn you, Devon."

"Oh, I see." I try not to flinch as my heart takes the jab his words deliver. I nod toward the barn. I want to keep going forward to see if McKennon is inside still chasing her ghost.

"Up there," JD directs, pointing at a ladder attached to the side of the barn. "We'll go in through the hayloft. See, the door is open."

"Why don't we just go in through the front?" I ask.

"I'm not sure what McKennon is planning to do, but I do know that he doesn't much like me meddling in his business. I don't want to set him off for no reason. I figure we can step in if needed."

"I suppose that makes sense." I shrug.

"Come on, just trust me. I've known McKennon a long time. Anyways, I used to take my women up there when I was a youngin'. It'll be fun to show you around," he snickers, elbowing me in the upper arm.

"You'll never change, JD," I groan, poking him in the gut. "Think a woman will ever tie you down?"

"Nah, unless you've had a change of heart. Then we can just get gettin' to what I used to do up in that hayloft and forget about all this McKennon drama."

I give him a look.

"OK. OK. Let's go. Come on, cowgirl."

We scramble up the ladder and disappear inside. It is dark, but JD knows his way. On our hands and knees, we crawl across the hay-covered loft, careful not to make a sound. Out in front of me, JD moves swiftly like a superhero. I am less graceful, bringing up the rear. JD drops to the main level through an opening above the tack room and motions for me to follow. Mustering up my courage, I drop into his able, open arms. He catches me easily.

"You're light as a feather," JD whispers as he sets me down on my boots. "Come on this way."

JD leads me along a hall adjacent to the main aisle. We tiptoe to the end of it and peer around the corner. It is then that we see

McKennon. The moonlight spotlights him from the hayloft door. He looks stoic. I can tell it is McKennon by the build of him and the illuminated contours of his face. He is lingering outside of a partially open stall door.

As my eyes adjust, I can see McKennon better. He appears rattled. My heart aches. He is still beautiful to look at, but his appearance is disheveled. He has grown almost a full beard, and his eyes look tired, even more weathered. They are angry. McKennon's presence is icy, and his mouth is set in stone, a scowl. I start to move toward him, but JD presses my belly and warns me back.

"Can't be sure what condition he's in, Devon," JD murmurs, caution in his eyes.

Just as JD finishes his sentence, the overhead lights flick on. A startled McKennon redirects his pistol away from the stall and toward the heavy boot steps that are coming toward him on the paved aisle. I gasp. JD puts a finger to his lips and shakes his head. He tucks me protectively in the crook of his thick arm then leaps from the shadows with me in tow.

He is going to intervene, and he is going to drag me with him.

CHAPTER 51

MCKENNON

I am prepared to end him, but a switch flips on, and the aisle lights burn to life above me. I squint in the brightness and take a new aim with my pistol.

Suddenly, JD comes out of nowhere with Devon in tow. Her eyes are wide, confused.

"What's she doin' here?" I growl, lowering my gun.

"Figured she'd be able to talk some sense into you."

"You're wrong, JD. My mind's made up." My sights blaze past both of them and drill into Sterling McCall making his way down the aisle toward us. He's carrying a rifle.

"How did you know I'd be here?" I bark.

"A little bird told me," Sterling replies.

"You tell him I was coming here, JD?" I ask through clenched teeth.

Kid doesn't know how to keep his mouth shut.

"No, McKennon. It's not like that. I don't want to see anyone hurt. Horse or human." JD motions toward Demon.

"You're a traitor, JD," I grunt. If Devon weren't beside him, I'd punch him straight in the nose for meddling.

"Can't blame the boy, McKennon. He may not be my biggest fan, but he certainly looks out for you. I hear you're planning to put an end to my stallion here? Is that true?" Sterling asks, gripping his rifle tighter and nodding toward the horse.

"I can't go on living knowing he's alive, and she's dead, Sterling! I have a debt to settle with this devil," I hiss, raising my pistol again. I alternate pointing my gun between Sterling and the horse. "Problem is I don't know who I want to shoot more right now, you or this demon here."

"Come on now, son," Sterling begins, reaching out to touch my shoulder.

"Don't touch me!" I shout, swatting his hand away. The commotion is making the horses restless. They are pacing in their stalls, nervous with our energy. I aim my pistol at Sterling's forehead. "Give me one reason why I shouldn't put a bullet in your head and then his?" I sliver my eyes and slowly start to squeeze the trigger.

"Stop! *Please,*" Devon shrieks. Her panic is evident. She puts her face in her hands. "JD, do something!"

In reaction to Devon's plea, JD comes at me like a freight train before I can make my move on Sterling. He thrusts my arm in the air, and the gun goes off.

Bang!

Trapped in their stalls, the horses scurry furiously at the sound and call out to each other in waves of uneasy whinnies. I hear Devon scream. JD bulldozes me into the wall with his beefy shoulder. He takes us to the floor and wrestles me into a headlock. I writhe beneath him like a wild animal.

I've still got the gun.

I swing with my free arm trying to land punches anywhere I can. I connect a few times, and I am satisfied when I hear JD groan. He loosens his grip around my neck, and I twist myself free. I am blinded by my hate for the damn horse and for Sterling.

I start to scramble down the aisle on all fours, but JD grabs my boot and tugs me backwards. He is back on top of me before I can escape. I release a wail when he slams my hand against the cement floor. JD pounds my fist on the floor again. Pain shoots through my knuckles, and I lose my grip on the pistol in the scuffle. We both clamor for it as it spins out of reach, but Sterling rushes in, knocks me back and puts a knee in my chest before I can reach it. In an instant, he has me pinned, barrel of his rifle pressed into my throat. I struggle to catch my breath.

"Calm down! JD and I loved her too, son," Sterling snarls above me.

"You sure had a screwed up way of showin' it!" I yell in his face. Sterling presses his rifle harder against neck. I gasp for air. JD pins my arms and puts a knee in my chest, too. I'm no match for the two of them at once. I can't get them off of me.

"Stop it! You're hurting him!" Devon wails. Out of the corner of my eye, I see her scurry for my gun. "All of you stop it! Now! JD let go of his arms and get your knee off of his chest! Mr. McCall take that rifle away from his throat, NOW!"

We all go still and look at her. Devon's breathing is erratic. There's a wild look in her wide eyes. She is trembling, holding my pistol in her grip. Her knuckles go white, aiming it at the three of us.

"There has to be a better way to work this out!" she shouts. "I'll not have any killing happen on my watch. Behave like grown men! All of you!"

"You going to settle down, McKennon?" JD asks.

I nod, but I'm furious. I'm not sure I won't explode if they let me up. Sterling hesitantly removes the pressure from my neck, and JD tips back on to his boots.

"I like her. She's got grit," Sterling adds. He's amused.

I am not.

I eye Devon as I get up. Attempting to swallow my pride, I rub my throat, sure of the mark the rifle has left there, then dust myself off.

"I know you're angry, but listen to him, McKennon. For me? Please," she begs, meeting my bitter stare and still pointing the gun.

Daring Devon.

CHAPTER 52

"She's right, son. Just listen to me. Give me a chance to explain. I don't want to fight anymore. Let's settle this once and for all. There's some things you should know," Sterling begins, stepping out of the aisle to rest his rifle in the corner of the tack room.

"What is there to know? I know that you never cared about Madison! All you ever did was make life more difficult for us," I shout after him.

"I've turned a new leaf," Sterling continues, returning to the aisle palms up.

"The hell you have," I roar. I want to fight – for all of the pain he caused us, caused her, our business. My face is hot, and I can feel the veins pulsing at my temples. My hands are free. I shove one into my pocket and retrieve my pocketknife. I flip it open, ready to lunge. Devon steps forward and jabs me in the back with my pistol.

"Put it away, McKennon," she commands. I know she won't pull the trigger, but I oblige anyway. I grind my teeth and glare at her as I close the knife. I tuck it back in my pocket.

"For heaven's sake! Settle down, boy. You're right. I tried to trip up your new business. I am not going to defend myself or argue that point with you. I'm an ass. Madison was a good daughter. I know I treated her, you, both of you, all of you, wrong ... JD, too. I've taken revenge on an animal before, and let me tell you it didn't do anything to ease the pain. I'm trying to save you from making the same mistake. Let me explain, McKennon."

"I'm listening," I mutter, folding my arms across my chest. I take several deep breaths. It's an attempt to calm down. I'm only lending an ear to this nonsense because Devon's here.

"Did you know Madison still called me occasionally?"

"She still talked to you?" I ask, narrowing my eyes. This is news to me.

"Yes. She checked in to see how I was doing even after I'd been so awful."

"I don't believe it," I grunt. I feel betrayed.

"Believe it, son. Madison helped me see that I'm the one that turned the family upside down after that damn bull killed my brother. It turned me cold. I was controlling. I was an angry bastard. I see that now. I was just trying to steer her clear of getting hurt. Truth is, I didn't want Madison to leave the way her mother did. I didn't want to see her get her hopes up with the likes of you."

"Is that so?"

"I was wrong though. You weren't the leaving kind. In fact, I'm pretty impressed by what you accomplished together."

I wince at the compliment, especially after everything he did to try and derail our little start-up.

"I wanted to earn Madison's forgiveness. Our conversations stirred hope of a reunion, a settling of the past, a bridge that I might one day be able to cross. She called me that day ... well, that's neither here nor there anymore. She sure loved you. And she loved this damn horse. I knew that much from our last phone call. You were stupid running off and getting married like you did. I was just plain stupid. I can't believe I didn't give my daughter away on her wedding day. At least I had the chance to apologize for keeping Cash. I was planning to return him to her when you got back from Congress."

"Madison knew this?" I ask in disbelief.

"Yes, McKennon. Madison and I were on the road to a truce. I'd like to extend that to you now. Let us try to put this behind us. Let the horse live, and let's let her finally rest in peace. I know Madison would want us to put our differences aside."

I furrow my brow and consider his offer.

Can I forgive this man?

I meet Devon's eyes. She nods to me, lowers my gun and hands it over to JD. Hastily, JD snatches it, secures the safety and tucks my pistol into the waistband of his jeans.

"This one here," Sterling continues. "He's a pretty good horse, you know. Great with his offspring and gentle with the mares. He has calmed down in his maturity, but he's still a bastard under saddle. I don't even try to get on his back anymore."

"You're breeding him? How can you?" I shoot the animal an evil eye and ball my fists at my side. Demon is no longer in the shadows. I see him clear as day.

"You two actually had a good eye together," Sterling says, ignoring my question. "Shame on me for not giving you credit for that. M&M Quarter Horses showed a lot of promise. I'm sorry for all of it, son." He stretches a hand to me. I don't take it.

My gaze drifts to Devon again. JD has a firm grip on her shoulder, and his other hand is on my pistol at his waist. This is a lot of information for her to absorb. I want to comfort her, but then the pang of guilt comes back to me like it always does. I remind myself that I'm standing here in Madison's family barn with her father and brother.

"How —" I start.

"How'd I wind up with him?" Sterling asks, reading my mind. "Madison … she invited me to the show. She wanted me to see what you were capable of. I was in the stands that day rooting for the two of you. I was planning to shake your hand after the class. She asked me to make amends, to welcome you to the McCall family, but I never got the chance, McKennon. After everything happened … well, I followed JD. I bought the horse from the auction after he left him behind."

"Why? Why would you buy this killer?" I ask, waving an angry hand toward his stall.

"Because this damn horse is all I have left of her!" Sterling bellows. "I knew how much she loved him. Do you have any idea what it was like for me to track down her mother, tell her the news and see her grieve at the funeral? I am responsible. I drove everyone away. I lost my family. It's all my fault."

I watch Sterling put a hand over his mouth in an effort to contain his grief as he reaches toward Demon. I am stunned. It is a moment of sensitivity, a rarity for Sterling. I mull his words over as he strokes the horse that caused all of this.

"I couldn't believe my ears when they told me Madison had sustained fatal internal injuries from the accident. I was foolish to think that the rodeo is the only place where someone would get hurt living this lifestyle. Let's both move on, forgive. It's time, McKennon. I'm man enough to know that I need to make amends. It's time to put this behind us. Please?"

Sterling extends his hand to me again. I eye it hesitantly, but this time, I take it. All I ever wanted was his approval. I'm tired of being angry. I'm sick of fighting this battle with the past. We both loved and lost her. He suffered, JD, too, just the same. I never thought about them – what they might be going through. I never considered that their loss might be similar to mine.

CHAPTER 53

"Somewhere along the line, someone got rough with him," I say, releasing Sterling's hand and gesturing toward Charming.

"Yes, I reckon so," Sterling replies, adjusting his cowboy hat.

"Then I came along and didn't help the matter any. I was too busy trying to prove myself to everyone. I pushed too fast, too hard, too far. His mind wasn't ready. Worst of all, he didn't trust me, and I didn't trust him. The whole human-horse relationship is built on trust. I doomed us from the start. It's we humans who do it to 'em, make 'em mean, or scared or whatever. We do it to win, to be the best. We don't think of the animal. I'm guilty, too, but at least I can see it now. Madison tried to tell me. Hardest lesson I've ever learned. I owe all of you for keeping me from doing something foolish. I've already got enough regrets."

Exhaling, I turn on my boots and walk to his stall. He is lingering in the shadows at the back. I can barely see him. He rustles inside, and my heart clenches as he approaches me. His nose pokes out the door and he nickers, clearly remembering my scent, remembering me after all this time. I put my hand to the cool metal handle, and I open the door further. Charming pushes his head out into the aisle and into my chest. I meet his big brown eyes, and suddenly a rush comes over me. It wasn't his fault, no more than it was mine. He's happy now, obviously a different horse. He's a sire. He's retired. He was never meant to be a show horse. With the life Sterling provides him, Charming is able to just be, running free with his herd and covering his mares. It's as nature intended. I suddenly feel warm toward Sterling, grateful even, for stopping me, for saving Charming, for preserving Madison's memory and her love for the horse.

"I pushed you too hard," I confide to the stallion. "It was all because I wanted to win so badly. I forgot my roots. I ignored my training. I'm sorry, big guy. I should have listened to you ... to both of you. Can you forgive me?" I ask near his ebony ear.

Charming pushes his broad forehead into my chest again, and I can't hold it any longer. A sob escapes me. Devon places a reassuring hand to the center of my back.

It is time to move on.

I stroke the stallion's head and close his stall door. I turn, open my arms and motion for Devon to come to me. I'm nervous that she'll reject the invitation after all I've put her through. I am relieved when she settles into my arms.

"Why do you go wasting your time on me?" I whisper into her hair. "I've got a lot to say to you, but I'm scared that if it doesn't come out the right way that I'll seem like a monster, and you'll want to get away."

She lifts her face to look at me and shakes her head.

"I'm right here," she murmurs.

"I've been scared to let myself feel for you," I continue, stroking her soft cheeks with my thumbs. "I thought letting you in would cause my memories of Madison to slip away. I felt like I was betraying her. I couldn't focus knowing this horse was alive. The thought of him still breathing mixed with the memory of her death made me feel furious and incomplete all the time. I thought if I ended him, it would free me, set things straight, but I realize now that killing him wouldn't have fixed things. I don't want to make the same mistakes Sterling did, and I'm not going to push people away anymore."

I feel Devon let out a sigh of relief against my chest.

"Your arrival at Green Briar changed all my plans. The feelings about staying alone for the rest of my life started to fade. The way I had it mapped out doesn't make sense anymore. It's all because of you, Devon."

I look to Sterling, to JD with his arms folded across his chest, then to my gun in his waistband. I don't care that we have an audience. I hug Devon tightly and rock her gently. She clings to me as I bury my nose in her hair.

"Thank heaven," I breathe. "I was afraid I might have lost you running away like I did."

"Never," Devon whispers in return, breaking from our embrace to look at me. I cup her face with my palms and search her eyes. I kiss each cheek, her forehead, then quickly on the lips. I am fully aware that she has one eye on Sterling and JD the whole time.

"You win, brother," JD utters. "Devon belongs with you. Now will you stop acting like a stallion that's just lost his family jewels and get on with things? Are you gonna get back in the saddle or what, cowboy?" Devon blushes as JD's heavy hand slaps down on my back.

"All right, then." I shake my head, rub the back of my neck and give Devon a weak smile. "Devon meet De-, I mean, Charming. I used to call him Demon," I explain, peering into the horse's dark stall again.

"Hi, Charming," she coos, softly giving his velvet nose a stroke. "More importantly, hello *you*. I've missed you." Devon puts her hand in mine. When she gives it a squeeze, I feel a small electric current pass between us, and Charming whinnies as if he experiences it, too.

Some might think the timing of Charming's nicker is a fluke, but I take it as a sign. It's Madison telling me to go on. I press my lips together. After all of this time, it happens when I am here, in her barn with her horses. I glance over at Cash, his head hung over the door.

Of course, Madison's guidance would come this way.

It was always about the horses with Madison. She wants me to make peace with Charming, with her father and with her death. A small smile creeps to my lips. I look up and point to the sky. Devon puts her hand on my heart. I look deeply into her eyes. This woman unexpectedly entered my life, changed my path, and I'm interested again. Interested in life, in horses and in her.

"You know, a man sure is lucky to find love twice in a lifetime," Sterling interjects, slicing through the moment. "I'd hold onto that, McKennon. She'd want you to. Come on, JD. Let us have a whiskey." I acknowledge Sterling with a nod. He tips his hat to me, rubs Charming on the nose and leaves me alone with Devon in his barn aisle.

JD meets Devon's eyes. It seems he's still unsure about my intentions. I don't blame him really. She gives him a faint smile and mouths 'I'm OK.' JD shoots me a look of warning. It reads 'you better be good to her this time or else,' then he follows his father out into the moonlight.

CHAPTER 54

DEVON

After Sterling and JD are gone, I wrap an arm around McKennon's taut waist and put my head on his shoulder. I feel his chin touch the top of my head. We watch Charming in silence for a while. My heart pounds in my chest because there's still one question left. I'm not sure I'm ready for the answer, but I've grown tired of the waiting game.

"Are you coming back?" I whisper.

McKennon stops watching the horse, puts his hand beneath my chin and lifts my head toward him. I can feel his beautiful blue eyes on me, but I'm nervous to meet his gaze. I steel myself for his response.

"Yes."

It's a simple reply, but it's one that doesn't require any additional explanation. I know it's the truth. McKennon grins as he slings his arms low around my waist and pulls me to him. He pats my back pocket, taking notice of my journal stuffed there.

"Been writing have you?"

"Yes," I say, smiling up at him. "Poems mostly. I've been writing them a lot since my cowboy's been away."

"I'd sure like to read one of your poems someday," he responds, tipping my chin toward him again. He searches my eyes for a stitch in time, and then he presses his lips to mine. There is a promise in his tender kiss. "Come now. I'll drive you home."

Home? I don't want to go home. I want to go home with you!

I feel deflated as McKennon takes my hand and leads me out of the barn. My mind is its usual tornado of one-way conversation with myself, but I hold my tongue. I've only just gotten him back, and I don't want to spook him with a barrage of questions. We walk silently across Sterling's land. Reaching his truck, he helps me inside and lingers at the door for a moment.

What happens now? When will I see you again? Take me with you!

"Devon?" McKennon asks.

"Yes?" I respond, anticipating his next words from the edge of my seat.

I hope he is reading my mind right now!

"Will you ride with me tomorrow?" he murmurs.

"Yes. Yes, of course," I reply quickly. I'm immediately relieved, but also a little sad because he didn't read my mind. My hope was for an invitation to his bed.

I suppose a ride will do ... for now.

McKennon closes the door on me with a satisfied smile. Seated in his passenger seat, I open my journal to a blank page and write five words.

McKennon came back to me.

CHAPTER 55

MCKENNON

I've been looking forward to this ride. It feels good to be back at Green Briar. Sitting atop of Star, my eyes settle on the beautiful woman riding her painted pony beside me.

She has certainly weathered my storm.

I love observing women with their horses. Women – they are meditative when they're with horses, in a calm, otherworldly place. I especially love watching Devon. There's this quiet determination about her, a commitment to do everything the right way and all by herself. She bites her lip and furrows her thin eyebrows when she focuses on Faith.

Gosh, it's sexy.

I loved watching my wife with the horses, too, but Madison grew up with them, and she had the best-trained horses. It was easy for her. Working with them was effortless – she just knew what to do.

Devon, on the other hand, is learning, and so is Faith. It's the earnest way she does things that I enjoy. Devon always wants to know more, go farther. That's what is so intriguing to me. I like that this city girl has *try* and that she doesn't even know it. On the rodeo circuit, we use 'try' as a noun. *Try* is what got me on the back of the rankest horse and then back on my boots after I got bucked off. *Try* is the part of a person that just won't quit. *Try* is what always keeps me going even in my darkest hours. Devon has *try*. She is going to make Faith *the one* no matter what it takes. And I'm determined to help her achieve that dream.

It's her turn now.

Devon's presence at Green Briar awakened something in me. I'm beginning to rediscover the man I used to be – not the rodeo man, the good-time lovin' man, but the man who was married to Madison. The one who loves looking after a woman, protecting her and coming home only to her. I was fond of Devon's looks from the beginning, that's for sure, but I yearn to know her more deeply.

Who is she when I'm not around? What really turns her on? Does she wear silk pajamas or sweats to bed?

Her city side inclines me to think silk, but the way she just fits in on the farm suggests something more casual. My mind wanders to what she might look like in one of my white T-shirts. I don't know if I deserve to be happy again after what happened to Madison, but I'm determined to earn this happiness I've found with Devon.

I am ready to make peace with the past. I am ready to love Devon.

"Devon?" I ask.

"Yes, McKennon," Devon replies sweetly, turning just the slightest in her saddle to meet my gaze.

"I've been thinking," I pause to clear my throat.

"Go on. You've been thinking?" Devon coaxes.

"Well, it's just I've been thinking … there's been too much room in my bed for far too long."

"OK … and?" I like how my statement makes her blush in her usual way. She still maintains eye contact though.

That's good.

"And … I wanted to know if you would join me tonight?"

There, I'd said it. It's our start.

"Oh," she gasps and bites her lip as the redness in her cheeks deepens.

"Before you answer though, know that this would mean more to me than just a night's vacation from reality. It would be so much more. It would be the start of somethin' real for you and me."

"I want you with every fiber of my being, McKennon."

"I want you, too. I want someone real … alive. Flesh and blood, no more ghosts. This time around, I know I can be true. No more leavin'. This time, Devon, it's going to be all about you. I want to help you achieve your dreams. Let's win you and Faith that buckle. I'm back in the business of training."

"Really? You'll help Faith and me win a championship?"

"I sure will."

I grin as Devon leans over her saddle horn so she can get near Faith's ear.

"Dreams do come true, Faith," she whispers, running a hand under her mare's white mane.

"Speaking of dreams coming true. What'll it be, Devon? Will you join me tonight? And … every night after that?" I ask, hopeful.

"Yes," she answers through a beaming smile.

It's all I need to hear.

"This cowboy is here to stay. No more going away, Devon."

A PREVIEW FROM BOOK THREE OF
THE IN THE REINS SERIES:
DEVON AND MCKENNON'S STORY CONTINUES

CHAPTER 1
MCKENNON

Devon is a beautiful disaster in the morning. She is tangled under the humid blankets, her skin hot and moist. I am intoxicated by her sweet scent. I love everything about her pretty mess, especially having her wake up in my arms. Finally, she is here in my bed. We've just spent our first night together, but we didn't sleep together.

I can't wait for that to happen.

I think the events of the last months had exhausted me to the point I only wanted to sleep and cling to her, hopeful for our future. I feel rested for the first time in weeks, and I am ready to take on the day.

The morning light is bright, and so is my spirit, but Devon's body heat is impossible to ignore. I have to throw the blankets off myself to continue lying next to her. I stroke her back, touching my T-shirt she had worn to bed. It's damp with perspiration, and her long auburn hair splays across her face. I swear I hear a little snore escape her in her last moments of attempted slumber. I pull her hair back from her face. She squeezes her eyes tight and releases a cute yet displeased moan.

"Hey, you," I whisper, pressing my lips to her soft cheek.

"I am so not a morning person," Devon grumbles, tossing an arm over her eyes.

"I'm gonna go check on the horses. Get 'em some breakfast."

"Stay," she says, clutching me to her. "You fell asleep on me last night. I think it was from the magnitude of it all – of finally letting the past go."

"Yeah," I answer, mulling those words over.

She's right. There's a lot to let go of.

"Don't worry. I'll be back. None of them horses are gonna keep me away from the likes of you for long, miss. I plan to tend to your breakfast, too."

"When?" she murmurs. "I want more of what we started last night."

"Soon, little lady." I say with a chuckle. "We've got the rest of our lives to get frisky. Don't we?"

Devon responds with a groan.

"Soon," I repeat. I run my thumb over her pouting lower lip. I want to assure her I'm interested. The truth of the matter is I like the wait. I want to bask in her want for me just a little longer.

Rising from the bed, I pull my jeans on over my boxer briefs, fish a clean white T-shirt from my dresser and start to ease on my trusty, lambskin work gloves. Looking one last time to Devon, I notice her pained expression.

"What's wrong?" I ask.

"The gloves," she grumbles.

"These?" I ask, raising my gloved hands and shrugging my shoulders. "I've owned them forever."

"Yes, those. They kind of bring up some unhappy memories for me," she says plainly.

It hasn't occurred to me that my gloves could be a pain point for her. I took the ring off a while ago.

"Well, then," I reply, giving her a wry smile and pulling the gloves off finger by finger. "Want to do the honors?" I ask, offering them to her and motioning toward the trash.

Devon smiles and leaps from my bed. A lovely embrace is my reward as she wriggles them from my grasp.

"Stay," she breathes again into my neck. Her lips are soft as satin on my skin as she utters the word.

"I'll be back soon," I promise.

"OK," she replies with a smile. She releases me and happily trots off to chuck my work gloves into a tiny trashcan in the corner. Devon hovers near the can for a moment before turning on the tips of her bare toes. "I can't do it. I'm not going to throw away your favorite work gloves."

I shake my head, unable to ward off my grin.

"Glad to hear that you've had a change of heart. I'm quite fond of those gloves. Takes time to break 'em in just right."

"Here, cowboy," Devon says quietly as she hands my gloves back to me. I take them with a smile and tuck them safely in my back pocket.

"Thank you for giving us a chance, McKennon," she whispers, looking to the floor. "I know you've been through a lot. I hope one day you'll be comfortable enough to talk with me about her."

"I will. In time ... just give it some time. Right now, I want to focus on Green Briar, our horses and startin' our future. I want to know what makes Devon Brooke tick." I pull her toward me and settle my hands in the small of her back. "I'm wonderin' something though," I hum near her ear. "Still got that trench coat of yours?" I can't help myself, and I'm eager to change the subject.

"Why as a matter of fact I do, cowboy," she teases, giving me a sultry smile.

"I'd sure like to see you model that for me again, pretty lady." I raise an eyebrow and bite my lower lip.

"Would it make you stay if I put it on?" she purrs, peppering my throat with kisses.

"I reckon it might."

"Alas, if only it weren't still at my apartment," Devon sighs, naughtily.

"Well, is that so? I guess we'll have to go pick up your things later then. I'm lookin' for a redo on that particular missed opportunity. I'll be seeing you in a bit, cowgirl," I say, lifting her chin and kissing her again. I chuckle as Devon reluctantly lets me go, pads back into my bedroom, flops into the bed and pulls the covers over her head.

"I'll be waiting for you," she calls. "Hurry back, will you? And bring some of those strawberries!"

"Yes, ma'am. Your wish is my command."

Shaking my head, I make my way out into the sunlight full of glee thinking about Devon's hands all over me the night prior. It's time to stop pretending that I'm not in love with her. Devon's it for me; her dreams are my dreams now.

I'll get that buckle for her if it's the last thing I do.

I stretch on my porch and grin at the rocking chairs we sat in together the first night a drunken Devon stayed in my house. I take a deep cleansing breath of Green Briar air and leap off the front steps.

I love mornings here – so much possibility.

I feel a renewed sense of purpose and responsibility to the horses now that I'm in the business of training again. I've already shown that I'm still capable of winning given my Congress performance on Star. Next, I'll remind the equine community what I can do with Devon and Faith in the show pen. I'm aiming to take them on a championship run. It might require some time to rebuild my reputation, but I'm prepared for the long haul. I'm ready to understand each horse. I want to know their strengths and weaknesses, where to push and when to hold off, so I can bring out the very best in each of them under saddle. Charming will always be my reminder to not put training over trust.

I tip my hat to JD as I enter the barn. I am glad JD decided to stick around to help us start up again.

"I got this," I tell him, shaking his hand.

"You sure?" he mumbles, sleep still rimming his eyes.

"Yep," I assure.

"Thanks, man. Was out a little too late last night," JD says, obviously relieved. Then he smirks and knuckles me in the shoulder.

I grimace thinking of the unlucky lady he likely bedded the night before. The thought repulses me when I have Devon, still keeping mine warm. I watch JD pull his hoodie up over his head and curl up like a cat on a pallet of shaving bales in the feed room. JD hasn't learned to play his cards right. He always goes straight for the easy catch. He isn't willing to bait the hook and just wait on a good one.

Like Devon. One that you don't want to toss back.

My insides suddenly go all warm, an unusual but welcome feeling. It is new and refreshing. In this moment, I can't wait to get back to Devon and am wishing I hadn't left so quickly this morning. I can't shake the intuition that I needed to be down here in the barn first thing today though. I move on to the task at hand. The horses are anxiously waiting their morning feeding. I reach into the feed bin and scoop Faith's grain as quietly as possible to not stir JD.

I'll take care of my cowgirl's horse first.

I section out two flakes from a hay bale and stroll toward Faith's stall. As I approach, I hear the clear sound of struggle. I peer inside and drop her breakfast in the aisle. I know instantly that something is wrong with Faith, and I am yelling, but I can't feel it.

Not now! Not when things are going so good for Devon and me. Not Faith!

"JD – Go get Devon! NOW!"

"What? What's happening?" JD calls lethargically, peering out of the feed room.

"Just go! Ask questions later. She's at my place. Hurry!" I shout.

Swallowing hard, a sick knot grows inside me. I slide open the door and slip into Faith's stall. I hear JD's boots fast on the gravel outside of it. Assessing the situation, my eyes follow the line of Faith's patch-worked neck to the slope of her withers to the shoed hoof that likely began this ordeal. Dropping to my knees beside her, I put my hand to Faith's sweaty, tense neck. It feels familiar.

Damp just the way her mama's was this morning in my bed.

Faith groans. It is guttural from somewhere deep inside. It's a sign that she's clearly in pain. Her breathing is labored. Something wicked clutches my heart in its fist, tightening with each racing beat. My insides ache for the horse. My heart is ready to break over what this is going to do to Devon. Faith's crazed eye is on me waiting, begging for me to intervene. I bow my head for a moment and then reach for my pocketknife. I open it and run a finger over its cool, sharp edge. The stainless steel blade glints in the overhead lighting, and I question what I am about to do.

"Shhh ...whoa, now, girl. It's gonna be OK."

That's what I'm saying right now, but I don't know if it's true.

ABOUT THE AUTHOR

Carly Kade is an award-winning author from Arizona who enjoys competitively showing her registered Paint Horse. In her free time, Carly works on her next novel, reads voraciously, and spends time with her husband and two adopted dogs.

Feeling Social? Join the herd and connect with *Carly Kade Creative* on Facebook, Instagram, YouTube or Twitter.

Can't wait to find out what happens next for McKennon and Devon? Visit Carly's blog at carlykadecreative.com for sneak peeks, updates and release info.

Reviews are golden! If you enjoyed this book, please leave a review on Amazon or Goodreads. Your readership and support is greatly appreciated!

ACKNOWLEDGEMENTS

Thank you to the readers. When I learned that *In the Reins* had broken into the Amazon Equestrian Fiction Top 100 (then the Top 25, then the Top 5), my heart grew a thousand times its size because I knew it meant that my writing was resonating with **YOU**! You are the audience I wanted to identify with and write for. You know who you are ... you're the bookworms, the horse lovers, the cowgirls, the connoisseurs of cute cowboys! I couldn't have done it without <u>YOU</u>.

To my husband, my cowboy, my first editor, my business partner, my one and only. Without your endless faith in my writing, this series would never have seen the light of day. You keep me going when I am stopped.

To my current horse, Sissy. You are the inspiration behind the *In the Reins* series. You've taught me that good horse(wo)manship is a journey, not a destination. Thank you for keeping me on my toes and perpetually teaching me something new.

To my editor, Ann. You make my books better and are an irreplaceable friend. Thank you for being such a positive contribution to my creativity.

To the EQUUS Film Festival for recognizing *In the Reins*. I am honored that *In the Reins* is an EQUUS Film Festival WINNIE Award recipient. I met so many amazing fellow equine authors, filmmakers and readers in New York City. The EQUUS Film Festival is an excellent platform for bringing the storytellers of the horse world together through films, documentaries, videos, art, music and literature.

To the fellow equine authors and equestrian bloggers who have supported *In the Reins* and me. It makes my spurs jingle when authors and bloggers unite. I've learned so much from other writers and appreciate how unique each of our writing journeys is. I think it is so important to support each other and share knowledge among us. We are stronger working together to expose this "niche" genre of ours. Let's hear it for horse books and blogs!

Made in the USA
Columbia, SC
20 March 2019